PRAISE FOR *HEART IN*

BOOK 1, ON VICTORY'S W ᵢᵥₒₛ ₛₑᵣᵢₑₛ

A sweet and compelling romance that doesn't shy away from the difficulties of war. Heart in the Clouds is beautifully researched, based on Jennifer Mistmorgan's grandfather's experiences as a pilot in the RAAF. Perfect for both World War II buffs and for those who simply enjoy a lovely story and characters who feel like friends. Don't miss this one!

~**Sarah Sundin**, bestselling and Christy Award–winning author of
The Sound of Light and *Until Leaves Fall in Paris*

Jennifer Mistmorgan soars into the world war fiction scene with a debut that will steal your heart. Characters that are flawed but compelling, a plot that keeps you turning the pages, and writing that will have you coming back for more makes *Heart in the Clouds* a must-read for historical romance fans!

~**Roseanna M. White**, bestselling and Christy Award–winning author
of *Yesterday's Tides*

An enthralling historical romance set against the backdrop of WWII Britain when the heroic men of RAF Bomber Command took to the skies night after night and courageous women did their part for the cause of victory. From their witty banter to the heartache and hope of their unfolding love in a perilous time, Alec and Maggie's journey is one readers will long remember. Jennifer Mistmorgan's expert research infuses every page in this compelling and inspiring novel. Highly recommended for fans of Sarah Sundin and Kate Breslin.

~**Amanda Barratt**, Christy Award–winning author of
The Warsaw Sisters and *Within These Walls of Sorrow*

The
MAPMAKER'S
SECRET

The

MAPMAKER'S SECRET

JENNIFER MISTMORGAN

Cover design by Roseanna White Designs.

Paperback: 978-0-6458566-6-8

eBook: 978-0-6458566-5-1

AUTHOR'S HISTORICAL NOTE

During the Second World War, country homes across England, including Winston Churchill's own, were requisitioned to accommodate a wide range of military uses. Although loosely based on Hillside—the wartime name for Benjamin Disraeli's country house in High Wycombe—Bartondale is fictional. For more historical notes, see the author's note at the back of the book.

For Paul, Lydia, Miriam, and Leo. Love you lots.

CHAPTER ONE

RAF Medmenham, Buckinghamshire, England
21 June 1943

"You want me to do what!"

Lieutenant Jack Marsden wasn't using the polite, respectful tone he usually took with his superiors. But considering the idea just presented to him, there was nothing else to say—and no other way to say it.

"It's unconventional, I know." Lieutenant Colonel Robert Lewis, the most senior American officer at this British photographic interpretation unit, should have been on Jack's side. Instead, he leaned back in his chair and continued laying out his argument. "But most of the time you'll be involved in the same kind of work you do here. And from what I've seen, you are well suited to the task, Jack."

"Well suited? Sir, I do this photographic intelligence work to serve my country, but my real training is in medicine, not espionage." In front of his superiors, Jack usually kept quiet about his former life as a doctor, worried he might get pulled away from a desk and put in a clinic. He had no intention of returning to medicine anytime soon. Nope. He'd boxed that part of his life up and buried it six feet under when his wife died.

Two British civilians—military Intelligence, he suspected, from the way they were talking—stood behind his commanding officer, bestowing such stern looks he wanted to laugh. One of them, introduced with the single name of Petrie, looked at least ninety, with white-gray hair covering his solid head. The younger one, Wilson—although Jack didn't know if that was his first or last name—stared with merciless, foxlike eyes.

"Lieutenant, you are an urbane, single, intelligent man who knows all about cartography, and right now that's what we need." The older man compensated for the perfect stillness of his body with the deliberate energy of his precise Edinburgh accent.

"I'm not single, sir." Jack indicated the wedding ring on his left hand.

"She's dead, Jack." Warrant Officer Alvin Harris, his *supposed* friend sitting in the chair beside him, piped up.

Jack glowered at him.

"It's been four years." Alvin spoke more gently this time.

So this was an ambush. That was why Alvin was here. There was no other reason for him to be at a meeting like this, other than to get Jack to play ball.

"Your country is asking this of you, Marsden. You did sign up to serve your country, didn't you?" the lieutenant colonel said.

"Not as a spy," Jack muttered. Intelligence reports were one thing—what they had just proposed was completely different. "Don't we have some kind of euphemistically named department—Strategic Services, isn't it?—that can help you out?"

He wanted to keep protesting, but by the way the others stared at him, he faced a losing battle. He looked down at the unopened dossier in his hands and sighed. "Explain it to me again."

"Bartondale is a new cartography facility set up by the Air Ministry." Wilson spoke for the first time, his sly eyes studying Jack from behind round spectacles. "Hitler began preparing for war as soon as he took power. But he wouldn't allow maps to leave the country. Up-to-date maps are very hard to come by. As a result, the accuracy of our bombing was compromised. You've seen the results in your work here. Bartondale is the fix. Similar to this place, it hosts a range of specialists on site—intelligence officers, cartographers, artists—all of whom make sure our maps marry up with the most recent information, and in a form that is easy for the pilots and navigators to use. I should say that all this is top secret, and everyone in this room"—he looked at Alvin directly—"is bound by our Official Secrets Act and the Treachery Act, both of which you signed on the way in, not to mention a word."

Everyone nodded without thinking. Secret keeping was a matter of course these days.

Wilson continued. "In the months that it has been open, the Germans have anticipated several of our air raids. They've been ready for us with extra antiaircraft measures and have brought dozens of aircraft down. Lives have been lost." He paused to let the gravity of that statement sink in. "We've traced the link back to Bartondale."

"And you have a suspect?" Jack ignored Wilson's dramatic flourish.

"Open the dossier and you'll see."

Jack flipped open the file, and his attention zeroed in on the photograph paper-clipped to the first sheet of information. A woman with Rita Hayworth–style good looks and golden-brown hair. She smiled elegantly at the camera in a studio photograph, wearing a Women's Auxiliary Air Force uniform.

"Who's the broad?" Alvin leaned over Jack's shoulder and gave a low whistle.

"Grace Deroy. She's a WAAF corporal." Wilson motioned to the file. "As you know, we have requisitioned the country houses of wealthy families all over Britain for this kind of work."

Jack needed no more proof of what Wilson was saying than to look around him. RAF Medmenham was a grand house with glorious views out toward the river Thames. Lewis's office had probably once been some old lady's sitting room.

"Bartondale was recently requisitioned from Grace's family, but she insists on working there. Actually, she lives on site in a caretaker's cottage."

"We think she could be working with the Nazis." Petrie lobbed the comment into the conversation like it was a precision grenade.

Jack raised his eyebrows as he flipped through the dossier. His eyes skimmed the typed report about Grace Deroy, understanding a little more about her home and family. Then he came across a photo of Grace, younger this time, grinning up at an athletic young man. His dapper suit and shiny Oxfords told of elegance and breeding.

Jack frowned at the picture and looked closer. "I know this face."

"That's Andrew Hastings, otherwise known as the Duke of Clarence," Wilson replied. "Although he wasn't the duke when that picture was taken in forty, because his father was still alive then."

Jack remembered. He'd seen this guy walking with the King in newsreels several times since Jack had been posted here. Jack couldn't recall all the details, but the guy was some kind of businessman or art dealer as well as having all the privileges of being a member of British nobility.

"His father was openly sympathetic to the Nazi cause before the war." Petrie took up the story. "He was one of the peers to urge negotiation and even capitulation to the Germans. We suspect his son inherited his views when he inherited his land and title. That picture was taken while the couple was at Oxford, when the pair were close."

Jack had been on English soil long enough to understand that "close" was a euphemism. "Can't you just transfer her away if you are suspicious of her?"

Wilson glanced at his white-haired colleague, Petrie.

"Not to put too fine a point on it, but her father is a high-ranking officer in the RAF," Wilson said. "Her brothers are also in the air force. If she is up to something, it may go further than just her, and we don't want her relatives getting wind of our suspicions."

"They want to embed you in the mapmaking facility, Jack." The lieutenant colonel came to the point. "You'll work there, just as you do here, but your real job will be to get close to her and work out if she is the traitor."

Hopefully, the lieutenant colonel wasn't using the same euphemism as the Brit.

"With respect, sir, isn't there someone else? A surveyor or engineer, even someone with a little more experience in espionage?" That was a much more acceptable question to ask aloud than some of the others firing through his brain. Ones like, *Is this really how we plan to defeat the Nazis? With harebrained schemes?*

His CO shrugged. "I already told them that and suggested several other candidates, but they seem to think that you are the kind of guy she might go for, which will make things go faster. They think she'll open up to you, especially if you get *close*."

He did not like where this was going. Not one bit. He scrambled for another excuse, one that Lewis could appreciate. "Doesn't the Air Ministry hate us? Resent us for having the firepower but not being under their command? What makes you think they'll just let me in?"

"They'll do what I tell them to do." Petrie's tone left Jack in no doubt of his power to pull strings behind the scenes.

"I'm sorry, but you've chosen the wrong man for the job." Jack closed the file and pushed it back across the desk.

"We aren't ordering you to seduce the girl." Wilson was backpedaling. "Although, you have permission to try."

Jack hoped his stone-faced expression told Wilson how he felt about that. He doubted he could help with such a scheme. Since his wife had died, he was out of practice when it came to romance. She was the only woman who'd ever fallen for his charm anyway. Even then, they'd both been so bashful on their wedding night. He was literally the opposite of a Casanova.

Not that he would say that here.

"Your CO tells us that you have deeply held religious convictions. They might help you tease out some of the contradictions in her character."

Jack ignored the pang of guilt that description caused.

"Your work here will help you in your day-to-day job there, and you already know the whole mapmaking process. You understand the technical side of the work there. You are a unique combination, Lieutenant."

Jack tried objecting in a new way. "My father was the surveyor. He ran the mapmaking business, not me. Are you telling me there isn't anybody else in the US Army with more qualifications—one of the navigators maybe—who could do this job?"

"We want you, Lieutenant Marsden." Petrie's uncompromising stare skewered Jack.

He had no way out. "I don't have a choice, do I?"

Everyone else in the room, including Alvin, shook their heads.

"You'll be serving your country, Marsden. And there are worse ways to do it." The lieutenant colonel looked toward the door. Jack nodded, said his farewells, and pivoted toward the exit, hoping his grimace remained private.

"I'll be in touch with more about the specifics next week," Wilson said as Jack left.

Once outside, Jack turned on Alvin. "How could you do that to me, Alvin?"

"Do what?" Alvin feigned innocence too well.

"You were part of an ambush!"

"C'mon, Jack. Live a little. An English country house. A pretty girl. It's not every day you get orders like that! And did you see her, Jack?"

Alvin's whistle left Jack in no doubt what he thought about the picture of Grace Deroy, but Jack's own stomach churned. How could he possibly be the right man for a job like this? Besides, the ring on his finger reminded him of his promise to his wife. Not many men wore a wedding ring, but he had been delighted to accept the gift. He happily weathered the jokes about being shackled to her—because he was, heart and soul.

"You aren't cheating on anyone," Alvin said.

Jack didn't even know he'd been playing with the thin gold band on his left hand. He changed his tone to playful to shake Alvin off.

"I'm just disturbed this is the Allied plan to bring down a Nazi stooge, maybe even a whole ring of them. It relies on me, a widowed ex-doctor and definitely not a spy, whose sole romantic interest includes one woman, 'getting close' to someone who may or may not already have the Duke of Clarence as a lover."

He paused so that Alvin understood he thought the whole thing was incomprehensibly foolish. "What could possibly go wrong?"

———•◆∞◇———

'Bartondale'
Lincolnshire, England

Grace Deroy straightened her blue Women's Auxiliary Air Force uniform jacket before rapping her knuckles on the door. The irony of doing this was never lost on her. The room she was about to enter had been, until a few months ago, her bedroom. Now it was the office of Group Captain Richard Carter. Something he never failed to mention whenever she was called in.

"Enter."

She took a deep, fortifying breath, clutching the file in her hand tighter to remind herself to take an indifferent attitude to whatever she was about to see, and opened the door.

Group Captain Carter sat ramrod straight at his desk. In his forties, the years had not diminished his natural good looks. If anything, the smattering of salt and pepper in his hair increased them. But the smile she once thought friendly now made her skin crawl.

Carter had the bearing of a man in the military all his life. She wasn't intimidated by that, as some were. However, the way his eyes followed her put her on edge.

"I have the files you asked for, sir." She approached his desk and handed them over.

"Always sorry to have to ask you into this room, Grace. I know it used to be your private quarters once."

There it was. Hopefully, that would be the only reference to her bedroom and they could get on with the meeting.

Once her family's estate had been requisitioned by the Air Ministry, it had taken two weeks for the invasion of her home to begin. The whole thing felt like the RAF were conducting their own blitzkrieg on her family.

"Isn't it enough that I have to give up my husband and children for this war? Now they want to take my home too?" Her mother had moaned in her overdramatic way when she'd heard the news. No one had listened. Her father, stoic as usual, had helped Grace coordinate the whole process of relocating.

For Grace, having to give up her bedroom to a CO who made her skin crawl was a small price to pay when entire neighborhoods had been bombed to oblivion. She should bear her lot.

"Will that be all, sir?"

Carter looked up from the files, his brow still furrowed. "Well, there's one more thing."

She tried to smile serenely and not let on that she was holding her breath. In the short weeks she had worked with him, there had been several "one more things." *Can you help straighten my tie?* As if a man in the military for over two decades couldn't do that himself! *Would you be able to work with me over supper tonight?* As if it were appropriate for a man of his rank to ask such a thing of a young woman in her position! Luckily, endless etiquette lessons from her mother gave her the tools to politely and firmly put him in his place. From what she understood, not every girl in this building was able to.

"Sir?"

"We are expecting a liaison officer from the US Army to join us in the next few days."

"An American? Here?" Were they going to overrun her home now too?

"Yes. I'm afraid it's part of an agreement to share information to speed things up over Europe. I was hoping you could show him around, make him feel at home." He looked her up and down. "I'm sure you are the right person to give him the best impression of the place."

Grace fought against a shudder of disgust. "Of course, sir."

She turned to leave. His gaze followed her out of the room, attached, she was sure, to her backside. His usual habit.

Once the door was safely closed, she made her way down the stairs to her father's study. Not a study, she reminded herself as her hand caressed the banister. The library, as the new plaque on the door announced.

She glanced at the drawing room, now called Room Six, as she passed, trying to recall the happy memories the room held for her. Laughing with her brothers, watching her mother sewing in the sunlight, seeing a dear friend fall in love at last year's Christmas party. Cramming as many friends as she could into the room for the same friend's wedding breakfast and toasting with contraband French champagne. She tried to hold these things in her heart.

In the library, four functional desks with sturdy typewriters had replaced her family's ornate and antique furniture. They banged, clattered, and pinged under the hands of the other women who worked with Grace.

"All clear?" Susie Morton asked from the desk to Grace's left as she sat down. It was the code the girls used to check on each other when they returned from seeing the group captain.

"All clear." Grace nodded.

Before Broughton become Bartondale, this room had been little more than a hallway that led into her father's mighty book room. Now it was the place where all requests for information were processed. She envied the artists who worked in the drawing room, next to full-height windows. But Grace and the girls here simply didn't need the same quality of light to do their cataloging, filing, and tracking of the requests.

It took four of them—another WAAF corporal like Grace and two civilian girls—to manage the work of retrieving the reference materials from the extensive catalog and redistributing them around Bartondale. Some materials were kept in a room off their office, but others were stored in the bedrooms at the end of the hall upstairs. Often they reached their daily quota of exercise simply by running about between rooms to fetch and deliver the required documents.

Grace missed having a room to herself to work in, as she had in her previous job when she'd worked in the Map Room of a nearby Bomber Command airfield. The airmen had called her their "Map Queen" because she'd ruled the library of maps required to mount the offensive against the Germans. But she had requested this transfer, determined to take care of her family's home.

She carefully avoided talk of the changes when she wrote to her mother, who'd always blanched at the sight of women in uniform in her home. Lady Elaine Deroy could stand military men in her house, but she had insisted Grace and her friends discard their WAAF uniforms and dress properly for dinner when they visited.

The thought of her mother flying through the room and insisting all the girls change into something more refined made her hold in a smile. How her new friends would love to swan about in elegant dresses here! Should she tell them they were about to add their first American to their ranks? She decided not. They would probably all go giddy. As it was, Grace herself could barely concentrate.

She sighed, hesitating over her work, contemplating another change for her beloved home. Broughton—no, Bartondale—had seen so many changes over the past few months that this one shouldn't matter. And yet it did. Because every change to her home—even if it was just adding another staff member she had to give a tour to—felt personal.

Deeply personal.

And she didn't like it. Not one bit.

CHAPTER TWO

28 June 1943

"I've brought your tea, miss."

Grace slowly opened her eyes at the clink and shuffle of Sarah setting the tea tray down. She came face to face with a full pot of tea and jammy toast as Sarah threw open the curtains so the summer sun could stream in.

"Too bright." Grace turned over, moaning under the covers, almost spilling the tray.

"You're running late, miss."

Grace groaned and sat up, reaching blindly for the tea Sarah poured while Grace's eyes adjusted to the light.

"I was reading until late." She yawned, sipping the strong black brew and letting it bring her to life. "Do you think they'll miss me if I don't show up to work?"

"You say that every morning, miss, and you always go in."

"Hmpf. You know me too well, Sarah."

When her mother had retreated to the seaside, the staff who could gain security clearances stayed on to meet the needs of the new workers at the big house. Grace had arranged the new jobs for as many as she could personally. Sarah, who'd worked with her family for ten years, had taken up the role of live-in housekeeper for Grace.

Not that a housekeeper was strictly necessary for a place this size. Family history said this simple stone cottage, with a sitting room and kitchen downstairs and two cozy bedrooms above, was built sometime in the eighteenth century for the master of the house's valet. But Grace didn't mind how humble it was when Sarah made it such a lovely home.

Not many single women in the WAAF had their own servant. But Sarah happily took care of all the cooking, cleaning, and laundry while Grace worked long hours at Bartondale. Not that Sarah would call it that if she could help it. Her loyalty to Grace's family meant she couldn't bring herself to call it anything other than Broughton. Grace could change the name easily enough but not the feeling of responsibility she held for the house, even after she'd overseen the erasure of her family's history from every nook and cranny.

Sarah also took care of Olive, the precocious eight-year-old evacuee Grace's family had accepted at the beginning of the war. Olive was a full-time job in herself, one that Grace was glad to hand over to Sarah while she was at work. When Grace had lived in the big house with her mother and father, the decision to house an evacuee from London had been simple. They had plenty of room and many families in London's East End had none, thanks to the Luftwaffe. Grace had collected Olive and her single dusty suitcase from the railway station. She had hoped her mother would so enjoy having the child as a companion that they might invite a few more children to live with them. Olive, however, proved too precocious for Lady Deroy's nerves.

Hearty, healthy, and thoroughly enlivened by the country air, Olive lived to make trouble. She drove Grace crazy with make-believe games about pirates and seafarers. Olive's family had written regularly at first, but when Lady Deroy had relocated to the seaside, the letters had abruptly stopped. Not wanting to add to her mother's distress, or Olive's for that matter, Grace had kept Olive with her when the living arrangements changed.

Together the three of them—Grace, Olive, and Sarah—made an unusual trio.

"Time to get a wriggle on, miss."

The tea took effect. "How late am I exactly?"

"It's already gone half past eight, miss."

"Blast! I forgot! The American!"

Grace's brain slipped into gear and was off at a flying pace. She raced around the room, peeling off nightwear and slipping into her WAAF uniform, leaving a trail of clothing behind her. Anticipating this, Sarah followed behind, picking up the pieces as they dropped. Since they lived so close to the main house, Grace probably still had plenty of time to make it out of the little stand of trees that concealed their cottage and up the long drive before her day officially began. However, she didn't want to be late to meet her guest.

"Where's Olive this morning?" Grace called from in front of the mirror as she pinned her hair above her collar.

"Gone into the village to use her charm on the butcher."

Mr. Filby had a soft spot for the little girl. When Sarah had realized his portions were more generous whenever she sent the child to fetch the order, she'd made it Olive's regular job.

"Tell her I expect to see her times tables completed and on my dressing table when I get home."

They heard the kitchen door open, then slam closed. Olive. She could not shut a door quietly to save herself.

"Never mind. I'll get the gossip before I go." Grace grabbed her toast off the tray and took a hurried bite, then barreled down the stairs two at a time, in the way her mother had always said was unladylike.

"What news from the high seas?" Grace leaned into the girl's perpetual fantasy that she was a pirate captain. She had a good ear for gossip, and people were often unguarded in front of someone they considered to be an ignorant child. Often Olive would learn more in the queue listening to a conversation than any ordinary person would participating in it.

Olive reeled off the usual list of rumors she'd heard while Sarah came down with Grace's breakfast dishes.

"Mrs. Johnston has an *American* staying with her." Olive added special significance to *American*. She always reported things exactly as she heard them. "She says he's too young for her, but she thinks he might be right for Nancy Filby!"

Grace could well imagine the machinations in Julia Johnston's mind and the lengths she would go to once she decided to set up the butcher's daughter with an unsuspecting GI.

"Anything else?"

Olive shook her head.

"Good. I'm late to deal with an American of my own. I'll tell you how it goes tonight." Grace waved toward Sarah. "Thank you for getting me out the door, Sarah!" At the doorway, Grace turned back: "And, Olive, I want to see your times tables when I get home!"

Olive's groan followed Grace's fast pace up the garden path toward the big house.

——————◦◦◦◦

Jack didn't think his experience as a doctor-turned-intelligence-officer would qualify him in any way for a career in espionage. He was wrong. A year of dealing with patients as an intern at Springfield General Hospital was the perfect practice for dealing with his new landlady. In Mrs. Julia Johnston's delight at having a fascinating American in her house, she forgot to leave the doorway of his tiny upstairs bedroom when she showed him up to it. Jack's ability to keep a benign expression, nod politely, and gently suggest her time was up came in handy.

Perhaps I can do this job after all.

"Much better to have an American than a WAAF here," she said as she was leaving.

"Oh, why's that, Mrs. Johnston?"

"It's just lovely to have a single man here. For the village, I mean." Then she flounced back down the stairs.

Jack almost protested. He had removed his wedding band before he'd left Buckinghamshire. He should have known it would set every village matchmaker worth their salt onto him. It had been like that before he'd met Dorothy too. All the gossips in his town and every old lady at church had tried to set him up with their daughter, goddaughter, niece, or sister. Until Dorothy Delaney walked into his father's store, looking like sunshine after a rainy day. Then the shoe had been on the other foot, and he hadn't rested until he'd secured an introduction.

Since the day he'd met with Lewis and the MI5 men, he'd had several more briefings from the English and American sides. Both had offered him crash courses on how to get the information he needed without giving the game away—tell the truth when you can and only lie when you absolutely have to.

That was what he did at breakfast this morning when Mrs. Johnston peppered him with questions to double-check the facts he gave her yesterday.

Yes, he enjoyed his work in the army.

No, he couldn't say what his work was at the big house.

Yes, he was a widower. No, he wasn't attached to another woman. (She was keen to clarify the facts around that point.)

Yes, he was born in Kansas City.

No, that wasn't the same place as in the Wizard of Oz. He hated the quirk of fate that meant every Briton he came into contact with inevitably mentioned his dead wife by name whenever he told them where he was from.

The toot of a car horn interrupted the Trial by Breakfast. Jack escaped to the car waiting to take him to his first day at Bartondale. He'd walk or cycle normally, but Group Captain Carter had insisted on sending a car for his first day.

The driver, an older man in tidy civilian clothing, introduced himself as he held the door open for Jack. "I'm Martin, sir."

Jack warmed to him immediately. Not just because of the man's kind manner and easy demeanor. Jack suspected a chatty civilian driver could prove useful, especially one who had worked at the house since he was a child, as this man had.

"You're not military then?" Jack asked.

"That's the beauty of this new arrangement. I lied about my age during the first war but barely saw any action before my lungs gave out. No one would have me for this war, so I stayed with the family. Thought I was going to have to find a new position, until Miss Grace arranged for the staff to keep their jobs. So I'm serving the military without being in it."

"That was nice of her." Or a clever idea to keep her network of trusted accomplices close by.

After deciding he had no other choice but to do his job diligently, Jack studied the dossier about the Deroy family. Snippets of text ran through his mind, like study notes during a final exam.

The Deroy family is one of the richest in Lincolnshire, with a name that stretches back as far as the Battle of Hastings. . . . The surname is derived from the French for "of the king."

Last night he had spent several hours studying the titles and ranks of the British upper classes, trying to understand where the titled Sir Henry Deroy and his children sat in the order of precedence. It bamboozled him. After taking an aspirin for his headache, he'd concluded that, as a baronet, Henry Deroy was somewhere toward the bottom of the aristocracy. Jack still had to address him as *Sir* and his wife as *Lady*. His title would pass to Grace's older brother, Peter, when he died. But for now Jack wasn't to use a title for Grace or her brothers. That kind of courtesy title was only used for the older children of dukes, earls, and marquesses.

Whatever they were.

"Is the family close?" It wouldn't hurt to do some primary research of his own.

"I'd say so. Lady Deroy can be a bit strange at times, but she is

French, so I suppose she can't help it."

"Suppose not." Jack concealed a smile.

"Are you married, sir?"

"Widower."

"Ah, well. No doubt Mrs. Johnston will try to fix that during your stay." Martin grinned at him in the rearview mirror. "This is it."

They turned off the main road and entered the property through gates that, Jack suspected, would have once been made of wrought iron if the whole country's supply hadn't been removed and melted down for armaments. Jack absorbed the view as Martin drove along a picturesque lane lined with overhanging trees, before the roadway opened into a formal drive and revealed the house in all its grand symmetry.

Jack gave a long, low whistle, trying not to be overawed. The Deroys must be even richer than he'd imagined after reading the dossier. And with money came power. No wonder Wilson and his cronies were concerned about a plot within the family.

"I've driven with Lady Deroy enough to be able to tell you the particulars that she gives about it," Martin said. "It was built during the Reformation but before the Baroque influence truly caught on. The family employed the finest builders and used the best local stone. We've always had lots of visitors interested in the place."

"Good to know." Jack nodded. "Who's that?"

A woman in uniform ran along a path toward the big house, with athleticism and ease despite the way her clothing must have restricted her. She was heading for the drive, looking as though she expected to run along it. She paused when she saw the car, long enough for Jack to see the rosy glow across cheeks he had studied in the dossier.

Grace Deroy.

Martin slowed the car to a stop in front of an armed checkpoint and greeted the guard with a friendly grin. Then he leaned across the passenger seat and awkwardly wound down the window. "Miss Deroy, can I offer you a lift to the big house?"

"Oh, thank you, Martin." Breathless, she opened the front passenger door and hurled herself into the car. "I'm late, and I have to meet this new attaché before I start. It's thrown out my whole morning. Oh!" She exclaimed when she saw Jack.

"Your new American attaché, you mean? Pleased to meet you. I'm Jack Marsden." He stretched out a hand to her.

"Hullo, Lieutenant. I'm afraid you've caught me out." She matched his smile in an endearing way that made his grin even broader.

As she reached for his hand, the morning sun filtered through the summer leaves of the avenue, casting a golden light over her face. Her skin already glowed with vitality from her run, but the sunlight dancing on her honey-colored hair made her radiant.

Jack's breath caught in his throat. Not very professional for someone employed as a spy. If he weren't worried she could be an evil genius planted by the Nazis to sabotage the Allies' work, he would be in trouble.

Big trouble.

CHAPTER THREE

"Actually, the place is quite easy to understand. King Charles and his cronies liked their symmetry, so all you have to remember is anything to do with mapmaking is on the right as you walk in. The artists need the best light, so they have the rooms with the best windows. Interpretation and analysis are on the left, including you and the other checkers. The bigwigs are all upstairs." Grace summed up the tour she'd just given the new American liaison officer.

"I'm sure I'll get used to it." The lieutenant glanced around the room, as though determining the fastest route out.

He was a strange one. He'd barely strung a sentence together all morning, hardly looking at her and forcing her to do all the heavy lifting in the conversation. Although, when he did speak, the warmth of his accent sounded friendly, and so different to the clipped quality of her own.

"I'm in the library, and we're basically shut away in the cupboard under the stairs." She grinned, but her usual charm must have deserted her, because he looked terrified. He went to speak but seemed to think better of it. Getting words out of him was like prying water out of a stone. A pity, because he wasn't bad looking.

She endured the awkward pause. "Do you have any questions, Lleutenant?"

"No. Your tour was wonderful." He sounded earnest, then looked annoyed at himself for having done so.

Even though his sandy-colored hair was cut in the military-style so many GIs wore, it suited him. She suspected he was older than many of the US servicemen in England. The tiny lines forming at the corners of his dark-blue eyes told her as much, as did his straight, confident posture. No signs of gangly-ness at all.

Yes, he would be quite a catch . . . if he could just form words.

"Right, well. You'll be working through here." She led him into what she knew was once a sitting area, decorated with yellow wallpaper her mother had insisted be custom made for the space. It was now furnished with three desks, one of which held the stereoscope contraption used to inspect aerial photographs.

"Lieutenant Charles Worthington. This is Lieutenant Marsden from the US Army."

She was sorry to have to hand him over to Worthington, who was, quite frankly, a pig. With blond hair and a crooked nose, he had the face of a man who'd played one too many rugby games. He made some of the girls here all giggly, but she disliked the way he walked around her house like he owned it.

"I'll be in the library—"

"Under the stairs, right?"

Now the lieutenant smiled, like he was relieved to be getting rid of her. She matched the smile with her own polite one.

"If you need me for anything, I'm at your disposal, Lieutenant."

"Does that go for all of us, luv?" Worthington called after her when she turned to leave.

Grace ignored the look of shock followed by apology that passed over Marsden's face at the other man's rude comment. She was used to fighting this battle. "Don't be a beast, Worthington," she said over her shoulder as she headed toward the door. "Besides,

I wouldn't touch you with a ten-foot pole." She slammed the door on the way out.

When she returned to her desk, Charlotte Evans was the first to ask about the new man in their midst.

"Well? Tell us everything!" Charlotte demanded from her desk next to Grace.

Susie and Betsy Cartwright leapt from their desks and crowded around, eager to hear Grace describe the American.

"Is he as much of a dish as they say?" Susie asked.

"He's all right, I suppose. Nothing striking," Grace said. "He's quiet and a bit older than us, I think."

Charlotte sighed dreamily, leaning her head on her hand and accidentally striking the space bar on her typewriter with her elbow. "Oh blast!"

"The all-important question is, is he single?" Betsy leaned on Grace's desk, one hand on either side of her typewriter.

Grace could sense the girls holding their breath. She'd predicted this conversation and had made a point to notice the light line on his tanned left ring finger, where a ring might once have been. "I think he might have worn a ring once, so make of that what you will."

"A widower!" Betsy said. "How tragic!"

"Maybe he's a divorcé." Susie's arguments were ever pragmatic.

"Maybe he's a hopeless philanderer who had a ring but took it off as soon as he saw Grace so she would fall helplessly into his arms." Charlotte, the youngest of them, also had the best imagination. Her speculation sent them into a fit of giggles.

"If this is gossip, I want in!" Margot Monteroy, one of the artists from Room Six, where the maps were drawn up, strode into the library and joined the conversation. Her loose-fitting civilian clothing gave her a bohemian appearance that contrasted with the many military uniforms, but her garments were entirely impractical for her job. She always had paint on her cuffs or in her carelessly tied hair, which made her seem like absentmindedness personified. Grace found she couldn't ever be annoyed at Margot for long.

"Well, like most things here, Margot, it's need to know. We could tell you, but—"

"Let me guess. You'd have to shoot me?"

The others dispersed back to their desks as Grace got to work on Margot's request.

"What am I doing?" Jack had spent half the night mulling over his interactions with Grace, until he threw off the covers to pace his room.

How had the lieutenant colonel described him? Urbane and intelligent? Not today when Grace Deroy showed him through Bartondale.

He wished he could say that such a thing had never happened before.

But that was the problem.

It had. With Dotty. His wife.

When he'd tumbled head first in love the moment he'd seen her. No other woman before or since had turned him into such a monosyllabic fool, until Grace Deroy climbed into that car.

He should have protested harder that day in the lieutenant colonel's office when Wilson and Petrie had suggested this espionage project. He just wasn't a spy, and all the briefings and dossiers in the world couldn't turn him into something he was not. But he was here now. The orders were signed. He had no choice.

So he dug his notepad out from underneath the false bottom of his suitcase. Wilson had given that luggage to Jack as a precaution, saying he could hide any notes or evidence in there. He also stressed that Jack should write his notes in code in case his work was discovered. Both decrees reinforced the madcap nature of his task. Alvin called it a dream assignment, but it was a nightmare as far as Jack was concerned.

"And don't be afraid to get close," Wilson had said during the briefing. He'd stressed several times that national security and Allied victory were at stake. The pressure of that felt worse than when Jack had a patient on the operating table. Not that he'd done that since joining the army.

In his four years of service, when he'd managed to reinvent himself as a competent photographic intelligence officer instead of a doctor, he hadn't had a romantic thought about another woman. Never had his head turned. Never even dared to picture himself married again. Until Grace Deroy exploded open something inside of him that had been safely locked since Dotty died. Of all the compromises he'd figured he might make as part of joining the army, this was not one of them.

Once, he'd believed that God had cast a pool of golden light over Dotty the first time he'd seen her, as a sign she was meant for him. That was when he was young and fervent, a faithful disciple praying unceasingly and seeing signs in everything. But he hadn't so much as uttered a prayer since the night Dotty had died. What was the point? God had ignored him when he'd prayed the most ardent and earnest prayer of his entire life. And so he and God were in a silent stalemate. Or so he'd thought.

Jack flung himself back on the bed and opened the notebook. Why couldn't this have happened with a social acquaintance from whom he could turn the other way and run a mile? Or one of the women at RAF Medmenham, where he could hide behind Alvin? Why did this have to happen now, when he was meant to be playing the spy?

He forced himself to relive the entire exchange with Grace, several times. Each time he tried to focus less on his own embarrassing monosyllabic conduct and the strange looks she'd given him as a consequence. Instead, he wrote down what he had learned about her.

Goldilocks. He christened her in his notoriously bad handwriting, a reference to the way the sun had glinted off her hair when he'd first seen her. He shook his head to remove that image from his mind. But it wouldn't budge. She was much more attractive in person than in any of the files he'd been given. About his height, with a strong, athletic figure. Lots of British women had pale, wan complexions after hard years of war. But not Grace. Especially after her cheeks had been flushed with the exertion of running up the path.

He groaned, pushing his pen across the paper, forcing himself to concentrate as he wrote *clever* underneath her code name. He'd enjoyed her witty recount of the history of Bartondale, even if he couldn't formulate questions. She'd done her best not to sound wistful when she'd mentioned the former function of each room. Each entertaining story had been followed by her pointing out something dull, like the typing pool or storerooms, but the pride in her voice as she spoke about the building's connection to her family was unmistakable.

Well liked.

He put a line through his second point after a bit of reflection. Not everyone was happy with her. Worthington called her a "bitter hag"—but that was after she'd put him in his place for his offensive remarks, so that might not be an unbiased opinion. Jack liked the way she'd shut him down.

She took jibes from others too. Subtle ones about her being the lady of the manor or taking too much care over The System she had put in place to keep track of the files checked out of the library.

The System?

He underlined the words, feeling another twinge of guilt. What would his father think if he could see him now? Cartography was his father's vocation, not Jack's. Before he'd died, he'd done his best to equip Jack for the family mapmaking business. But neither the surveying nor the store was enough. Jack had preferred the hospital. His father had eventually relinquished him to medical school, swelling with pride at the fact his son had earned a scholarship. He'd been devastated when Jack had joined the army without even mentioning that he'd completed a medical degree.

"Enough."

He snapped the notebook shut and readied for the workday ahead. As well as having half his mind consumed with Grace Deroy, he also had to learn more about the photographic work from Worthington. So he'd need extra coffee to assist his concentration and make up for his lack of sleep.

The man in the mirror looked back at him like he was a fool as he shaved. Out of nowhere, a cold breeze tickled his neck, and his hand slipped, cutting himself under his jaw. Just a nick, but it was an unsettling reminder of Dorothy's gentle hands when she'd shaved him. Guilt surged through him, resolving itself in a ball of dread in his gut.

At breakfast, he couldn't eat, but Mrs. Johnston's gossip about the Deroy family meant that at least he didn't need to talk.

"They've always been a bit high and mighty for me," Mrs. Johnston said as she placed the coffee she had made in front of him. "Sir Henry brought the lady of the house back from the last war, and the twins followed *very* quickly afterward."

"Is Grace a twin?" He took a sip of coffee, forcing himself to swallow the poorly made brew under Mrs. Johnston's gaze.

"Yes. Peter is her twin brother. He's a pilot down south. Fighters." She paused, perhaps waiting for his verdict on the coffee. "You've taken a liking to her, have you?"

"Just interested in the family. Great coffee, Mrs. Johnston."

She beamed at the compliment and offered up more hearsay, as he'd hoped she would.

"I'll warn you not to get your hopes set on any of the Deroys. They are a proud family. Too proud for their own good, if you ask me. Lady Deroy will expect her only daughter to marry someone with a title."

"Thanks for the warning, Mrs. Johnston."

"Nancy! How lovely to see you!" Mrs. Johnston looked to someone over his shoulder.

A young woman with straw-colored hair and a decent sprinkle

of freckles stood at Mrs. Johnston's back door. One hand fiddled with the buttons on her pretty floral dress, while the other clutched a parcel.

"Mum wanted me to bring your order over." She spoke to Mrs. Johnston but was looking at Jack.

"Well, come in and meet my guest. Lieutenant Marsden, this is Nancy Filby."

A familiar feeling crept over him. The kind that came when a well-meaning aunt introduced him to her single niece. He glanced at his watch. "I should get going." He still had plenty of time to get to Bartondale on the bicycle provided at the end of yesterday, but neither of them knew that. "Thank you for breakfast, ma'am. Nice to meet you, Nancy."

Relieved that his charm and ability to make conversation hadn't gone completely AWOL, he collected his bicycle from near the front door and set off to Bartondale, determined to find out more about Grace and get out of this ridiculous circumstance as soon as possible.

CHAPTER FOUR

1 July 1943

W‌hen Grace arrived home from work at the big house, she saw her little brother, Teddy, facing a cunning foe at the back of her cottage. Olive saw the whole garden as her own make-believe version of the high seas and had convinced Teddy to play swords with her. Grace watched them play from the kitchen window, hoping it was doing Teddy good. He'd grown so serious since joining RAF Bomber Command.

"Olive mounted a surprise attack when Mr. Edward arrived." Sarah grinned as she arranged tea and biscuits on a tray beside Grace. "I think she pressed him into serving under her pirate flag."

"Well, Olive can be very convincing."

"En garde!" Teddy held out a wooden sword fashioned from two sticks. A long one made up the blade and handle, and a shorter one was laid across it to serve as the hilt. The two pieces were tied together with kitchen string that Olive had no doubt swiped from Sarah's stash.

"Pirates don't say that, Teddy." Olive admonished him through narrowed eyes.

"Well, what do they say, oh Pirate Captain?" Teddy kept his makeshift blade high to ward off attack by his tiny but passionate aggressor.

"They say . . . Shiver. Me. Timbers." With each word Olive lunged with her weapon.

He blocked her until the final blow, when she stabbed her sword under his arm. He feigned a painful, gurgling death against the wall of the greenhouse, which she relished to watch, eyes gleaming.

"You've been reading too much Robert Louis Stevenson, Olive!" Grace called out as she came from the house.

Sarah followed her, carrying the tea tray. Teddy struggled to his feet and dusted the grass off his uniform before greeting Grace with a friendly kiss on her cheek. He flung himself down on the wicker sofa nestled under a magnolia tree.

"Come on, Grace. We used to have grand escapades once! Where's your sense of adventure gone?"

Teddy winked at Olive, who grinned back through a mouthful of scone that she had grabbed from the tea tray when Sarah rested it on the table. He swiped one too. Good, he needed more meat on his bones. He'd grown skinny since joining the air force.

Grace poured the tea and offered Teddy a cup, settling down on the sofa next to him.

"Are you staying with us?" She meant it as an invitation as much as an assurance that if he ever needed a place to stay, he had one with them. She offered him another scone.

"No, heading to London for my six days, but I missed the old place and wanted to take a look around."

"You won't get close to the house, I'm afraid. There's heavy security at the gate. But when we shut ourselves off down here, we can almost pretend that the Air Ministry isn't there."

"You're lying, aren't you? You can't really be happy working in that place, with strangers overwriting memories of the things you hold most dear."

Was that how he felt too? She shrugged. "Everyone has to do

their bit. And at least our house is still intact."

She made side eyes at Olive, hoping Teddy would get the hint and not be insensitive to a child whose home had likely been turned to rubble by German bombs.

Teddy's eyes traveled to Olive and he turned ghostly pale. He stilled and stared at the child for so long that she squirmed under his gaze.

"Teddy, are you all right?" Grace furrow her brow in concern.

Teddy deflected her question. "I was just thinking that the fields don't look like mud anymore now that there's something growing in them."

Grace maintained the polite conversation, all the while worrying about her little brother. Her eyes never left him as she commented airily on the way more and more of the countryside was being turned over to grow food. She should have been more circumspect, because he abruptly stood and made to go.

"Thanks for the tea, Sarah. Good to see you, Grace. And you, my pirate captain." Teddy addressed Olive with a dramatic bow. "I salute you and pledge my undying fealty."

Olive's face said she wasn't quite sure what fealty was but was happy to take it anyway.

Not so fast, little brother.

Grace wouldn't let him rest. She chased him out to the front of the cottage and grabbed him by the elbow, stopping him in his tracks. "Teddy, you'd tell me if anything was wrong, wouldn't you?"

"Of course. Everything's fine, Gracie."

She didn't believe him.

———••◀︎∞◗

The more Jack saw of Bartondale, the more impressed he became at the collection of talent in the building. The Air Ministry employed artists, draughtsmen, architects, graphic designers, even a cartoonist. Civilians and military alike. Anyone with good attention to detail was hired under the strictest code of secrecy. Still, most workers only saw information directly relevant to their own jobs. People like Worthington, who had been promoted through several departments, saw the bigger picture. As a sign of transatlantic cooperation—and probably at the behest of MI5—the group captain gave Worthington permission to speak to Jack about the totality of the work.

"We are just one part of a chain." Worthington paused at the door of what might have once been a dining room but now said *Processing and Interpretation* on the door sign. The men and women working at the dozen desks were collecting and synthesizing information from aerial photographs and intelligence reports. Every head tilted down as they studied their materials and made notes in the books next to them. Jack was familiar with this kind of work from his time at Medmenham.

"They work in pairs or threes on the same location. Any photos, maps, or other materials they need are checked in and out from the library."

"Under the stairs, right?"

"Yes. Run by the former lady of the house herself."

Jack picked up on Worthington's scornful tone. It wasn't like he hid it. "You don't like her?"

"She's a bit high and mighty if you ask me. Very proper and can't take a joke. Likes to lord it over the rest of us."

Jack frowned. "How can she lord anything over anyone from the library under the stairs?"

"Trust me, she manages. The whole filing system is her own devising. She kept us all on our toes trying to learn it in the first place and comes down on anyone like a ton of bricks if you get even the minutest detail wrong."

Jack's frown deepened. If Grace was purposefully leaking information, devising her own filing system would be a neat way to conceal the paper trail.

The overwhelming smell of oil paint hit his nostrils as soon as

Worthington opened the door of the next room. Jack had already heard the rumors about Room Six.

Kooky.

Crackpots.

Mad as hatters.

Eight tilted draughting desks sat drenched in the light that flooded in through large windows. Men and women perched on stools in front of each desk, surrounded by pencils, paints, and other tools of an artist's trade. None of the workers here wore military uniforms. A man in the far corner sported a beret and painting smock, a modern caricature of a Renaissance painter. A woman wore an elegant, draping robe that couldn't have been practical. Definitely a room of artistic types.

"This is where the real magic happens. We cobble together new maps from a combination of the old ones, new intelligence reports, aerial photographs, and the like. Then people like Margot do them up so that they can be read in the dark. See?"

He walked Jack over to where the woman in the draping robe worked with delicate precision and surgeon-steady hands, painting magenta details onto an otherwise simplistic black-and-white map. She didn't flinch at the too-familiar hand Worthington placed briefly on her shoulder. Worthington either had a poor understanding of personal space, or the pair had a more intimate relationship than either were letting on.

"It's the best color for the dim light in the bomber cockpits. She's only painting on the details that will be relevant to the pilots at night—rivers, lakes, mountain heights. They don't need the rest."

He was right. RAF aircrews didn't need their attention drawn to the churches, markets, schools, hospitals, and houses that were under their bombs. The US boys, who flew daylight raids, couldn't assuage their consciences so well, not when they saw every detail lit up by the sun.

Jack didn't see any point in asking the artist what she was working on. He knew from his briefing that she wouldn't even know the name of the place that the map below her hand described. Or at least she shouldn't.

"Our job is to check the maps." Worthington concluded his tour back in their small office. "Since nobody knows what anyone else is doing, the process can be fractured. We reconcile the painted maps with the aerial photography and give the final sign-off that they are accurate. Then they are handed over to dispatch riders, who courier them to Bomber Command HQ, who send them to the air stations."

Jack felt the weight of his job in the tingle that ran down his spine. This was different from interpreting reconnaissance photos. These were the actual maps that guided the pilots in, told the bombardiers where to drop their bombs. A failure from him could have serious consequences, either in the air or on the ground. In a way, lives depended on his accuracy. Not unlike when he'd had a patient on the operating table.

"So where do I start?"

"Not so fast. First I have to teach you the stereoscope. Have you ever used one?"

Jack nodded. A tool of his trade at Medmenham.

"Aren't they absolutely brilliant!" Worthington seemed excited, like a kid wanting to show off a new toy. He handed two aerial reconnaissance photographs to Jack, of the same structure and in the same scale, but one of the pictures must have been taken farther to the south. "These are of the Möhne Dam."

"Before or after?"

"Take a look."

Jack placed the images under the stereoscope, aligning them to get a three-dimensional view. He marked out the dam wall in each with his finger, then looking through the scope, placed the photos in such a way that his view of his fingers lined up through the viewfinder. The photographs now appeared to jump up at him. The buildings had height and seemed to have more detail than when looking at a single photograph.

This was a view of the Ruhr Valley, the heartland of German industry, after the Brits had crippled it. They'd used specially designed bouncing bombs to blow a hole in the massive dam the Nazis used to generate electricity. He'd seen this photo in his work before. His team at Medmenham had written the report that estimated thirteen hundred casualties, not counting the people who might have died as a result of the flooding.

"So we check the final maps against the aerial images?"

"More than that, we reconcile everything. Which means that we have access to something that most others in the building don't—the name of the place in the map."

Jack nodded, feeling the weight of responsibility.

Worthington dropped his tour-guide tone and became serious. "Guard your words while you are here, Marsden. We don't need some loud-mouthed American letting the name of our next target slip."

"Noted." Jack's jaw tightened at Worthington's characterization, but he accepted the warning. "So what's first?"

"You need to go to the library and speak to the lady of the manor about this." Worthington scrawled some numbers on a piece of paper, handing it to Jack with a sarcastic smile. "You, my friend, now get to learn 'The System.' Good luck."

He suppressed a groan. He needed all the luck he could get.

In the library, Grace was nowhere to be seen. But three other young women were falling over themselves to answer his questions. He sure hoped they couldn't smell fear.

"Lieutenant Worthington told me you are the people to explain the filing system to me. I hear one of you ladies devised it."

"That was Grace. But I can help you." A breathy young girl in civilian attire approached with a smile. "I'm Charlotte."

"Jack Marsden, ma'am." He smiled back.

She dissolved into nervous giggles, so a woman in uniform stood and shook his hand. "I'm Susan Morton, but call me Susie—everyone else does. That's Betsy." She indicated the third woman, who waved from her desk. "And I believe you know Grace?"

"We've met, yes." No need to mention his bedtime reading was a dossier all about her.

"The System isn't that difficult, no matter how hard Worthington finds it to grasp. If everyone fills out the right information every time they borrow something or transfer it between rooms, we are able to locate any one of our resources wherever it is in the building in an instant."

"I take it Worthington doesn't do much of the filling out?"

"There are other culprits too. Don't be one of them." Susie gave him a stern look, then grinned. "Here's the lady herself to explain."

"Explain what? Oh hullo, Lieutenant! What brings you here?"

His mouth went dry, and the words that had been on the tip of his tongue vanished. "I was asking about the filing system."

That didn't sound strangled, did it?

"Well, it's better you learn it from us than Worthington!"

"We told him it wasn't hard."

Jack wasn't sure which of the other girls was talking, because he couldn't take his eyes off Grace. He tried to listen and not get distracted by the highlights in her honey hair or the perfectly kissable shape of her mouth. Oh boy. Where did that thought come from?

Get a grip, Jack.

"Do you have any questions?"

He blinked.

Charlotte's giggle floated over his shoulder.

Be suave.

Be flirtatious.

Be something other than mute.

He should ask follow-up questions, should use this as an excuse to somehow get close.

"Thank you, Corporal, for your help." He pivoted to rush out of the room.

He was a terrible spy.

CHAPTER FIVE

4 July 1943

"You look ridiculously happy." Grace sat with her friend, sipping tea and eating Sarah's carrot biscuits in the sitting room of the cottage.

She and Maggie had worked together for two years at a nearby Bomber Command air station, inseparable pals. Now they only had rushed cups of tea on Sunday afternoons after church to share updates on their separate lives. Last winter Maggie had fallen head over heels in love with an Australian pilot. Grace cherished the memory of the drawing room at Broughton, full of happy people at the pair's wedding breakfast, because the next day she'd begun preparations to convert it into offices.

"I am." Maggie still glowed with incandescent newlywed bliss. "Alec got another six days of leave, and we toured Scotland. We had to show our wedding certificate at every bed and breakfast because the landladies wouldn't believe I was married to an Australian. They all thought he was another airman trying to have his wicked way with a nice British girl."

"Which, of course, he was." Grace winked at her.

"We're married, Grace! There's nothing wicked about it." Maggie blushed all the shades of red and changed the subject. "How are things going here, anyway? Any more strange behavior from Our American Friend? Great code name, by the way."

"I think OAF must be incredibly shy. He often comes to the library and looks like he wants to speak with me, but can't quite get the words out." Grace laughed. "It happened three times this week."

"I thought he looked like he wanted to speak with you after church too. Maybe he likes you."

Grace rolled her eyes at Maggie's glinting ones. "You're worse than the girls at work."

Jack was the talk of all the girls in the office too. There was wild speculation about his past. Every day one of them came up with a new theory or tragic story about him. Maggie raised her eyebrow as she took a bite of biscuit.

"Don't you give me that 'I'm married now, so I know everything about men' look, Maggie Thomas!"

Maggie's eyebrow stayed right where it was.

"I suppose he might have a bit of a crush. But it seems unlikely, unless I've dazzled him from afar!" She laughed again. "I can count on my hands the number of conversations we've had."

"You're a beautiful, intelligent, kind woman, Grace. It's not that unlikely." Maggie's look became thoughtful. "You know, it hasn't escaped my notice that you've had a front-row seat to my entire love life. But you've never told me exactly what happened to you at Oxford."

Grace made light of Maggie to avoid having to spill that tightly held secret. Some things you couldn't even tell your best friend. "You know, I don't think that I like Married-Woman Maggie very much." Grace narrowed her eyes. "She's pushy."

"Well, you can't avoid her for much longer."

Grace often pondered telling Maggie about why she left university. But Maggie looked up to her, and Grace couldn't bring herself to reveal just how unworthy she was of Maggie's esteem. Besides, letting her friend in on her secret would mean opening that box inside her that she had nailed shut by starting a new life in the WAAF.

"Not today." Maggie seemed satisfied with Grace's soft response. "For now, just know that I am doing my best to avoid the wrong kind of men."

"How do you know OAF is the wrong kind of man? Wouldn't you have to get more than two words out of him to find that out?"

After Maggie's too-short visit, Grace mulled over her friend's words. How the tables had turned from a year ago, when Maggie's heart was all aflutter and Grace was the one doling out advice. She couldn't bear to have Maggie discover that Grace's own wisdom was born from extreme foolishness.

She could still so easily bring to mind the streets of Oxford and the city's distinctive stone buildings. The thrill of her first class in one of the university's hallowed halls had never left her heart. She'd been bright eyed and eager, ready to be dazzled by the world.

Until she'd met Alexander Blakey.

The Artist.

She closed her eyes and could still see his fine Gallic features, blond hair, and wolfish grin. And his eyes. The deepest brown she'd ever known, but at the same time on fire with energy and possibility.

And sadness, but she hadn't seen that until later.

She'd been infatuated within a second of meeting him. Theirs had been a secret affair, conducted mostly in the bedroom attached to his studio. She should have known better, but the thrill of being with him had made every inch of her feel alive, like electricity coursed through her veins, not blood. But electricity could be dangerous. It had powered his frenzied creativity, but it had hollowed her out. Slowly, without her noticing, until she finally found the strength to leave.

"Enough." She wrenched memories of Alexander Blakey from her head and sighed out a prayer asking God to not let her dwell on that time of her life. When she looked up, Sarah stood in front of her, holding out a steaming teacup.

"That American has been asking questions about you in the

village," Sarah said matter of factly once Grace had collected herself with a sip of tea.

"Not you too, Sarah."

"Julia Johnston is trying to set him up with the butcher's daughter. I'm just saying you'd be doing him a favor if you took the pressure off."

Grace laughed and leaned back on the sofa cushions. "Perhaps I will."

———•◄∞⟩

There could be no denying Julia Johnston in full flight. She had been adamant—he worked too hard and needed to make the most of his days off. He hadn't seen any countryside around the village, and it was such a lovely day. Nancy Filby liked to picnic by the river after church on Sundays. And look, here she was with a picnic basket. What better way to enjoy the sunshine on a day like today? That was how he had been railroaded into walking down to the river with Nancy Filby instead of striking up a conversation with Grace after church.

With all his rehearsing in his head, he'd barely listened to a word the preacher had said. His throat had been dry in the hymns. Grace had sung with gusto and listened attentively to every word of the sermon. Would someone leaking military secrets be able to put on such a convincing display of devotion? He knew the answer. His own displays had been pretty convincing for the past four years, even though his heart felt empty. Far, far away from God.

He'd watched his chances of a conversation slip away as Grace had hurried off after the service on the arm of a friend. So here he was with Nancy Filby. She barely said a word as she led the way along the narrow path by the river. Every time she turned back to look at him, he thought she might speak, but instead she giggled and drew the words back into herself, like she was scared of releasing them. He concluded she was shy, which was probably why she'd needed Mrs. Johnston's help to invite him on a date.

He'd had patients like this once. With them he'd found the best thing was to tell them about himself so they would feel comfortable opening up. Of course, then it had been easy. He had Dorothy to talk about or the baby they were expecting. Somehow, he didn't think it would be appropriate to mention any of those things now. He couldn't talk about work either—not the work he did at Bartondale or his real reason for being there.

He looked around him for inspiration and compared the countryside around them—quiet, apart from the thrum of an aircraft every now and then—to his home.

"What are those flowers?" He pointed out a purple-flowered shrub. "We don't have those back home."

"What's it like?" Three eager words emerged from her mouth before she bobbed her straw-colored head. Then he remembered something that Alvin had told him. Alvin, who was always bragging about his romances with local girls. "I could be from Tiny Town in the state of Backwater and to them it is as exotic as New York City."

Forgive me, God. I'm about to take Alvin's advice on dealing with a woman.

He launched into a detailed description of the two places he knew best: Kansas City, Missouri, where he was born, and Springfield, Illinois, where he once worked. Alvin was right. She listened with rapt attention.

They reached a bend in the river, where Nancy spread out her blanket and set out the small meal she had prepared. Corned beef sandwiches with early tomatoes, carrot cake, and some lemon cordial to drink.

She offered him a sandwich and nibbled away at hers, mouselike, while he kept talking until he had exhausted his supply of facts about Missouri.

"All right, Miss Filby, it's your turn now. I have to eat my lunch."

She dipped her head and brushed a crumb off her cornflower-blue dress.

"What can you tell me about the village? I bet you know a bit.

Everyone has to use the butcher shop, after all."

When she grinned, he saw for the first time what might have been making her keep her mouth shut. She had terrible teeth. Every one of them stuck out at a different angle. He had seen plenty of jagged mouths in his time, but Nancy's was one of the worst. Still, he didn't let on. Keeping a straight face was one of the first things he'd been taught at medical school. If only he could manage to do that with Grace.

Once she warmed up, Nancy was a valuable source of information about the village and its inhabitants. As someone who didn't talk much, she listened well. She retained all the bits of gossip shared in the queue at the butcher shop and gave him the rundown on all the virtues and peccadilloes of the village inhabitants.

She had something on everyone.

The doctor? "A little too fond of the sherry."

The magistrate? "His wife says he snores terribly."

No one escaped. Even Mrs. Abling, who ran the Women's Institute and, according to Nancy, made the best blackberry conserve in the whole of the midlands, had aspersions cast on her good character. Nancy even told him about the time Mrs. Johnston had accidentally set fire to her mother's cat.

"Pebbles is always sneaking in where she shouldn't. She jumped up to explore what was cooking, scorched herself, then caused the soup to go flying. Mrs. Johnston didn't know what had happened until she found a singed cat in the garden! Pebbles still hisses every time she walks into the shop now."

Jack chuckled. "What about the family who lived in Bartondale?" He knew he shouldn't encourage her gossip, but this had suddenly turned into work.

"Sarah Michaels won't hear a bad thing said about them. But that's because she's been with the family since she was my age. My parents think Lady Deroy is as mad as a hatter. She couldn't tell the difference between this war and the last one, so Sir Henry had to ship her off to the seaside to take some rest."

"And their daughter?"

She paused. "Do you like her?"

"I work with her." He was careful to sound casual. "And yes, I like her. She seems like a kind, hardworking person." Hopefully, that was detached enough to encourage information out of Nancy.

"Did you know she was engaged to a duke once?"

Jack stopped chewing his sandwich.

"Or maybe not engaged, but very close. Everyone from the house was abuzz with the news. Said all Lady Deroy could talk about was that her daughter was spending time with royalty or that she expected her to become a duchess any day now."

"Do you know who the man was?"

His fingers itched to jot down what she was saying in his notebook.

"No. It was while she was at university."

"Nothing came of it?"

"I suppose not. Whatever went wrong was sudden, and no one wanted to talk about the fact that she came home from university and never went back."

"Was she brokenhearted?"

"Nobody would say. But the whole village knew that she stayed in her bedroom for months on end, crying all day. Lady Deroy wasn't happy when Grace joined the WAAF. The gardener said they had a terrible row about it."

Gossip about Grace spilled from Nancy's lips. In any other circumstance, he'd want to stop her, but right now this information was too useful. *When it becomes outright slander, I'll get her to stop it.*

"She doesn't come into the village much anymore. People say she thinks herself too good for us. But I think she's just busy. She must work long hours. And my father changed his tune about her earlier this year. Says it was very loyal to stay on when the Air Ministry requisitioned the house."

Loyalty or something else?

"Thank you for a lovely lunch, Miss Filby. It's been very informative," Jack said as they walked back into the village.

He tried to ignore Nancy's crooked grin, shining with an admiration for him he didn't deserve.

CHAPTER SIX

7 July 1943

Cataloging. Alphabetical order.
Having a place for everything.

Those were the things Grace adored.

The numbering system that protected the secrecy of each location that Bartondale dealt with was her own stroke of genius. Not even the artists painting the maps knew the names of the cities they were drawing. For secrecy's sake files, photographs and maps couldn't be labeled *Munich* or *Stuttgart* because it might give the game away. So she replaced names with alphanumeric labels.

Some people railed against having to learn the code for each new resource they borrowed, but it wasn't hard. If people just filled out the logbook every time they moved a file, she could locate any item from the catalog within minutes of it being required, no matter where it was in the building. But today she couldn't.

And there was hell to pay.

Judging from his thunderous expression, the group captain was in a bad mood. He caught her at the bottom of the staircase, declaring that he couldn't find the file he needed. His roaring words bounced off the tile floor and floated through the house so that most of Bartondale was privy to his unwarranted criticism.

She tried to explain, with regard to his rank rather than his manners, that it wouldn't be a problem to locate because of their well-designed system. But the group captain didn't give her a chance to speak. His full-force rant about how the library let the whole country down with its incompetence ricocheted through the halls. Grace set her jaw with steely endurance until he stormed back up the stairs to his office.

"I want that file on my desk by the time I get back from my meeting with Harris at HQ, Deroy! No more excuses!"

The WAAF at the desk in the entryway shot her a sympathetic look as the other staff, who crowded at doorways or leaned over the banister, dispersed back to their jobs. There was nothing for it. She would have to backtrack through the records to discover where it had got to.

She groaned when she opened the register that kept track of all the movements of files in and out of the library. Worthington had checked out that file three days ago. He was the single biggest offender when it came to losing things. It was probably languishing on his desk.

The American stood when she walked into the office. He looked pained and remained mute, but she appreciated the politeness.

"To what do we owe the pleasure, Gracie?" Worthington said.

She fumed. Her brothers could call her Gracie, but no one else was allowed to. Worthington repeatedly ignored her requests that he stop. Reminding herself of her mother's insistence that a woman could catch more bees with honey than with vinegar, she pasted on a smile.

"Do you have D67168 on your desk, Worthington?" Grace asked with all the reserves of sweetness she could muster.

"Why don't you come and take a look for yourself?"

She marched to where he sat, leaning back in his chair, and rifled through the mess strewn across his workspace while he watched on, seemingly amused by her desire simply to do her job.

"Your desk is filthy, Worthington."

"So are you," he said, so only she could hear. "If rumors from the art world are true."

Her breath caught in her throat as her hand froze on a pile of papers at the sudden reminder of something that she'd thought was long past. Her eyes moved up to his smirking face, and heat rose into her cheeks.

He licked his top lip, studying her. Then he raised his voice, likely for Jack's benefit. "Are you finished, Deroy? I need to get back to my work."

The smug look she'd like to slap off his face said Worthington was satisfied with the reaction he'd provoked in her. She took in a breath to retort with an insult for his boorish behavior, but Jack spoke first.

"Cut it out, Worthington. Let her get on with her job."

She spun around. He didn't catch her eye because his gaze was firmly on Worthington, who straightened in his chair at Jack's challenge. She managed a polite smile for the American, horrified he might have overheard. When she turned back to Worthington, she didn't meet his eye. Her attention caught on a brown cardboard folder under a glass of water.

Just what she was after.

She extracted the file. It now sported a circular stain, thanks to Worthington's slobby behavior.

"Just return things next time," she said as she left, keen to exit.

"You okay?" Susie said as Grace sat back down at her desk in the library. "You look pale."

"I'm fine. Worthington just got under my skin."

It was more true than usual. The nasty undercurrent of the comment about rumors bothered her. It could have been a simple expression, designed to unsettle her. But it was quite a specific thing to say. Perhaps he knew something about what she kept hidden in this house.

She shook it off. Worthington couldn't possibly know anything incriminating. He was probably just trying to rankle her, sensing she was vulnerable after Carter's dressing down. It was just like him to go in for the kill on someone who was already wounded.

Grace put the file to the side while she regrouped, still deciding if she should march up the stairs and fling the file on the group captain's desk herself or send one of the others. She sighed. She usually tried to shield the younger girls from him. It would be cowardice not to go herself. But she wasn't about to head upstairs before lunch.

"I will say that I think OAF is a friendly." She told the others about Jack's defense of her over sandwiches in the cafeteria. "He stood up for me just now."

"He's so polite," Betsy said. "It's so lovely to be called ma'am! Blokes where I come from wouldn't call me that."

"He asks a lot of questions about you, Grace," Susie said, with a knowing singsong in her voice.

"Really?" Grace paused mid-sip of tea. This was the third time someone had mentioned this. "He's barely said a word to me directly."

"You intimidate him." Charlotte nodded as wisely as an eighteen-year-old could. "Men don't like that."

"How would you know?" Betsy, who had two years on Charlotte, scoffed.

"*Women's Illustrated*," Charlotte said, as though referring to a sacrosanct and revered volume of knowledge. "Clare Rutherford's advice just last week was not to let a man know that you are his intellectual equal because it hurts his self-esteem."

Susie—the same age as Grace and with the same amount of good sense—shared a look with Grace.

"Someone has to get these silly notions out of your head, Charlotte. This is the twentieth century, for goodness' sake! I've a good mind to march up and invite him out for lunch just to make a point."

"Go on then," Betsy chimed in.

"Yes. Go on, Grace," Susie agreed "We dare you!"

Grace laughed, shaking her head at her friends, before heading up to face the music with Carter.

The group captain wasn't in. Neither was his secretary. Grace entered his office, strode up to his desk, and left the file right in the center of his workspace so he couldn't miss it. She had already updated the register in the library to indicate the file had been returned by Worthington and then checked out again by Carter.

Her eyes fell on a stack of blank notepaper with a black fountain pen sitting on top. Impulsively she took a blank piece of notepaper, uncapped the pen, checked her watch, and wrote *Returned 1400 hours*, then signed her name with a flourish.

She allowed herself a glance around the room, even though she knew the details in the patterned wallpaper by heart. All her beautiful furniture was long gone except for a large, ornate wardrobe that had been too heavy to move. Her throat tightened as she remembered the way she'd cried the day she had to empty it of all her things.

Her fingers itched to open it and see how the Air Ministry was using it now. She'd once hid something precious behind a secret panel and now fought the urge to peek in the door, just to check if it was still safely hidden away from the world. But she had promised herself as she'd secured the panel and handed the room over to the Air Ministry that she would forget all about it. Checking on it now would break that vow—not to mention look suspicious.

She turned on her heel and left the room.

On her way back down the stairs, she passed Worthington and Marsden.

"Safely in the hands of the group captain?" The American paused momentarily even as his colleague kept on course up to the second level.

"Yes. The system is only as good as the people using it." She raised her voice, making sure Worthington would hear.

The giggly lunchtime conversation she'd shared with the girls rang in her ears, making her hope that Jack would say a little more, but he gave an apologetic smile and continued up without another word.

———— ⋈∞⟩

Espionage was a complicated business.

Every two days Jack had to phone in a report from a telephone booth in the village. He would ask the operator for London 692. After that, the conversation would be short and cryptic.

"Good morning. How's the weather where you are?"

He'd say "No changes in the air" if everything was going fine, but "fine" if he had something to report. "There are more clouds than expected" was the line if he needed to meet with someone. He was only to say "sunny" if he was in imminent risk of being discovered. Only the English could develop such an elaborate code involving just weather-related phrases.

Remembering which weather pattern signified which response had confused him at first. Fortunately, years of study to be a doctor, committing the names of bones, body parts, and diseases to memory, meant that he caught on easier than some might. But rather than reassuring him, the codes reinforced the outrageous nature of his role.

If he heard the words "a great season for bird watching" amid the pleasantries, he then had to wait at the bus stop until he saw a man reading a newspaper from the previous day. If either of them said "The ducklings are having a fine time in this weather" and the other responded "Really? I thought they didn't come out until the spring," he knew he could trust the stranger.

Today he didn't need any code words to recognize friend from foe. Wilson Weathers, who'd been at that first meeting with Lewis, was waiting for him at the bus stop. The pair shook hands and strolled to the pub like old friends.

Since morning light streamed in through the windows, they were unlikely to be overheard. To be on the safe side, they chose a table far away from the counter, where the publican stood polishing his beer glasses.

Wilson shot straight to the point. "What have you found out?"

"Nothing really." Jack didn't like to disappoint him but had to report what he'd discovered. Apart from the few who felt Grace was above them, she seemed to be a model officer going about her duty. "A file went missing a few days ago, but that's the only remotely suspicious thing that's happened."

He recounted the fuss. How Grace had found the file on Worthington's desk and returned it to Carter's office with time to spare. "She ended up proving that her system worked."

Wilson considered Jack carefully from under his spectacles. "Have you searched her house?"

"No! Why would I do that?" Alarm made Jack's voice louder, causing the publican to look up at them.

Wilson waited to speak until the man had gone back to his work. "It's part of the job, Lieutenant."

Jack rubbed his jaw. He didn't like this one bit. "I thought I was just here to discover whether or not she was a threat, not ransack her room."

"You're here to find out whether she's hiding something."

That feeling of dread pooled in his stomach again. The one that told him he was in over his head. After he'd had so much trouble actually speaking to her, he'd convinced himself he could do this from a distance.

"You have two weeks, Lieutenant. Be thorough."

CHAPTER SEVEN

12 July 1943

*R*epulsive was the first word Jack used to describe Charles Worthington in his notes.

Jack accepted his invitation to the pub, hopeful a change of scenery might uncover some redeeming features. However, Jack was disappointed. Despite having every possible privilege—family connections, good education, good health—Worthington still complained everything and everyone was out to make his life miserable.

"Take Grace Deroy." He slurred his words after several pints of the Blue Pig's best. "She's poisoned the others in the library against me."

Somehow, buddy, I don't think you need any help to poison people against you. You're doing fine on your own. Jack refrained from speaking the thought aloud, but only just.

Despite making repugnant comments about most of the women they worked with, he seemed to have caught the eye of Margot Monteroy. Worthington didn't flinch when she'd joined them at their corner table and leaned in to give him a kiss on the cheek. In fact, from the goofy grin he wore, Jack guessed the man was smitten.

He could see the appeal to Worthington. Although Margot smelled like Room Six, all paint and turpentine, she had pretty, wide eyes and a smile that made you feel like you were the only man in the room. She used it on Jack as she questioned him about his home, as Brits usually did. When he asked questions of his own, she told him stories about how her art had taken her across the continent. Her presence made time pass quickly, and Jack decided Worthington must have some redeeming features if a creative mind like Margot's was attracted to him.

Jack's sympathy didn't last long. Once they sat in the office the next morning, Worthington was back to his under-breath mutterings and insulting chauvinist comments about the girls from the library.

"Put a sock in it, Worthington." Jack fled the office they shared, tired of sitting through another tirade about how useless Grace's System was.

Apart from that, he didn't have a real reason to leave the room. He loitered near the bottom of the staircase, wondering if it was too early for lunch or if he should walk by the library. He had to make up his mind soon. The woman who staffed a small reception desk at the door was giving him strange looks. He'd just steeled himself to approach Grace's desk when the lady herself appeared on the staircase.

"Lieutenant Marsden." She called out like she was purposefully trying to get his attention.

He spun around, sure he looked like a guilty child. His heart also hammered in his chest when she addressed him directly.

"Would you like to have lunch with me?" she asked when she got to the bottom step. "The sandwiches at the cafeteria barely have any filling, but they are much more enjoyable when eaten outside. And I know the best spots."

Jack gaped like a goldfish for a moment. "I'd like that very much, Corporal."

He hoped the relief that flooded him didn't show.

"You're right on both counts." He swallowed a mouthful of dry bread. "There isn't much else but bread to these sandwiches. And you do know the best spots."

The stone bench in the center of the formal rose garden was surrounded by fragrant flowers blooming in more colors than Jack thought possible. Their delicate perfumes drifted through the air. He couldn't help but take a deep breath in to enjoy the scent.

Why, despite being able to manage any number of erudite conversations on a given day, could he not manage one with Grace? It hadn't been like this with Dorothy. Although, when he'd finally been able to talk with her, he hadn't had to lie through his teeth about his motivations and purposes. He only wished he could be that direct here, especially when she studied him so intently.

"Do I displease you in some way?" Luckily, she was direct enough for the both of them.

"No. Why?"

"You're chatty enough to everyone else, but you always look rather pained whenever you have to talk with me."

He chuckled at her insight. She had seen to the heart of him. In that moment he decided to follow the advice he'd been given in his briefings—tell the truth as much as possible.

"You remind me of someone. Someone I loved very much . . . once. Still do. And so when I see you, there's a battle going on in my head about what I should say."

Mostly true.

"Divorcé or widower?"

"Widower. How did you know?"

"I saw that you used to wear a ring. The girls and I have been trying to guess your story since you arrived."

"I only recently took it off, though it's been four years."

Silence filled the space between them for a few moments.

JENNIFER MISTMORGAN

"Do you want to tell me about her?" Grace offered. "You don't have to, of course, but if it will help, I'm happy to hear."

Tell the truth where possible.

"Well, sure. Although there's not a lot to the story." He paused, looking over the garden as he chose a place to begin. "I was a student, working in my father's store in Kansas City during the holidays. He used to make and sell all sorts of maps and surveying equipment. One December day this gorgeous girl my age walks into the store, looking for a birthday present for her dad. I didn't know her or anything about her, but as soon as I looked into her eyes, it was like the sun broke through the cold December sky and sunlight streamed into the windows of the store. I just knew in that moment that was the woman God meant for me to marry."

"How romantic!" Grace's hazel eyes beamed in a way that shouldn't have sent the warm thrill through him the way it did. Not considering what they were talking about.

"Well, there was still the problem that I didn't know who she was. I couldn't manage, you know, actual words when she was in the store." He laughed at his own foible.

Grace returned the smile, encouraging him on.

"So when she left, I didn't know anything about her except that she was my future wife. I finally found out where she was staying and got someone to introduce us."

"What did you say to her?" She leaned in.

"I came clean about her being my future wife, and she didn't sock me in the nose."

Jack recalled how he'd told Dotty that God had given him a sign that she was the one he was going to marry, so if she didn't mind, he would like to hang around until God showed her the same thing. Fortunately, she didn't mind.

"She agreed to let me write to her when she went home. When she wrote back, I found out how clever she was, and not someone likely to be impressed by a stranger claiming to have a sign from God. She had such a bright mind and a faithful heart. Eventually she agreed to marry me. Her family thought I was a little crazy. Understandably, I think. They said we had to wait until I finished medical school before we could make it official. I wanted to marry her the day I graduated. I would have worn my cap and gown as a wedding suit if she didn't object!"

"You've been to medical school?"

"Fat lot of good it did me." He shouldn't have let that detail slip. If Grace really was a traitor, she might use it against him. But it was too much part of the story. A story which should have ended there, with a happily ever after like in the fairy tales.

Grace waited for him to continue.

"She died giving birth a few days shy of our first wedding anniversary. The child died too."

He couldn't say the words without a rasp in his voice. There was so much to say, and yet that seemed to say it all.

"War was brewing, so I joined up." Better not go into that too much, in case he gave away more specifics than he should. "Long story short, here I am."

Tell the truth, they'd said. He'd sure done that. One big truth.

Eventually, Grace broke the silence, tears in her eyes. "I'm so sorry, Lieutenant."

He breathed in deeply, letting the complex scents of dozens of varieties of rose fill his mind. Trying not to think about Dorothy and what she would say about this stupid caper. Fighting the urge to cry. He was sure successful espionage didn't involve breaking down into tears in front of your target.

Grace gazed out over the garden, probably as a way to give him time to collect himself. Once he had, he studied her delicate profile, the kind that got carved in agate and mounted in a cameo brooch. She couldn't look more different to Dotty, who'd had jet-black hair and plump features. He turned his attention to the countless roses around him and took another deep breath of their perfume. Dotty had loved roses. She'd loved flowers of any kind. Jack used to make a point of bringing them to her once a week, at least.

"I'm sure our marriage was a gift from God. I don't think I'll ever understand why it had to be so short."

"I suppose God gives and He takes away."

"I suppose he does. But knowing that doesn't make it any easier."

———◦∞◦———

"Well, girls." Grace sat down with a pile of papers she had brought down from the group captain's office. "I have some answers about OAF."

Betsy, Charlotte, and Susie all spoke at once.

"Answers?"

"How?"

"No?"

"You didn't?"

Grace waited for them to finish before she continued. "He walked me home yesterday."

She paused for dramatic effect, looking at each expectant face. Her spine had tingled when he'd told the story about his wife. Such a romantic and tragic tale and told in his own raw, faltering words. After their previous halting conversations, it was a lot of information all at once. But the privilege of being the one he trusted with it weighed on her heart. She felt woven into it somehow. After his revelation in the rose garden, Jack had seemed lighter. He'd turned out to be quite affable.

"Well, don't leave us hanging," Betsy said. "What happened?"

"What do you think happened, Betsy? He walked me home. Sarah was there, so we had some tea, and then he left."

"Did he kiss you goodbye?" Charlotte asked dreamily.

"Charlotte, really?" Susie chimed in. "You and I really need to have a chat about all the romantic nonsense you fill you head with!"

Grace laughed. "We talked about his home, mostly, and the people he knew in Missouri."

"Missouri." Charlotte sighed. "So exotic."

Susie shook her head at the younger woman.

Grace didn't tell them how much she'd enjoyed Jack's company. Now that his reticence had vanished, he made a good conversation partner. Clever and lively without being a show-off.

Jack's new confidence around her had relaxed his features too, which made him quite handsome. Once or twice he'd grinned at her in a way that had made warmth bloom through her middle. For the first time since The Artist, she'd felt the twinge of attraction to a man. It wasn't the same instant magnetism as with Alexander, but she still recognized the feeling for what it was.

She remembered how Jack had hesitated before entering the cottage. He was less than an inch taller than her, so she didn't have to tilt her head up to look right into his green-brown eyes. Just as they were about to step over the threshold, she'd caught a tortured kind of look flash through those eyes. Somehow that propriety endeared him to her more. A man who questioned the appropriateness of being alone with her in her home was definitely made of different stuff to The Artist.

She'd reassured him. "I live with my companion, Sarah, and Olive, who"—she'd spotted Olive hiding up a tree over his shoulder—"is our resident pirate." She'd winked.

He'd played along. "A pirate so far inland? That must be a challenge."

"You have no idea."

The memory of him sitting in her favorite armchair, delicately balancing a teacup and glancing around her sitting room like it was an alien planet, made her lips quirk up.

Susie, who'd been watching her carefully for the whole conversation, didn't miss a beat. "So when are you two going on a date?"

Grace bit her lip to contain her smile.

"Please, Susie. It's a little too early for that." Then she couldn't help the grin that broke across her face. "But if he asks, I wouldn't say no."

She barely had the sentence out before a squeal erupted from her friends.

CHAPTER EIGHT

21 July 1943

He was a fraud. A guilty, lying con man who'd tricked a girl into inviting him into her home purely so he could scope out how he was going to sneak in and search her bedroom. He tried to comfort himself with the idea that Grace could be working with the Nazis to bring down the Air Ministry from within. It wasn't working. The more time he spent with her, the more he thought that Wilson got his wires crossed somehow.

Last week he'd had a meeting in the group captain's office, Grace's former bedroom. Jack had taken in the details, wondering what clues they'd give him about her. But apart from the wallpaper and a heavy-looking armoire, no real sense of femininity permeated the room. Grace's history had been erased by the military man's presence. His gut told him Grace was simply an intelligent, good-hearted woman concerned for the welfare of her family home. But could he trust it? The men who'd sent him on this silly quest didn't think so. They still wanted a thorough search of her house.

He chose a time when Grace was at work. When he'd had tea with them, Sarah and Olive had mentioned they had an errand in the village this afternoon. He guessed he had about an hour.

The cottage was concealed from the road in a copse that also gave it a quaint English charm. The haphazard country-style garden hummed with life and burst with color. Dotty would have loved it. Flowering plants and herbs at their peak lined both sides of the white gravel path that led to the front door. Purple foxgloves reached high on both sides of the path. Nasturtiums sprawled along the ground by his feet with cheerful yellow and orange flowers among their flat, round leaves. What seemed like a hundred other plants he couldn't name crowded into the merry chaos of the garden.

Get a grip, Jack. You're here to rob the place, not smell the roses.

The pale-blue door of the cottage sat under a bower of climbing roses that crawled up the stone wall. His knock went unanswered, as he knew it would, so he made his way to the back. During his fretful sleep last night, he'd figured that would be the best place to stage this burglary.

He peered through the kitchen window, making out the sitting room where Sarah had served tea. Grace seemed perfectly used to being waited on, but he'd found it jarring.

"Lady of the manor." He tried to make sense of the contradiction. Here was someone who worked independently in the library at Bartondale, as happy as any of the other girls to ferry documents around. Yet the girls she worked with probably went home to flats like his or billets in farmhouses, while Grace had this place to herself, with a live-in servant and orphan evacuee.

Olive, who'd taken quite a shine to him, was the one who'd pointed out how the branches of one particular chestnut tree reached right up to the windows on the second floor of the cottage. She'd even pointed out which window belonged to Grace's bedroom. Olive had praised this tree for its sturdiness, claiming it was the best one on the whole estate to climb.

He'd soon test that for himself.

He was strong and fit, but it had been years since he had shimmied up a tree. Even then he'd done it unencumbered by a uniform. His conscience wouldn't let him pray that no one saw him, but he considered it a minor miracle that the branch held his weight with all his unathletic shifting and shuffling.

The window sash lifted easily. Good, because he'd climbed up here with no tool to jimmy it open. Although it wasn't one of the grand windows at Bartondale, he had no trouble fitting through it into Grace's bedroom.

That was when his palms began to sweat.

He pushed down his discomfort, making a clinical study of what he saw as he glanced around the small space, with a gabled ceiling just barely high enough for him to stand upright. The neatly made bed with a rose-patterned coverlet dominated the room. He flicked through the books stacked on her bedside, a curious contradiction of American classics, like *The Scarlet Letter*, and several popular mysteries by Agatha Christie. His eyes traveled over the pale-green kimono draped over a hook on the back of the bedroom door. He felt like a creep, committing all these intimate details to memory.

Wrestling away guilt, he focused on the task at hand. He was searching for things that might connect her to leaks at Bartondale. Although what that actually looked like, he wasn't sure.

"Things that might somehow seem out of place with the story she's given you."

Wilson's words rang in Jack's head but still failed to provide guidance. He didn't want to be thinking about Dotty while conducting this terrible invasion of another woman's privacy, but he brought her to mind while he prioritized where to explore. After Dotty had died, he'd discovered she kept her most treasured possessions in the drawer next to her bed. So he started there with Grace.

No luck. Grace's bedside only contained handkerchiefs and small pieces of soap to help fragrance them. Next he tried the wardrobe, determined not to think about the clothes and how much he'd like to see her wearing them. No secret panels that he could see.

He moved on to the dressing table.

When he opened one of the small drawers, a small bundle of letters stared up at him. Tied carefully with red ribbon, Grace's package looked similar to the collection of love letters from him Dotty had once kept. A small tag, like one that would label a Christmas gift, hung from where the ribbon was tied with a bow. It had a red letter *A* stamped on it.

He hesitated.

The letters in this bundle did not look likely to contain Air Ministry secrets. But the faint scent that rose from them wasn't perfume. The bundle smelled more like the oil paint and turpentine in Room Six.

Any kind of letter could contain a code. That was why he was opening them. Nothing to do with his own burning curiosity. Nothing at all.

The six letters in the bundle, all in the same hand and still in their envelopes, had three-year-old postmarks on the front and no return addresses on the back.

As he undid the ribbon that secured them, a folded piece of paper fell to the floor. He picked it up. It was the kind of thick-quality paper that was nowhere to be seen in England these days, the kind artists used for sketching.

His eyebrows shot toward the ceiling when he saw the sketch. A naked woman, in charcoal outline, sat hugging her knees, her head buried in her crossed arms. Jack didn't have much experience with art, but if it was meant to capture feeling on the page, then this was definitely a skillful drawing. Melancholy jumped up at him from the dusty black and white of the paper.

Was this Grace? He couldn't see the woman's face and wouldn't let his mind compare and contrast the naked body on the page with what he'd seen of Grace's. But if it wasn't her, why did she have it? He refolded it and took up the letters, hoping for answers.

With the letters laid out on the bed, he saw they were all definitely from the same person and written over a two-week period in 1940.

Jack had written enough love letters to Dotty to know that there was more than a little desperation among the extravagant claims of passionate love. He had the feeling that the guy writing them had done something wrong and was trying to make up for it by cramming three or four pages with overwrought prose. Jack assumed they were written to Grace, but each letter was addressed to *My love, My heart,* or *My sweet dove.*

He only had one side of the correspondence, but he could tell that the first five letters had gone unanswered. The sixth was different.

> *My sweet muse,*
>
> *Do not torture me with letters like your last one: too few words containing too many protestations. These last few weeks, not having you to myself, for myself, have been torment, and your letter only heightened the need that courses through my veins. My need for you.*
>
> *I don't believe that it is over, that you would give me up for a place among the angels. I can't believe it, because I can't exist without you. I can't work, I can't feel, unless you are near me. Every day I can't touch you is torture. Put simply, I crave you like air, like water. I can't think of anything else but you. God cannot love you more than I do! No being, in any realm, feels more for you than I do.*
>
> *If you won't come to me, I will come to you. I will blaze through that little town and declare my love so boldly that it will eclipse whatever else you think you feel.*
>
> *I promise, my love, my light, that you will never doubt my heart. It is, and always will be, yours.*
>
> *A.*

Jack swallowed hard after reading it through. He wasn't sure if his heart was racing from the letter or the fact he was reading it illicitly. He needed to focus.

The letters were all signed with a decorative *A.*

Andrew Hastings? He assumed so. That fit with Nancy's story about a duke as well as the evidence that MI5 had collected.

But the letters read like a love affair gone wrong, not some kind of espionage pact. Grace had left the guy, and he couldn't let go. It sounded like she'd had some kind of religious epiphany, which fit with the Grace he had seen at church. But the final page was covered in splotches, as though it had been read in a shower of rain. Or possibly tears.

Hating himself for invading her privacy, he rubbed his hand

over his face. It came away slippery with perspiration. Whatever this was, it wasn't a threat to national security. He bundled everything up, tying the envelopes together as they were when he'd found them and putting them away in the drawer. His watch told him that he had spent too long reading. Sarah and Olive would be home soon. He snooped under the bed and knocked on walls for secret compartments, but couldn't find anything else.

"Because there is nothing to find." He muttered the report he'd give Wilson next time he saw him.

There was no time to look downstairs now. He slipped back out the window the way he'd come in, closing the sash carefully behind him.

"There was nothing there." Jack told Wilson the whole story when they next met. This time, they walked along the river and sat on a stone bench that someone, forgotten by history, had once installed on a picturesque bend.

"No photos or film. No maps or paints. Nothing. It was just the bedroom of a normal young woman."

He'd already decided not to mention anything to Wilson about the love letters. They were just proof of what MI5 already knew. She had been close to Andrew Hastings once. She didn't need them poring over the particulars. It might be wrong to feel so protective of her, but that was what they got when they sent him in to do the job.

He'd been unable to face her for the past few days. When she'd made a point of walking out of the building with him just before he'd headed out to meet Wilson, the easy, companionable chatter they'd found in the rose garden evaporated under the strain of his guilt.

"I know I said I'd show you that river walk this weekend, but I've been summoned to London to meet with my father."

He'd almost looked her in the eyes but couldn't quite manage it. He did see the way she grimaced at the idea of going into the city.

"You don't want to go?"

"Not exactly. It will be lovely to see him, and hopefully he will coax Mother out of hiding, which will be nice. But London makes me sad at the moment." She seemed to realize her feelings as she spoke them. "The city is a shadow of its former self, a broken place. When I go there, I miss what it once was."

"I never saw it before . . . all this." He gestured to the military uniforms around them.

"Perhaps we can go next weekend. On the walk, I mean?"

"Sure. I'd like that."

His wretchedness meant his expression lacked any enthusiasm. Even now the strange look she gave him made him want to kick himself.

He told Wilson what he'd learned. "She's going to London on the weekend."

"We know."

The words gave him chills.

"In fact, you're going too." Wilson drew an envelope from the inside pocket of his suit jacket. "This should be everything you need."

"What's this?"

"See for yourself."

Jack opened the envelope and glanced at the contents. Train tickets, reservation information for a hotel in the West End. Some bank notes. Jack groaned inwardly at the thought of more spying business.

"We want you to 'accidentally' meet with Grace in London and observe the family dynamic. It will be a good way for you to gather more information about her that you can use later on . . . to get closer."

Jack shook his head, exasperated. "I don't like all this talk about 'getting closer.' Makes me feel like some kind of creep."

"If you think she's innocent, then we need you to prove it. Either way you need to gather evidence, Lieutenant." Wilson had an all-too-practiced calm about him. "And you don't have a choice to be part of this. Your train leaves at eight."

CHAPTER NINE

23 July 1943

"Two Coca-Colas please, sweetheart."

Jack would never address a woman he didn't know like that, but Alvin had no qualms flirting his way through Rainbow Corner, the club serving US GIs in London. It didn't seem to matter to Alvin if they were local girls hired to be listening ears for men far away from home or volunteers from the American Red Cross. Alvin gave them all winks and broad smiles.

After the short, rosy-cheeked girl at the soda fountain handed over their drinks, they found a place to sit in a corner, where there was less risk of being overheard. Alvin might have the morals of a tomcat, but he was the only one Jack could talk to about his real purpose at Bartondale without breaking any laws.

"I don't understand you. You're given the best job of anyone in this war—get close to a beautiful woman—but you can't bring yourself to do it. Are you really such a prude?"

Jack took a sip of his Coke. It tasted like home. A home he'd made with a beautiful woman. A home that had been shattered in an instant.

"I'm just not that guy. I can't just waltz in there and sweet talk her. Besides, I don't think she'd go for that, no matter what they say about her."

Whatever Wilson thought Grace had been at university, Jack had seen nothing—zip, zero, zilch—to suggest she would simply fall into Jack's arms now.

"Oh, Jack. I see what's happening. You're falling for her."

"I'm not falling—" He cut himself off. It was a lie.

"Haven't you read any of the pulps? She's a femme fatale! She's played you without you even noticing."

"I just don't think she's an evil mastermind, Alvin."

"You wouldn't. She's duped you."

Jack shook his head. "I've done everything they asked. They want evidence that she's behind leaked information, but I don't see anything other than a young woman trying to make the best of a bad situation."

"Then tell them that."

"I have, but they just keep saying I need to get closer. Like I'll learn something more if I just hang around her like a bad smell."

"I don't think they mean—"

"I know what they mean, and I won't do it." Jack's raised voice attracted a few glances, so they were silent for a few moments, sipping on their Cokes.

"You're not cheating on someone if they're already dead, Jack." Alvin spoke like he knew, but he didn't understand the whole picture.

"I'm not worried about Dotty." It hurt to say it, but it was true. Grace consumed more of his mind than his wife did these days. "There's more to it."

Alvin shook his head, as though Jack were a helpless cause. "I don't understand you. But if you feel so strongly about pursuing anything romantic, don't go there. Just don't trust her either. There is a reason the Brits are snooping around after her."

They sat in silence until they had drained their glasses.

"So what's your play?"

"Apparently I have to meet a friend for dinner at The Savoy tonight."

In ordinary times Grace loved trips to The Savoy. She clearly recalled her first taste of the hotel's elegance. She'd been no more than six or seven, taking tea with her mother, sitting rod-straight in front of the elaborate service, scared her mother would be let down by the tiniest slouch. By the end of the afternoon, her bones had ached from the effort, but she was in love with the place. As a child, Grace didn't know the sumptuous and scandalous stories about the hotel, as she did now. And yet she'd somehow always known them. Such tales pervaded the atmosphere.

That day was the beginning of regular visits to London she and her mother had taken to indulge in the finer, feminine things of life, while Grace's father and her brothers practiced their shooting. Dress fittings. Hair appointments. Trips to Covent Garden. Any occasion to visit the city was also one to visit The Savoy. Often they stayed in one of the opulent rooms, but sometimes her father booked them a suite.

Grace had met all manner of important people at The Savoy, from Hollywood starlets to royalty. She'd even met Elizabeth and Margaret, the young princesses, on one of their regular visits.

But that was another time. As Martin drove her through the sand-bagged streets of London, those memories felt like they were from another city. The journey into town was taking twice as long as usual because of road closures and bomb damage. Martin navigated through several detours before arriving at the doors of the hotel, tucked away at the end of a small driveway off The Strand.

A man in a black top hat and tails greeted her with a friendly smile as he held the door open, returning her nod as she passed. She entered the lobby and made her way to the understated reception desk, leaving Martin and the doorman to worry about her luggage.

She announced herself to the clerk. "Grace Deroy. I believe Sir Henry and Lady Deroy have a suite for the next few nights, and I'm with them."

"Of course, Miss Deroy." The fresh-faced young girl with a hint of an East End accent smiled politely through over-red lips. "Toby will see to your things. If you don't mind waiting a few moments?" The girl extended her hand to indicate two cozy armchairs around a low table, where guests could be comfortable while they waited.

Grace took her seat in one of the leather wingbacks, smoothing out her deep-burgundy skirt. Since this trip was considered home leave, she relished being out of her WAAF uniform, one of the least flattering things a woman could wear. At least it was blue and not a ghastly khaki like the ATS girls had to wear. *Some* people might look good in khaki and olive green—Jack Marsden, for instance, cut a fine form—but she was not one of them.

She'd relished picking out this outfit. The wine-colored skirt with a single pleat up the center matched her jacket, buttoned up over a forest-green blouse. The deep-green gem stones in her brooch dazzled on her shoulder. The magnificent felt hat tilted to one side added fashionable elegance befitting her surrounds.

She sighed with contentment, careful not to display in public her delight in her surroundings.

"Now, children, remember what I said earlier?"

Grace watched on as a statuesque woman, hair perfectly coiffed into a double victory roll, guided two equally angelic-looking children toward the lift. She wafted with practiced elegance, but the boy and girl, scarcely older than Olive, looked bored by their plush surroundings.

Grace smiled, wondering if regular trips to The Savoy would be in store for her children in the future. The thought surprised her. She'd never been one to dream about marriage and children. Not even at the height of her affair with The Artist. But as she watched the family disappear into the lift, a sliver of her began to dream of that kind of future. She sat so transfixed by her imaginings that she barely noticed the man approaching until he spoke. As he did, a cold hand ran down her back.

"Gracie! What a pleasure to see you."

She looked up into a face she knew well and reviled more. Andrew Hastings, the Duke of Clarence. Although he hadn't had the title when she'd first met him. Then, he was just a debonair duke-in-waiting with too much money and too little care for it. By the time they were at university together, he was playing patron to an aspiring artist.

She sprang to her feet out of gut instinct, avoiding the vulnerable feeling of being towered over by him.

"Andrew! How lovely to see you again." She hoped she sounded polite, even though her words were the opposite of her feelings. She leaned backward so he wouldn't feel encouraged to move any closer. His caramel-colored hair, dark eyes that knew too much about the world, and well-cut suit were a powerful combination. In fact she'd once used that to her advantage. But now he reminded her too much of The Artist to want to be anywhere near him.

"And you too. Although I have to say, it's actually 'Your Grace' now."

Of course he would say that. He always wanted what he thought was due him, even if it was just the correct form of address.

"Yes, of course. I was so sorry to hear about your father." She refused, with another lie, to concede to his obvious desire that she use his formal title. The last Duke of Clarence had been a rabid supporter of Hitler's ideas, in private at least. She had dined with his family several times and seen how enthusiastically he'd espoused ideas about genetic purity, as though it were just another hobby of his.

"Very sad business." The Duke did not look remotely sad. "What are you doing here anyway? I thought you'd run off to join the navy."

She glanced at the reception desk, hoping for a clue that her room might be ready soon.

"It's my mother's birthday tonight. And I'm on leave from the WAAF, not the navy. We all have to do our bit."

"If only I could. Doctors say my asthma makes it too dangerous to get in there and fight."

She'd never heard him cough during the whole time she'd known him. "And I'm sure there is nothing else you can do away from the front lines to assist." She nodded sagely in her sarcasm.

Please, God, let them call me soon.

He narrowed his eyes. "My, you have come over all high and mighty, haven't you? I remember what a firecracker you were at Oxford."

"I'm sure I don't know what you mean, Andrew." She fought the urge to fidget. She did not want to be having this conversation in the foyer of The Savoy surrounded by the elite of London society.

Holding her chin defiantly, she willed herself not to look away from his eyes, even though doing so made her want to squirm.

A doorman interrupted them deferentially. "Excuse me, Your Grace. Miss Deroy, room 821 is ready for you."

Thank You, Lord.

"Thank you. Goodbye, Your Grace." She spoke his title with the contempt she felt for him.

As she walked past him to follow the doorman, he grabbed her arm so firmly it hurt, and leaned close to her ear.

"Don't play the prude, Gracie. I know all about you and Blakey."

Only she could hear his vicious whisper in her ear, and she wasn't about to show any onlookers how the words made her stomach clench. She had too much training in polite society for that. She shook herself out of his hold and pushed past him, eyes set on the lifts.

She was concentrating so much on holding back tears that she barely registered how the man in the blue suit reading his newspaper stood to follow the duke back to the hotel bar.

All the arrangements were outlined in the papers Wilson had given Jack. His cover story was simple: a professor from his medical school had heard Jack was in England and wanted to meet him for dinner at The Savoy. Jack was to wait for him in the lobby at a quarter to seven and "accidentally" run into Grace. During the "what an amazing coincidence" conversation, a doorman would produce a note saying the professor had telephoned to say he was too ill to make the dinner. At which point Grace would effortlessly invite him to dine with her family.

It all seemed too easy, outlined in the note. He was sure it couldn't possibly be that smooth. Except it was. Only one thing hadn't gone to plan. The way his heart leapt out of his chest at the sight of Grace Deroy in an evening gown.

He'd waited in the foyer, pretending to read the evening newspaper while keeping an eye out for Grace. Every time the elevator announced its arrival with an energetic ping, he'd glanced up.

The newspaper had dropped the same way his jaw did when the opening doors revealed Grace in a floor-length emerald-green dress. It made her look like a goddess from one of the stories he'd read as a kid about Greek mythology. Perhaps it was the way the fabric draped across her torso and gathered at her hip with some kind of a ruche or tie before it fell all the way to the ground. Maybe it was the gold jewelry that made her look regal. Or the sophistication in the way she walked—like she was exactly where she belonged.

She was breathtaking. Literally.

Go to her, whispered a voice in his ear. One he hadn't heard in four long years. Dotty's voice.

He jumped out of his chair and dropped his newspaper, glancing around like a madman, frantic to see where that voice had come from.

He calmed. There was no Dotty. Of course there wasn't. But there was Grace, and she was coming his way. This was not the "accident" he had been planning.

"Lieutenant? Are you all right? You look like you've seen a ghost."

Close, but not quite. Heard one maybe.

"I'm here to see a friend." He barely got the words out. "But then I thought I saw someone else."

"Do you know someone staying here?" she inquired politely but giving him an odd look.

Get a grip, Jack. There's no such thing as ghosts.

"A professor of mine is in town, actually. He wanted to meet me here for dinner."

The porter arrived on cue.

"Excuse me, sir. Are you Lieutenant Marsden?"

Jack nodded, knowing what was coming.

"I'm afraid Professor Adams just called. He is feeling unwell this evening and won't be able to make it for dinner. He sends his apologies."

"Looks like you've been stood up, Lieutenant!" Grace said. "Would you like to have dinner with my family?"

There it was. As easy as they'd said it would be.

"Are you asking if I want to walk into that restaurant with the most beautiful woman in London on my arm?"

Grace glowed at his compliment. "Yes, Lieutenant, I suppose I am."

"Then absolutely I do."

Tonight might not be so bad after all.

———••◄∞⌐

"I know this place is called the American Bar, but speaking as an American, I don't know what any of these drinks are."

As he looked at the fancy names on the menu and long lists of exotic ingredients in each drink, Jack felt a long way from home. His mother was a card-carrying member of the Women's Christian Temperance Union, so he hadn't drunk anything other than communion wine until he'd been well into medical school. Even now he drank only an occasional beer.

The heady decadence about this corner of The Savoy was the exact opposite of his humble upbringing. Shiny furniture in fashionable shapes, with fluid curves, decorated the room. The cigarette smoke hanging in the air made the place feel darker than it was. A piano tinkled with merry gentility under the fingers of an expert showman, who played without looking at the keys. He'd nodded at Jack with a knowing smile when he walked by with Grace on his arm.

"The trick is to understand that it's not really about the drink." Grace explained the bar like she was explaining her System back at Bartondale. But what she said was hard to believe, considering the display in front of them was practically a shrine to hard liquor. "It's about the theater."

"What can I get for you, Miss Deroy?"

Should Jack worry that the bartender who approached them knew Grace by name? Once he saw the way Grace could chat easily with anyone—showing concern, listening carefully, making genuine connections—he wasn't surprised the bar man remembered her.

"Tell my friend about the cocktail you made for the RAF, Eddie."

"Well sure." Eddie sounded American rather than British, but Jack couldn't place where he was from. The man gave a short story about creating a bespoke drink for each of the branches of the armed forces.

"He's definitely an air force man." Grace ordered for Jack, and Eddie moved off to prepare the drinks.

She was right. This was a performance. Dressed in a dinner suit rather than The Savoy uniform, he moved with ease around the small space behind the bar, selecting the ingredients from the Great Wall of Bottles behind him and adding them to a shaker one by one. The guy was like a dancer effortlessly remembering moves.

"How do I know if he leaves something out?"

"You don't." Grace laughed. "But if you enjoy the show, you don't care."

He'd seen the price of the drinks and thought he would care quite a bit if something was missing from them, but he kept quiet. Jack couldn't keep up with what the guy was adding anyway. A dash of this, a slop of that.

With a flourish Eddie screwed a lid on the metal cocktail maker and shook it. He poured the drink into a wide coupe glass from an unnecessary height, then added three drops of something purple that twisted and danced through the rest of the drink, like ink added to water. With one stir, the final ingredient dispersed and the whole drink became soft purply blue.

It really was quite the show. Grace applauded, clearly delighted. Unable to disappoint her, he took a sip of the offered drink. He immediately tasted why it was named for the RAF. It was as strong as aviation fuel, scorching his throat as it went down before going straight to his head. Maybe she was a femme fatale after all, trying to get him drunk so he couldn't concentrate on his task.

He forced his mouth into a tight smile as he swallowed. One sip was enough.

"You really know how to make 'em, Eddie."

Jack offered to pay, but Grace insisted the drinks would be charged to her family's account. As they moved away from the bar to one of the stylish lounges, Jack took surreptitious glances at the other patrons. He'd read that this was a place where the rich and famous came when they were in London. He figured it would be good to have a story or two to tell when he got home.

His eye fell on a stout man with a round face and thinning hair. Jack couldn't see him well through the cloud of smoke that hovered around him from the cigar the man was smoking. He was speaking forcefully to three other men at the table with him, occasionally poking the air with his cigar before shoving it back into the corner of his mouth. The gesture sparked recognition for Jack.

"Grace, is that . . . Winston Churchill?"

Grace glanced in the direction he indicated, neither surprised nor excited that she might glimpse the beloved British prime minister.

"Yes. He has a suite here. Runs some kind of secret supper club, I'm told."

"You *know* him?"

"Father does. I've only met him a time or two."

Jack could add that to his growing list of things that fascinated him about Grace Deroy. But even in his admiration, he felt a pang of apprehension. If she was guilty of conspiracy to leak information, she had an awful lot of access to top people from whom she could steal it. He hadn't found any evidence, of course, but Wilson had sent him here, hadn't he?

"I'm meant to be meeting my brother Peter here. Not even Father could get Teddy tonight off, unfortunately. But it doesn't look like he's going to show."

"Oh ye of little faith!" a handsome man in a blue RAF uniform exclaimed behind them. He had the same honey coloring as Grace and remarkably similar features.

"Peter!" She leapt up and embraced him.

Enthusiasm like that in anyone else would send drinks flying, but Grace moved with such fluidity and control. He had to wrench his eyes off her to appear polite when she introduced her brother. Jack didn't need the introduction. He'd read about Grace's twin in the M15 dossier.

Flight Lieutenant Peter Deroy was a distinguished pilot. His family's wealth and his father's status in the RAF might have helped to push him up the ranks, but Jack didn't doubt Peter's tenacity and bravery. He'd made ace just three months after getting his wings and went on to have eight more kills during his career so far.

"So you're the Yank my sister has written to me about." Peter held his hand up to a waiter so he could order a drink. "How exactly do you fit into the secret squirrel business that goes on at Broughton these days?"

"He's the liaison between the Air Ministry and US Army. If we told you any more, we'd have to shoot you." Grace gave a ready-made answer.

Jack appreciated the dark humor that passed easily between the siblings. He also liked knowing that Grace had told her brother about him.

"Well, I hope your intentions with my sister are honorable. You've no idea the number of rogues who are interested in her."

"Peter!" Grace looked horrified. "He's my friend. Have some manners!"

Jack shifted under Peter's stare. He hoped it was just the penetrating gaze of a protective brother and not that Peter saw through Jack's cover story. He pushed the feeling away long enough to enjoy a happy half hour with them both.

"You seem okay." Peter spoke in a low voice as Grace led the way out of the bar and up to dinner. "But I'll be watching you."

Jack didn't doubt it for a second.

CHAPTER TEN

Grace wished her offer for Jack to have dinner with her family was purely magnanimous. As happy as she was to help a friend in need, Jack was also a means to an end. He was to be both her sword and her shield for the evening, her offense and her defense. Putting a good-looking, fascinating man at the dinner table was a distraction that would fight her parents off. At the same time, it would protect her from the worst of her mother's reproaches. Lady Deroy was simply too polite to mention private family matters in front of a stranger.

The first stage of Grace's battle plan was to make an entrance. She knew that some elements of Elaine Deroy's deeply French soul were not tamed, even after twenty-five years of living in England. Her appreciation for a handsome man was one of them. Grace would first dazzle her mother with her entrance, purposefully pausing at the top of the small set of stairs that led down to the dining area, in order to show off Jack, her unwitting accomplice.

"What are you up to, sister dearest?" Peter murmured in her ear.

He knew her too well not to sense she had an ulterior motive.

"Ensuring I avoid difficult questions." She spoke through her smile as her parents glanced their way.

Staff at The Savoy always sat the most interesting patrons in the center of the room, a policy she completely agreed with. Dull evenings went so much faster when one could people-watch the rich and famous. When she saw her parents at one of the most central tables, she suspected her father had arranged it so that her mother felt important.

She led Jack over to them.

"Grace, you didn't tell me you were bringing a guest."

Lady Deroy fluttered and fawned over their visitor. Grace could see why women of a similar age envied her mother's tall, slender figure. Even though fine lines crinkled around her eyes and her hair had silver streaks, she radiated sophistication. She welcomed Jack with open arms and a kiss on each cheek, something Grace could tell he didn't see coming. She pressed her lips together to conceal her delight at his surprise and subsequent recovery. The small worry he might get a monosyllabic bee in his bonnet subsided.

Food at an RAF Air Station could be surprisingly decent, but nothing compared to dining at The Savoy. Here, restrictions and rationing mattered little. They ate their fill of seven courses, including the most delicious soup Grace had ever tasted—an unctuous pot-au-feu with sizable pieces of beef, not the scrapings that Sarah incorporated at home to provide a hint of extra flavor.

Grace watched her mother's eyes close with pleasure after her first mouthful of soup. When she opened them, she looked directly at her husband, who was obviously sharing the memory the soup evoked.

"Happy birthday," Sir Henry murmured across the table to his wife, his eyes full of genuine love.

Grace glanced away, worried she might blush at such an intimate exchange between her parents.

While the war forced every chef in the country into a frenzy of inventiveness, nowhere did this better than The Savoy. They had even established their own poultry farm for a seemingly unlimited supply of meat and eggs. As a result, the roast chicken made Grace weak at the knees, and there was no mistaking the real egg custard served with dessert. The entire table sent their compliments to the chef.

Somewhere between the third and fourth course, the interrogation of Jack began, just as she had hoped. This was usually the point where her mother turned on Grace, challenging every poor decision she had made in her life so far, opening old wounds and sometimes creating new ones.

Instead, tonight her family used their Gestapo-like thoroughness to uncover every aspect of Jack's life from politics to religion. Grace was all too aware that her mother's questions were really designed to determine his pedigree. She'd once harbored hopes Grace would marry a duke with a family as old as theirs, so Grace supposed Mother would be disappointed by Jack's new-world lineage.

He didn't flinch. In fact, he greeted Lady Deroy's snobbery without judgment, answering her questions about his home, his career, and even his parents. Grace fell a little bit in love with his warm honesty and found herself leaning in, like the physical closeness would help her understand him better.

She'd been intrigued by his mention of medical school when they'd spoken in the rose garden. Why was he working with them if he had medical training? Surely a war required all the qualified medics it could get.

"You said you'd done medical school, Jack. Why aren't you working with a medical unit?"

For a moment that stunned look crossed his face. She worried her words had pressed whatever switch it was that made him go from eloquent to mute.

"You remember I mentioned my wife . . ."

Everyone at the table stiffened, as though worried she had brought an adulterer into their midst. She fought the urge to roll her eyes at her family.

"You mentioned how tragically she died," she said, to help her family relax, though she tried not to emphasize the final word.

"I couldn't trust myself as a doctor after that."

Like in the rose garden, his simple truthfulness drew Grace in. She was so transfixed she almost didn't notice how her father and brother had stayed stiff as boards after Jack's explanation. A polite interrogation campaign was one thing, but discussing matters of raw emotion at dinner was not what the English did. Her mother's French sensibilities were still enthralled and, Grace suspected, emboldened by the bottle of Chateau de Y'Quem they'd shared over dinner.

"How did she die?" Lady Deroy wanted to take the conversation somewhere Grace didn't think she, let alone the rest of The Savoy, could handle.

"Mother!"

But Jack didn't falter, explaining some of what he had already told Grace. Lady Deroy looked likely to be carried away by the romance of the story, but Sir Henry had been witness to more emotional outpouring in a single dinner than he could bear. He changed the topic so swiftly the women at the table reeled.

"So, Lieutenant Marsden, what do you know about the new P-51 Mustangs?"

Jack performed his role better than if she had handed him a script. Grace took the opportunity to glance at her mother, curious to know what she thought of Jack. She hadn't expected to care about her mother's opinion, but found her inscrutable face annoying. At least Peter, a notorious snob, seemed to like him by the end of the meal. Although it might have been the meal itself that put him in such a generous mood.

Peter leaned across Jack's empty space when he excused himself after the dessert. "He's not bad. A bit of a chatterbox, but Yanks usually are, aren't they? And you like your men that way, I think. You could do much worse."

"High praise, brother."

"And Mother certainly seems to like him. You have my permission to date him."

"I don't need your permission!" She responded to his provocation by childishly poking out her tongue.

"Did you know that Clarence is here?" Peter used a low voice so their parents wouldn't hear.

Grace nodded. "Yes. I saw him in the foyer earlier." She wanted to tell him more, but Jack returned to the table.

"Do you dance, Lieutenant?" A big band would strike up soon, and well fed and relieved they had both survived the interrogation, she was ready for some fun.

"Only the older styles, I'm afraid. I can foxtrot all you like, but please don't ask me to jitterbug."

"If you ask me, I won't ask you."

———∞———

Get closer to her, they'd said.

Well, now he was about as close as he could get in public. One arm threaded around her waist, with his hand resting on her lower back. The other held her hand as they swayed through the other couples on the floor.

All thoughts about this being a job fled the moment she'd taken his hand and let him lead her to the dance floor. Just for one dance he let himself be a man reveling in the feeling of holding a beautiful woman so close. She smelled divine, like the first flowers in spring. He could stay this close, with all his senses filled by Grace Deroy, for the rest of his days. No one else in The Savoy mattered apart from the woman in his arms. The king and queen of England could be dancing next to them and he wouldn't have known or cared.

He only realized that the Duke of Clarence had walked in because Jack felt every muscle in her body contract under his hands.

Fluid dance moves became rigid.

Her breath hitched.

An expression of alarm—or was it fear?—crossed over her face when she saw the man over his shoulder. She covered it with a benign half smile. But up this close he could see through the mask. Her footing stumbled.

"What's wrong?"

"Nothing."

"Do you know him?" Jack couldn't let her get away with her lie.

"I did. Once. He's a complete weasel."

Jack silently cursed the weasel for bringing the rest of the room into focus and his mind back to the job at hand—observing the Deroy family dynamic.

He'd taken enough mental notes at dinner to fill a whole notebook. Grace appeared serene, but he had the impression she was performing some kind of bait and switch on her parents, parading him in front of them as a distraction. But what was she trying to divert their thoughts from? He survived the questioning by relying on his tell-the-truth-where-you-can mantra. He didn't have to lie once when he spoke about Dotty.

Grace watched the Duke of Clarence—although apparently it was polite to call the guy Clarence or Your Grace—over his shoulder, while he studied her face. She was so distracted by Clarence she didn't notice how intently Jack looked at her, even though he was mere inches away. Worry lines furrowed her brow as the duke made his way to where her parents sat near the edge of the ballroom.

He recalled the tear splotches on the letter she'd kept tied with a red ribbon in her dressing table drawer, hating himself for knowing they existed. He'd never had an ex-lover, but if he had, he guessed he would be agitated if she sauntered across the room toward his parents the way Clarence was doing now.

"Is everything okay?"

"I'm so sorry, Jack, but I need to make sure he doesn't put his foot in it with my parents."

She broke off their dance to intervene. He followed her but lingered back. Without Grace consuming all his senses, he could concentrate on the interactions. An alarm bell rang in his head. How could he have let her divert his focus? Alvin's comment about the pulps resonated. Maybe he was some kind of a dupe unable to see what was really going on in front of him.

Grace approached the duke warily but covered it with a polite facade. When Jack edged closer to them, he saw what she would have already noticed. Clarence was intoxicated.

"Good to see you again, Your Grace." The British system of precedence meant Sir Henry, as wealthy and distinguished as he was, had to defer to the younger one.

"We were saddened to hear about your father." Lady Deroy put her gentility on full display.

"You were? I was happy to see the old codger off. Hullo, Gracie! Well, this is cozy, isn't it?"

He flopped down next to Lady Deroy and flung his arm about the older woman's shoulders. His behavior was so boorish that people stared. Lady Deroy glanced at her husband, horrified. Everyone bristled under the strain of their politeness. Apart from the duke, the people here valued that over just about everything else. Several of The Savoy staff, who apparently prided themselves on their discretion, were gathered in a group, heads together, intrigued by the ruckus at the Deroy table.

"Who's the Yank?"

"Andrew, this is Lieutenant Jack Marsden. Jack, this is Andrew Hastings, the Duke of Clarence."

"Pleased to meet you, sir." Jack added the last word out of custom, not respect.

"Actually, it's Your Grace."

The duke wasn't so drunk that he couldn't hold Jack's eye with a challenge.

"Is it?"

Back home we give our respect to people who earn it, not people who inherit it.

He bit the thought back. Saying that would be ignoring every rule of British etiquette written in the little book he had read on his boat ride over.

"I've come for a dance with Gracie." It was a demand from the duke, not a remark.

Jack's instinct told him to intervene, but knowing MI5 was trusting him to find out if the duke and Grace were still connected, he'd let it play out. Grace glanced at the staring patrons nearby and the neatly uniformed Savoy staff.

"Yes, of course. How lovely." Her polite words were flat. If she was conspiring with the duke, she was doing so reluctantly.

Grace held out her hand, pulled him out of his seat, and dragged his swaying frame to the dance floor. Jack's jaw tightened when Clarence's arm snaked around Grace, his hand coming to rest much farther down than Jack's own had. Whatever love had inspired the tears on the letters in her top drawer was long gone. Grace's eyes shot daggers at her dance partner as she reached behind her to drag his hand up to where it should be.

Jack's eyes followed them across the dance floor. He couldn't hear what they were saying once they were swallowed up into the other dancers, but from this distance it didn't look like friendly banter. Grace's polite facade only dropped once. A look of pure horror crossed her face, before she packed it away again behind her mask.

Peter appeared beside him.

"Friend of yours, I hear?" Jack crossed his arms over his chest and kept his eyes on the couple.

"Used to be. We don't see eye to eye anymore."

"Because of your sister?"

Peter's head snapped away from the dance floor to look directly at Jack. "She told you?"

Jack didn't know how to play this. Peter's incredulous reply confirmed his suspicions that the letters in Grace's bedroom were from Clarence.

"Well, anyone can see that he has some hold over her."

"She was young and foolish, but she found the power to walk away. The WAAF was the best thing to happen to her afterward.

Gave her purpose, new friends, and a desire to keep going." Peter shook his head at the man on the dance floor. "I would punch him to the ground and set the dogs on him if there weren't laws against it."

"Has she recovered, do you think?" Jack tried to fish for more information.

"Not enough to be toyed with again." Peter's dark words were directed squarely at him. "I saw the way you two danced. You make sure you don't hurt her, Lieutenant. Or you'll have me to deal with. I might not care so much about breaking the law when it comes to an American."

"Noted. But I—" The band's music came to an ugly-sounding end as an air-raid siren rang out. As a wearied groan rippled through the patrons, Jack turned to look for an exit.

Just in time to see Lady Deroy slide from her chair to the floor, hitting her head on the table on the way down.

CHAPTER ELEVEN

24 July 1943

"Can I help you, madam?"

Grace reeled round, surprised by the voice at her elbow. She came face to face with an elegantly dressed man with fine Gallic features and a gold Sotheby's badge pinned to his lapel.

She blinked through her tiredness.

Despite the comfort of The Savoy, Grace had slept poorly after their evening had ended so abruptly. The air-raid siren was a false alarm, but her mother's faint had been real. Happily, she hadn't been unconscious for long.

"Too much excitement" had been Jack's opinion once she'd been settled back in their suite.

Now, there was a mystery. Jack Marsden obviously had a natural bedside manner. Yet he wasn't using his medical talents for the military—he was analyzing maps and photographs. What a loss! The memory of Jack in his professional element—calm, confident, and caring—revealed a new side of him. One she would definitely be divulging to the girls when she returned to work. Unfortunately, he wasn't the man who'd kept her awake last night. And her thoughts about Andrew Hastings were much less pleasant.

She managed a tight smile for the Sotheby's attendant. Thank goodness Sarah had packed a day dress and another hat befitting this kind of outing. She obviously looked like she was in the market for an artwork and not just a curious onlooker.

"It's a masterpiece, isn't it?" The attendant indicated the painting in front of her, set in an elaborate frame next to the podium, where the auctioneer would soon stand. A small plaque on the frame read *The Blue Lady. A Blakey c.1939.*

She didn't need to look at the artwork to know it was. Well, the original was. This was a forgery. A good one. Good enough, apparently, to fool the experts of the hallowed auction house where she stood.

"Alexander Blakey was a rare talent." She fudged in order to gather her thoughts, still confused by what she saw. "But I thought this particular work was sold only a few years ago?"

"You know your art, Miss . . ."

"Deroy." She saw the flicker of recognition in his eyes.

"Of course, Miss Deroy. And yes, the painting was acquired by an anonymous collector in 1940 who said at the time he would never sell. But it seems he's had a change of heart."

The attendant gestured toward a gentleman holding court among several journalists who were milling around him.

The Duke of Clarence.

Grace froze as her worst suspicions were confirmed. She would have skimmed over the Sotheby's advertisement in the newspaper this morning had the duke not been mumbling threats, thinly veiled with innuendo, about exposing her to the world as they'd danced last night. She doubted he remembered much of what he'd said, given his state.

"He's the seller?" She sorted through her thoughts.

"One and the same. He has an extensive interest in art and a vast collection of modernist works from all over the continent. Are you interested in bidding?"

"In truth, I attended here today as a curiosity. I knew the artist, you see. And as you say, it is a masterpiece."

"It was such a tragedy to lose a creative genius so young."

Grace nodded. "Perhaps I can be swayed . . . I take it this work has been authenticated?"

"Yes. By the Blakey Trust as well as our in-house experts."

She suggested he give her some time alone to think, but when he left her with the painting, thought was impossible. Emotion of every kind flooded through her.

This painting was as familiar to her as if she had drawn it herself. The description in the auction catalog couldn't possibly capture the way every brushstroke exposed her, body and soul, to the world.

> The Blue Lady *is one of Blakey's most famous experiments blending post-Impressionism and Fauvism. It represents the culmination of his short but prolific Oxford period. Often compared to masterworks by Matisse and Picasso,* The Blue Lady *is an erotically charged portrait—thought to be Blakey's mistress—showing a nude woman with angel's wings reclining across a bed, her sad gaze directed toward the evening scene outside the window. This was Blakey's last known painting before his death in a Lincolnshire motor accident.*

She burned with shame at the description. The style of the artwork meant that she wasn't easily recognizable as the model, but that didn't assuage her memory of posing for it. She recalled watching Blakey at work, through her tears. She'd gone to the studio to tell him that it was over, intending to break the spell he had over her. But he had cajoled and she had acquiesced. One last time and then it was over. He'd painted in a frenzy of blue oils. He had never looked quite so desperate, like he was standing still on the outside but running for his life inside.

Even now as she stood in front of this copy, she relived the intensity of that day through the lines of color in front of her. Perhaps that was what elevated this work into greatness. He'd channeled all his feeling, as well as all hers, into this work, and it transcended everything.

"You said you knew the artist, Miss Deroy?" The attendant came back to interrupt her thoughts. "Do you know who his muse was? That's got everyone talking. She must have been quite the paramour to inspire him to this!"

Grace ignored his sly innuendo and mustered all the nonchalance she could. If her heart didn't feel like it was in a vice, she might laugh at the irony that this painting could simultaneously reveal her soul and disguise her identity.

"No idea. Sorry."

"Come now, Gracie—that's not true."

A cold shiver ran down her spine when Andrew approached.

"Your Grace," the Sotheby's attendant simpered, and left them.

Grace couldn't very well say what was on her mind right here on the front podium at Sotheby's, so she took Andrew by his elbow and dragged him to a more private alcove.

"What are you up to?" She hissed out her words. "This isn't the original!"

He seemed unconcerned about her accusation. "You know, he really was quite prolific during our Oxford days. I never knew quite what inspired him at the time, but I've recently come across some sketches from that period. His style there is so much more, shall we say, realistic."

She knew. She had one of those sketches at home among her letters. And she knew he'd once kept a notebook of much more compromising ones. He'd told her he'd burned it. The thought of anyone seeing those drawings, from a time when she'd been so infatuated with Alexander she would have done anything for him, made her worry she might be sick in the middle of polite Mayfair society.

"The faces, in particular, are so very lifelike."

Dread bloomed in her tightly clenched belly.

"You really were a wild thing back then, weren't you? I know this is a portrait of you."

She didn't think her stomach could clamp tighter, but it did.

"Just like I know you'll never tell anyone this is a forgery." He leaned so close that she could feel his breath on her face. "I can see it in your face now. The shame at the idea I know what you got up to on those long afternoons in his studio. In his bedroom."

She flinched at the truth in his words and the mocking tsk of his tongue against his teeth.

"Must have been quite a shock when it came up at auction the first time. A good little thing like you in nothing but your birthday suit, inspiring—what do the critics say?—unparalleled passion and sensuality."

She looked over to the painting on the dais, on display for everyone to see, recalling the humiliation of seeing the original mounted in the same way at an auction three years ago. How every snicker and sneer of a gallery patron felt like a burn on her skin.

"I wonder . . . Should I make an announcement now? Should I call everyone over and say, 'Look! I've found the real blue lady. It's Grace Deroy. Under the uniform she's quite a—'"

"Be quiet, Andrew! You keep the past in the past, and I will too."

He held her stare until she crumpled under the weight of his.

"No. You won't say anything. You've got too much to lose now. A churchgoing, morally upright thing like you isn't going to risk revealing she is the subject of a pornographic painting. Imagine if those grubby little drawings got into the newspapers. What would Mummy and Daddy have to say? What would the WAAF do? What about that American from last night? What would he say if he knew?"

He was goading now, evoking her every fear, making sure she knew what he would do if she said something. He must have known from her face he'd defeated her.

"You'll keep your mouth shut about this, Gracie, and I won't tell the world what I know. Now run along like a good little girl."

The fact that Jack didn't bat an eyelid when a note saying *Sotheby's, Bond Street, Mayfair. 11.30* was pushed under his hotel door was an indication of just how strange his life had become. The note was probably from Wilson, summoning him to turn up at the designated place at the designated time.

Sotheby's was an art auction house, wasn't it? One of those stuffy British institutions with a centuries-long history and prestigious connections. And Mayfair was the ritzy end of town. Although with the gray sky full of barrage balloons and the buildings lined with sandbags, nowhere in London felt particularly swanky right now.

His cabbie skillfully negotiated the damaged streets and dropped him out front.

Grace would be right at home in a place like this. For a second he imagined what it would be like to walk into a room like this with Grace on his arm. She would expertly guide him through the pitfalls of Britain's upper classes, just as she had done last night. He fought a smile.

A man at the door handed Jack an auction catalog as he walked in the door. He flipped through it, seeing that several paintings were being sold today, most of them modern. Not his taste. The room buzzed with anticipation about the impending auction. The headline item was a painting called *The Blue Lady* by an artist he'd never heard of.

He scanned the foyer, trying to work out why he'd been sent here. He didn't recognize anyone, so he meandered to the dais at the front, intending to review the artwork itself. He thought he was keeping his senses alert, but he was still blindsided by a woman dressed in elegant navy blue with a terrific asymmetrical hat—all angles and feathers—when she careened into him.

"Excuse me. I wasn't looking where I was . . . Jack?"

Grace. She looked miserable. She must have been flustered to forget her usual poise and charge into him the way she had.

"What are you doing here?"

That was a good question. One for which he had no answer. He gaped, trying to frame words. None came, but she was probably used to that by now.

"I'm here to . . ." Nope. Nothing.

"Jack, old buddy!"

Jack and Grace turned toward the sound of an obnoxious American accent cutting through the polite chitter-chatter. *A fake American accent,* Jack thought when he saw who it belonged to. Wilson Weathers approached, sporting a moustache that Jack had never seen on him before.

"Glad you could make it here to meet your old pal Brad Butler."

Wilson Weathers. Brad Butler. Whoever he really was, he liked to alliterate his code names.

"Brad? Yes. Of course. Um, it was great to get your note."

So this is what it feels like to be sinking in an ocean of lies. He winced at the look Grace gave them, like she thought they were crazy.

"Well, when I heard you were in town, I thought I'd combine business and pleasure. But"—he glanced toward Grace—"I wasn't expecting this kind of pleasure. Say, aren't you going to introduce me to your friend?"

"Sure." Jack tried to keep his head above water. "Grace, this is Brad Butler, as you heard. Brad, meet Grace Deroy. She and I . . . work together."

Whatever had caused Grace to plow into him was obviously still on her mind, sidetracking her enough that she didn't seem to notice the way he stammered out the flimsy cover story. He hoped. Either that or her politeness was instinctive.

"What brings you to Sotheby's today, Mr. Butler?"

"Oh, I am working in the family business. Art and antiques.

Doing a little transatlantic trade. This *Blue Lady* is quite the portrait. I noticed you looking at it before. Are you interested?"

Did Grace just blush?

"Alexander Blakey was a rare talent. I-I knew him and just wanted to get a closer look."

"I was just on my way over to see it." Jack smiled, trying to be compassionate. "But I know nothing about art. Would you tell me more?"

A wave of what looked like horror washed over Grace, but she seemed unable to think of a polite way to decline in front of Wilson. She led them back to the podium where the portrait was displayed.

As soon as Jack saw it, he understood why she had blushed. This was not the kind of thing that would hang comfortably at Bartondale . . . or any genteel place, for that matter. But it wasn't the provocative nature of the painting that struck him the most.

"She looks so sad."

Grace turned her head to look at him, as though he were a problem she was trying to solve. She looked that way at Bartondale sometimes, with the cutest furrow in her brow.

"I can tell you the sadness is not the first thing men usually notice."

Wilson snorted, as if to confirm what she was saying. She didn't bother to hide her contempt for him under politeness. She must be upset.

"Now if you'll excuse me, gentlemen, I was just on my way out. I'll see you on Monday, Jack."

She disappeared in a blur of blue just as the auctioneer called the room to attention. His heart left the room with her, but he still had to work out exactly why he was here.

"What on earth is going on?" Jack hissed as they took their seats at the edge of the crowded auction room.

"Not sure." Wilson had dropped the accent. "But we got word that an exchange is happening here today."

"And you called me as backup?" If it weren't so serious, it would feel like the game of cops and robbers he'd played as a kid.

"Just keep your eyes open, Lieutenant."

A palpable frisson of excitement shot through the room when the auctioneer declared *The Blue Lady* as the next item. Jack saw Clarence, apparently the seller, all smiles near the front of the room. Thin and serious, the auctioneer read the description of the painting from the catalog in a disinterested voice, then asked, "Who would like to start the bidding?"

"Ten thousand pounds." A red-faced man in a dark-blue suit started the bidding at a figure unfathomable to Jack. It escalated in a few bids to an astronomical sum.

"One hundred and twenty-five thousand pounds." The ball bounced back to the red-faced man's court.

"You're not going to bid?" Jack glanced at Wilson, whose eyes were fixed on the self-satisfied smirk of the duke.

Wilson grimaced. "Something feels wrong. I can't quite place my finger on it, can you?"

Was Wilson kidding? Jack had no idea about art and auctions.

When the auctioneer's gavel fell, the final figure made Jack's eyes water. The red-faced man had prevailed.

"Come on." Wilson stood to leave. "I want the full story from last night."

Jack gave it to him over coffee in a fancy Mayfair café. It almost alarmed Jack how natural it felt to sit across a table from Wilson's enigmatic gaze and spill every detail of every interaction with Grace.

"Anything else?" Wilson looked Jack directly in the eyes, as though he was keeping something back.

He wasn't. He'd told Wilson everything.

Well, maybe not everything. Not the way his heart had hammered in his chest when Grace had taken him by surprise with a grateful peck on the cheek after he'd helped her mother.

"I gotta say, they don't seem like Nazi sympathizers."

"Why? Because they didn't greet you with a Heil Hitler?" Wilson shook his head. "At this point in the war, anyone thinking kindly toward the Nazi regime knows to keep their mouths shut until they are sure of the company they are in."

Jack supposed he had a point. "The Duke of Clarence was a real piece of work. But Grace didn't seem to be his biggest fan." He gave a brief description of the dance the two had shared. "She has this polite mask she puts on when she wants to hide what she's really feeling. It slipped once or twice, and there was no love there."

"The next week will be the test," Wilson remarked.

"You going to give me any more details or just leave that hanging mysteriously?" By now he was used to the cryptic sentences of his handler's conversation.

Wilson grinned. "Leave it hanging. Your objective is still the same. Have you asked her out?"

"You sound like Alvin." He liked the thought of an afternoon at the movies with Grace. But the idea of spending it worming details out of her felt worse than his dread at having to search her room.

"You really are bad at this, aren't you, Jack?"

CHAPTER TWELVE

24 July 1943

Jack only realized the problem he had created for himself when he was safely back in his room above Mrs. Johnston's kitchen.

Nancy Filby had been having tea with Mrs. Johnston when he walked in after making the short walk from the bus stop. When he'd seen the pair in the small sitting room near the front door, he immediately regretted telephoning ahead to let Mrs. Johnston know the time his bus would arrive.

Nancy smiled as much as she could with her lips pressed shut. He had the terrible impression she was trying to be alluring. Her hair looked like it had been professionally set, and he thought the dress might be new.

"Won't you sit and have a cup of tea with us, Lieutenant?" Mrs. Johnston motioned to the spare spot on the sofa next to Nancy.

Jack glanced up the stairs to where his room was, doing the calculations. If he took the steps two at a time, it would only take seven strides to be safely in his room. But he couldn't be that rude. He put down his case and sat next to Nancy while Mrs. Johnston poured the tea.

"Did you have a good time in London?" Mrs. Johnston asked. "You left suddenly!"

"Thank you. I did." He accepted the offered cup and saucer. "I actually met the entire Deroy family while I was there."

Nancy looked crestfallen, but Mrs. Johnston was undeterred.

"I read *The Times*! Grace Deroy seems like such a genteel girl, yet there she was letting that man have his way."

Jack didn't know what she meant about *The Times*, but her subtext was clear—she'd known all along that Grace was not as respectable as she appeared.

"I met the duke too." Jack tried to repair Mrs. Johnston's tarnished respect for Grace. "Let's just say that he doesn't live up to the term 'gentleman.'"

"You must tell us, Lieutenant! But before you do, let me just fetch some biscuits. I have a fresh batch in the oven."

She dashed out of the room, leaving him alone on the sofa with Nancy.

That was the moment he'd created his problem, thanks to not having had his wits about him. He couldn't think of a thing to say. The easygoing Nancy, the one who showed her teeth and reveled in the gossip she'd heard in the butcher's shop, was replaced by the timid one who looked petrified of speaking.

He stared down at the satchel in his lap, hopelessly willing the brown military-issue canvas to bring forth a topic of conversation. Miraculously, it did just that when he remembered what he had stashed in there.

"I brought you back a gift."

He could kick himself now for saying it like that, but at the time it had seemed a reasonable segue.

Reaching into his satchel, he'd pulled out a thin cardboard packet containing a delicate pair of nylons. Alvin had given them to him before Jack had left America for Bartondale, insisting they would be useful in getting close to Grace. But Jack had seen the many pairs of genuine silk stockings in her dressing table drawers, so he knew nylons wouldn't be the way to her heart. Since then he'd let the packet jostle around in his satchel, thinking he might give them to one of the girls she worked with. The packet looked a little shabby now.

"For me." She blushed and couldn't keep herself from grinning, revealing her teeth. He froze when it hit him. This gift had probably led her along more than any picnic invitation ever could. He'd tried to repair the damage. "Now, don't go reading too much into them. One of the GIs I know gave them to me, and I don't really have anyone else who would use them."

"You really don't have anyone else to give these to?" She gave the word *anyone* special significance, but he was too slow in these things to understand what she was really asking.

"Nope." He shrugged, perplexed by the way her smile grew broader.

The satisfied delight Julia Johnston wore all over her face when she came back into the room with a tray of freshly baked gingersnaps should have told him he'd made a mistake. But it wasn't until he was in his bedroom that he slapped himself upside the head. Of course, neither Nancy nor Mrs. Johnston had any way of knowing he hadn't given them to Grace because she didn't need them.

He groaned, falling back on his pillows and dreading his next conversation with Nancy Filby.

"Tell us everything!" Susie pounced on Grace as she walked into the library on Monday morning. She leaned extravagantly on her final word.

Grace chuckled. "Good morning to you too."

Betsy and Charlotte followed Susie into the room and didn't even stop by their own desks before they crowded around Grace's.

"It's really not as exciting as you think."

"Not exciting?" Betsy cried. "You went to The Savoy and hobnobbed with the poshest people in the country, and that wasn't exciting for you?"

Grace softened. She'd made a point of memorizing the details of her room for Maggie, who loved to hear about every opulent particular. She recited them now for her colleagues as they listened with rapt attention. When she mentioned the food, she watched their mouths water.

"I just heard OAF say on the way in that he was in London too," Charlotte said. "Did you two have a secret rendezvous while you were away?"

Grace shook her head at Charlotte's naivety, remembering when Grace herself had been all romance and dreams.

"Actually, it wasn't secret. He met my entire family."

She ducked her head to avoid the oohs and aahs.

"You did have a rendezvous!" Charlotte cried. "How romantic!"

"Hardly. It was dinner with my parents and brother."

"Did you dance with him?" Susie asked. "Can he jitterbug? All the American boys I've danced with can. It's such fun to be swung around without a care in the world!"

Grace grinned. "No jitterbugging, I'm afraid. But a bit of fox trotting and a good old waltz."

Susie wiggled her fingers in a *more* gesture.

"All right, then. Yes. He's a very good dancer."

If only the dance hadn't been interrupted by Andrew.

As if just thinking his name brought him up in conversation, Betsy said, "Is the Duke of Clarence as handsome in real life as in the papers?"

Grace frowned at the mention of the newspapers.

"His good looks in no way make up for his bad behavior." Grace hoped the ice in her voice would shut down that line of questioning.

"Yes, but he's so dreamy." Charlotte sighed.

Grace didn't have time to be exasperated, because Worthington stalked into the room and the girls dispersed to their desks, trying to look like they'd been hard at work all along.

"Deroy! Where are the photographs I requested on Friday? I

told you last week I would need them on my desk first thing this morning!" His bluster made him red in the face, like some furious dragon in one of Olive's storybooks.

Indignation rocketed through her. She'd run a full fifteen minutes late for Martin on Friday evening, digging those out for him.

"I put them right in the middle of your desk before I left on Friday, Worthington. Don't blame me for your blindness. You've probably put something down on top of them."

"I tell you, Deroy, they aren't there! And if I can't find them soon, I'll make sure you are hauled in front of the group captain!"

The others sat at their desks, no doubt trying to escape his ire by avoiding his eyes. Social and military rank both prevented them from standing up to him.

Grace sighed pointedly, stood, and smoothed her uniform. Glaring at Worthington, she pushed past him toward his office, leaving him to trail in her wake.

Her heart skipped when Jack stood at his desk as she entered, but she wouldn't let him distract her. She expected to march straight up to Worthington's desk and triumphantly point out the blue manila folder containing the photographs, sitting right in the middle of his mess. Exactly where she'd put it on Friday.

But nothing lay there.

She checked the log at the door, which should be proof she brought the file into the room.

Her heart sank. In her haste, she must have forgotten to fill it out. Her own System and she had been the weak link in the chain.

She frowned, losing her gusto.

"Not in the log, Gracie? Believe it or not, that was the first thing I checked."

How she hated Worthington's sarcasm.

"I put them here on Friday. Have you seen them?" she queried Jack, though it came out more of an accusation.

"What's going on here?" The booming voice of Group Captain Carter filled the small room.

She and Worthington saluted before the group captain put them at ease with an irritated "Yes, yes."

Of all the times for him to be prowling past the door! He looked like he could take down the whole Luftwaffe with the force of his angry gaze scanning for the right target. He found one in Grace.

"This is unacceptable, Deroy!" Carter thundered at Grace after Worthington explained the situation.

"Three times in the last week I've been unable to find photographs." Worthington added fuel to Carter's fire. "And that's just me. Marsden has had trouble too."

She glanced at Jack. He held his hands up to protest. "I'm still learning The System."

"You told me this System of yours would allow us to find any of the information we need at a moment's notice, and we seem to be losing more than ever!"

"With respect, sir, I don't think it is The System itself that is to blame." She had to defend her work. "In the library we have noticed that there are certain *weak points* involving staff who don't fill out the record log."

The group captain look alarmed. "You suspect foul play. Espionage? That's a very serious accusation, Deroy!"

"I suspect that carelessness is usually to blame." She looked pointedly at Worthington. "I know that is why I didn't fill out the log on Friday afternoon. I was already late and in a terrible rush to get away." It was painful to admit, but it troubled her more that the file was gone. She had put it there. She remembered it clearly. "Perhaps you could send around a memo encouraging us all to be more thorough."

"Fix this, Deroy!" The group captain spun on his heel and left.

"Yes, fix this, Deroy," Worthington repeated, with such a snide look her hands ached to slap it off him. "Jack and I need that file."

CHAPTER THIRTEEN

31 July 1943

Grace sank into the bathwater that sloshed around the deep claw-foot tub. Sarah had drawn it to be almost scalding, just the way Grace liked it, before she'd left with Olive to visit a nearby relative.

"I'll get Olive out of your hair so you can rest."

The rising steam helped clear her sinuses of the dreadful cold she had been fighting a losing battle with since her return from London. She couldn't smell the scent of the rose petals Sarah had thrown in to fragrance the water, but she appreciated the touch. If her head hadn't been so entirely stuffed up with sickness, she would have relished the luxury.

Seeing the tub crammed into a little annex off the kitchen had been what convinced her she could stay on here after the Air Ministry requisitioned the main house. She didn't know why such a small, simple building had a tub of its own. Perhaps her father had installed it for his valet, who'd once lived here, with rheumatism. Right now, she didn't care. Few things felt better than a long soak.

Before climbing in she'd pinned her hair into a messy bundle on top of her head and tied a scarf around her hairline to keep the stray hairs from falling. But she avoided looking in the mirror, too scared to see how red her nose was from all the sniffing and blowing.

She knew her eyes must be red and puffy and gratefully closed them against the feeling, letting the water envelop her like an embrace.

She had been on edge since that day at Sotheby's. She didn't trust Andrew Hastings, Duke of Clarence, as far as she could throw him. Mortification tightened her chest every time she remembered his threats to tell the world she'd been Blakey's lover and would share the drawings as proof. At the same time, he was clearly up to something else. He seemed to want to use her secret against her to keep her from stumbling onto whatever he had going on.

Then there were the missing files. The others told her not to worry, but they still hadn't turned up. And she was sure she'd left them on Worthington's desk.

It was impossible to know how long she soaked, lost between sleep and deep thought. The water had cooled when she heard a noise from her bedroom, directly above her. A clunk, a thump, and the unmistakable sound of footsteps over creaking floorboards. Despite her foggy head, she grew alert, listening to every sound of the intruder above her.

She stood in the tub and grabbed a towel as she stepped out of it. The change in height and temperature made her head spin. She tried to ignore the dizziness as she briefly patted herself dry, took her robe from the stool where she had left it, and slipped it around her.

The footsteps made their way to the landing and started down the stairs. Coming closer. She glanced around for something to wield as a weapon.

She lifted the now-cold cup of tea Sarah had left with her from the stool and carefully placed it on the floor. Then she picked up the stool and held it by two of its three legs, ready to smash the intruder over the head with it.

She waited, breathing through her mouth, her throat dry.

The footsteps seemed to visit every room in the house but avoided the kitchen. It must be a burglar snooping around for things of value.

If so, offense was her best defense. Once the intruder was in the kitchen, she could throw open the door and run screaming toward him, brandishing the chair high before thumping it down on his head.

Suddenly, lightheadedness hit her with full force. She lurched to the side, dropping the stool to steady herself and sending the teacup clattering across the floor.

There goes my element of surprise.

The footsteps in the next room headed toward the kitchen.

She struggled to pick up the stool again. "Who's there? Show yourself!"

She tried to sound brave and strong, but her pulsing fear and blocked nose dampened the effect.

"Grace?"

The voice sounded familiar, but she had to be sure. "Step into the light!"

A man in an unkempt RAF uniform, who looked and smelled like he'd slept at the pub for the last three days, stepped into the light of the kitchen.

"Teddy?"

All the energy she had mustered to face her intruder left her when she saw her younger brother. She sagged against the doorframe. "What are you doing here? And why didn't you use the front door?"

"I didn't mean to scare you." Remorse colored his features. And uncertainty.

"I'm in a bit of trouble, Grace."

———◦∞◦———

Tea had been her first order of business, but the cups sat untouched in front of them.

"Got anything stronger?" Teddy asked.

"Just tea." Since he was unsteady on his feet and smelled like a brewery floor, she figured he'd had enough alcohol lately. She pinched her robe together at her chest, trying to hold herself upright at the table. "Are you going to tell me what's going on?"

"I can't go back," he said to his teacup. "I won't. I don't care what Vail and the others say."

"Did you do something?" She tried to be soft and gentle as a way to extract the full story. It seemed to work when she used that tactic on Olive.

He shook his head, then nodded. "I can't go back. I can't do it again."

Questions raced through her mind, but she waited, listened, hoping his story would come out in his own time.

When it did, it sounded like the disjointed sentences of a madman. "I'm not like Peter. All he sees is an enemy he needs to chase down. He's shooting soldiers out of the sky. This was sleeping civilians against thousands of tons of explosives raining from the sky. I shouldn't have come. I'm going to get you in trouble. It's not even smart to be here."

She tried to pull together the thought fragments he offered into something more coherent. "Are you on leave?"

She saw in his eyes that he understood the question behind her question. He shook his head. "AWOL."

Oh dear. Her mind raced through all the regulations she'd had to read as part of her WAAF training, while she forced her face to stay sympathetic and understanding. "Do you want to stay here while we sort things out?"

Teddy nodded, looking more like a boy than a man. "I don't want to get you in trouble. But I'm so tired, Gracie. So tired. I just want to forget."

"You won't get me in trouble." She might be lying, but that was a problem for another time. When her head wasn't foggy with a cold. "Why don't you tell me everything?"

He slumped at the table, his body clearly exhausted. The circles under his eyes seemed much darker as he sorted through his thoughts, trying to find a place to begin his explanation.

"I can't stop seeing it, Gracie. An ocean of orange that is actually a city on fire." In that moment, she saw it too, as though the burning city was right there in his eyes.

Teddy broke away from the eye contact suddenly. "I'm sorry. I should go."

"Not on your life! You stay here for as long as you need to."

Nothing on earth—not her father's rank, her duty as an officer herself, nor her commitment to king and country—could make her send Teddy away in this state. The British might not hang people for desertion anymore, but prison wasn't exactly an attractive alternative. She knew the penalties for being absent without leave grew as time passed. But before she could start encouraging him back to his station, he needed a good night's rest. "Have some tea and sleep on the sofa tonight. In the morning we'll talk about what we do next."

For the first time, Teddy picked up the tea cup and took a sip. Even though it must be stone cold, it did what good tea usually did: lifted the weight from one's shoulders.

"You look ill, Gracie. You should go to bed too."

She rubbed her forehead with her hand, half supporting her head as she did. "You first. Take the sofa."

His lips turned up at her sisterly kindness.

"Thank you."

He stumbled to the sofa and fell on it gracelessly. She sat with him until he fell into a fitful sleep.

———⋅◀∞⟩

Jack had as good as convinced Wilson that there was no connection between Grace and the duke that morning after Sotheby's. Still, Wilson had insisted Jack needed one more week at Bartondale, maybe two, to be sure.

"What happens after that?" Jack had asked.

"Why? You hoping to stay on there?"

"I'm not bad at my job, you know. The photographic interpretation, remember? The maps."

Wilson had simply shrugged. Maps were not his area, obviously. Jack knew he'd likely be transferred as soon as Wilson no longer needed him. With his days at Bartondale nearing a close, he made a plan. He'd ask Grace if he could write to her. Without any more interference from Wilson, they could slowly get to know each other heart to heart. It had worked the first time, hadn't it? He'd courted Dotty through letters.

If this was really his plan, then he had another letter to write before it could begin. One that needed to travel across the ocean and then across several states before it finally arrived in Robert and Maude Delany's Kansas City mailbox.

Jack mulled over his long-promised letter to his father-in-law for days before finally rising early one morning to put pen to paper.

Dear Mr. Delany,

No matter how many times Dotty's father had insisted Jack call him Robert, Jack had never managed to do it.

You once asked me to write to you if a woman ever came along that I felt as strongly about as Dorothy. At the time, only months after she had died, I remember me insisting that there would never be cause for me to write that letter. Four years later, I am doing just that.

I lost everything when Dotty died, like God picked me up by the ankles, turned me upside down, and shook me until all the things that made me who I was fell out and smashed on the ground. I think I've been picking up pieces of myself since that day, and I'm nearly whole again.

I'll be honest and tell you that the circumstances of the war mean that this relationship may come to nothing, especially since I have no indication from her about how she feels about me! But I wanted you to know first.

You no doubt knew this day would come, and I am sorry if it brings you pain to read these words. Please understand that this in no way diminishes the love I felt for Dotty. I still consider it an honor and privilege to have been able to call her my wife.

Yours sincerely,

Jack Marsden.

He slipped the envelope through the slot in the Royal Mail box in the village before heading on to Bartondale.

This week's work involved reconciling new reconnaissance images, sent from RAF Benson of the German U-boat pens in

Lorient, with the most recent maps produced by Bartondale. As he checked and cross-checked maps against their real locations, he told himself he was making extra trips to the library for reference materials in order to be thorough, not to casually check if Grace had recovered from her cold.

He wrote the code he needed on a slip of paper and handed it to Susie. She frowned when she saw it.

"I can't help you, I'm afraid. This is the file that's missing. Grace almost tore the place apart trying to find it before she got sick."

"How's she doing today? Do you know?"

"She's still sick, I'm afraid." Susie spoke before he even had a chance to get his question out. "If you are so worried about her, why don't you call in to see her on the way home?"

"I'm sure you'll cheer her up." Charlotte smothered a giggle.

Jack made a hasty retreat from the library, but once the idea was planted, it grew throughout the afternoon. He left work early so that he could call in at the cottage on the way to what he hoped was his final meeting with Wilson.

Jack strolled down the path that connected Grace's cottage to the main drive, pondering whether real spies yearned for their targets like this when they didn't see them for three days straight. He suspected not. It wasn't exactly professional. In fact, it felt mighty personal. Thankfully, he wouldn't be a spy for much longer.

Sarah gave a start when he walked around to the back of the house.

"Grace has a cold, I'm afraid, Lieutenant."

He couldn't quite put his finger on what was fishy about the stilted way she spoke. She kept glancing beyond him, toward the kitchen.

"You can go upstairs if you like." She spoke loudly, as though she had a bigger audience than just him. "But how about I just check to see if she is awake first? Let's go through the house."

Sarah guided him by the arm through the back door and up the stairs. He waited on the tiny landing outside Grace's door—barely wide enough for one person, let alone two—while Sarah spoke with Grace. He thought he heard someone scurrying about below him. Olive, perhaps?

"Have you come to check on me?"

Grace sat up in her bed, plush pillows supporting her, with the green robe he knew she usually kept hanging on the door around her shoulders. Guilt at having been in here before washed over him. A book lay in her lap, but she looked like she'd just woken up and didn't want him to know it. The pallor of sickness haunted her under her mussed-up hair. A sudden, powerful memory of Dotty lying pale and exhausted by a labor that wouldn't progress hit him, constricting his throat.

That was the thing about grief. It sneaked up on you, even when you thought you were done with it, in the unexpected assonance in everyday life. Grace didn't look anything like Dotty, but her vulnerability here, and the way it rhymed-but-not-quite with Dotty's after two days of agonizing contractions, caught him off guard.

"How are you feeling?" He put on his best doctor voice so the tightness in his chest wouldn't register.

"My head feels like a swamp of mucus, and my throat aches. I want to sleep until next week. Are they enough symptoms for you, Doctor?"

He grinned. "Sounds like you have a cold."

"A beast of one." She glanced at the open doorway, where Sarah stood.

"Did you see anyone else on your way here?"

Out of the corner of his eye, he saw Sarah gently shake her head in some sort of secret communication with Grace. She seemed to relax a little.

"No. Perhaps I'll try and find Olive on the way out." Olive had taken a liking to him once he'd started spinning stories about pirate captains for her. He was in the middle of an epic maritime saga, delivering it to her bit by bit each time he saw her. "I have a mind to kill off Redbeard in this episode."

"Oh dear, she'll be so sorry." Grace tried her best to laugh. "But he had it coming."

"What are you reading?" He indicated the book in her lap.

She held up an Agatha Christie paperback. "Just the latest from Mrs. Christie, I'm afraid. My mother would be shocked by my low tastes!"

"Well, I won't tell you how it ends then."

"You've read it?"

"I finished it last night." He didn't add that he'd started reading it because he'd seen it in the teetering pile on her bedside when he'd been searching her room.

They chatted for a few moments about books, but his professional eye told him that she needed rest, not company. He told her so.

"I wish you didn't have to go." She sighed, sinking into the bed covers.

So did he. The echo of Dotty's past vulnerability overcame him. Without thinking, he bent and kissed her head, her gold hair featherlight on his lips.

"Sorry," he murmured as he pulled away. "Sometimes you remind me so much of her."

He expected to be slapped, as he should be, but his lips turned up when he saw her eyes, rimmed with red, gazing back at him with a smile of their own. "Get better soon, Grace."

Suddenly, a great clatter penetrated up the stairs and into the room.

"What the . . ." Jack spun toward the door, but he was stopped from moving by Grace's hand gripping his with a strength that belied her illness. He looked back at her pleading eyes, urging him not to leave the room. Red, puffy eyelids couldn't conceal fear and desperation.

"It's just Sarah. She'll be fine."

Sarah burst into the room. "Sorry, miss, for the racket. It was just Olive knocking over some furniture in her pirate game."

"Do you need any help with it?" Jack asked.

"No. No. No. No help needed."

One denial would have been enough, but four? That felt suspicious. He looked from one woman to the other, certain they were lying about something. He could see it in their taut expressions, feel it in the sudden tension in the room. Their guilty faces spoke as loudly as a courtroom confession.

His heart ached. He'd been hoping to bid Wilson a fond farewell this evening. Instead, he'd have to explain he needed more time at Bartondale to discover exactly what Grace was hiding.

CHAPTER FOURTEEN

4 August 1943

Worthington murmured an awe-filled curse as he looked through the stereoscope. His features were a few shades lighter when he straightened up, inviting Jack to take a look too. His own eyes took a second to register what he was looking at, but once they did, Jack's response was the same as Worthington's, minus the expletive.

Previous photos of the aftermath of raids showed patchy damage. But every structure in every inch of this photo was a roofless shell. There were probably five hundred bombed-out houses alone, all lining streets filled with rubble. Bodies too, Jack was sure of it, even though the resolution wasn't high enough to see. This wasn't the only photograph either. There were dozens more of the same location.

His mouth went dry. Though not everyone in the building knew the name of the city or town in the maps they worked on, in this case there could be no doubt.

Hamburg.

The success of Operation Gomorrah was splashed triumphantly across every newspaper in the country and all over the wireless too.

Hamburg burns! screamed the headlines the day after the first successful night. *Germany's industrial heartland obliterated!*

The newspapers never published a count of the casualties, but looking at this damage, there must have been many, many thousands.

"Incendiaries," Worthington said. "They had to invent a new word to describe it. Firestorm."

"I'll bet." Jack straightened and changed the photo under the magnifier. At least this one showed shipyards and factories, not just houses.

"It's quite a victory, really. Hamburg will be crippled for months after this." Worthington put on a positive spin, even if the grim images made his face ashen.

In the biblical Gomorrah, the Lord destroyed everything living in the city and the land around it, rendering it uninhabitable. That was undoubtedly what the Allies set out to do to Hamburg. It was a victory, but it sure came at a cost. How many innocent lives were lost under those bombs and in the fires they set? How many hospitals, schools, markets had been reduced to debris? In a city that size there must be hundreds.

"Why do we even have these?" Jack was used to looking at photographs of targets *before* they were hit to check them against the maps Bartondale produced.

"Carter gave them to me. Seemed quite chuffed. Wanted us to see what happened when we get everything right."

The images didn't leave Jack's mind for the rest of the day. He left the building behind two of the workers from the art department, one of them with magenta paint on her cuffs. She chatted happily with her friend and with a tinkling laugh made plans for the weekend.

Did she know how her art was used?

Did any of the sensitive souls in that art room know the power they held in their paintbrushes?

Probably not. It was better that way.

Better not to think too much about what role your work played in the great machine of war. Better to just do your job, head down, without letting your emotions get in the way.

But who was he to chastise? He'd let his emotions get in the way with Grace, and while he still wasn't sure what she was hiding, he could only hope it didn't have the same devastating consequences as the maps they made at Bartondale.

"Charlotte! There's another mistake in this." Grace's temper lit at the simple error. Her pride still stung from the humiliation of having to admit to Worthington and Carter that her own carelessness had lost track of those photos. Carelessness she railed against in everyone else in the building. She would not let any more silly mistakes creep into their work. "You have to be more careful."

She now insisted they check and double-check everything that went in or out of the library. The cold that had forced her into bed for four days put them behind as it was. She didn't want to have to deal with a simple mislabeling.

"You've labeled this *M* when it should be *N*! What were you thinking?"

Charlotte sighed and took the file back from Grace. "Sorry." She opened it and made the correction.

"Go easy on her. Charlotte's finding it hard to think about anything other than Sergeant Millar at the moment," Betsy teased, pausing in her typing. "He finally worked up the courage to ask her to the pictures."

Charlotte's cheeks turned bright pink under her freckles as proof what Betsy said was true. Millar, a dispatch rider, had been trying to catch Charlotte's attention for weeks. Her obsession with romance was bound to be drawn to his persistence, even if he wasn't the most handsome of the men here.

"I don't care what you do with Sergeant Millar when you aren't working. I need you to concentrate while you are here, Charlotte." She knew she would have to apologize later for being so surly.

Ignoring the looks the girls exchanged, she went back to her desk. Her own concentration was lacking too. Her head was still stuffed with sickness, and her brain held a constant simmer of worry over Teddy. For someone who should be in hiding, he seemed to be doing little to conceal his whereabouts, taking long walks through the countryside.

On top of that, she hadn't seen Jack all week. Not since he'd visited her when she was sick. At the time Sarah's interruption and their clumsy attempt to stop him from discovering Teddy had eclipsed the sad beauty of the moment he bent to kiss her. But when she let the memory creep its way into the front of her mind, she became as dreamy as Charlotte.

She enjoyed a few moments of blessed concentration against the clicker-clack-click of Betsy's typing before the mail arrived, delivered by a sparrow-like young woman who worked with the dispatch riders. She gave a small stack of letters to Charlotte who, finished with her corrections, went about opening them.

"This one's for you, Grace." Apology colored her tone.

Grace took the letter, trying to smile her forgiveness at her friend.

Some people hadn't got the message that her family's living arrangements had changed. The post office was generally good about getting letters to her by way of the cottage or through Sarah, but some inevitably slipped through. Odd that this one didn't have a postmark.

Already fighting a losing battle with concentration, Grace let her curiosity win and opened the letter.

Inside was a single newspaper cutting from the society pages of *The Times* from the week after her visit to London. She turned to ice when she saw the headline: "Duke of Claret Cops Handful at Savoy!"

Grace felt bile rise in her throat. She angled herself away from the others while she read the rest of the story, aghast. Most of it was crammed with details about Andrew showing up intoxicated at The Savoy, written with lurid rhetorical flourishes. But the story also contained snide remarks about her. In fact, the only things it got right were the details of her dress.

Ambitious socialite Grace Deroy was not put off by the intoxicated state of the duke, insisting he dance with her to complete her opulent night of wining and dining.

To Grace's horror, the paper saw fit to use its rationed ink supply on printing a small photo of her dancing with Andrew, taken at a moment when he had his hand on her backside.

If the article itself wasn't bad enough, someone had cut the whole thing out of the paper and scrawled SHAMELESS in red-inked capital letters across it. They'd also scratched her name out of the story with such force the pen had ripped the fragile newspaper.

"What's wrong?" Susie asked, with her usual perceptiveness and concern.

"Nothing." Grace hurriedly folded up the paper and returned it to the envelope. "Just a note for my family."

She pushed the envelope under a blue manila folder on her desk so she wouldn't have to look at it. But, she was as distracted as Charlotte for the rest of the day.

CHAPTER FIFTEEN

6 August 1943

It wasn't technically a date, was it?

Grace debated the question in front of her dressing table.

She'd told the girls at work it wasn't.

It had been such a casual suggestion that it barely even counted as an invitation. And she was the one who'd done the suggesting, so he technically hadn't even asked her out.

Besides, Maggie would be there, so they wouldn't be alone. Thus, it couldn't be a date.

She'd just be going to the cinema with two friends—one new and one old.

Unless Maggie's husband, Alec, came.

In which case it might be a double date.

She pulled a face at her reflection in her dressing table mirror.

She was certainly getting ready as though it was a date. She'd soaked in a bath to feel fresh, shaved her legs, and rubbed precious drops of her favorite perfume on her wrists and behind her ears. She'd even dressed in her favorite bra and knickers—not because she expected Jack to see them but because they made her feel good about herself under the clunky uniform. WAAF uniform unless on home leave. Sigh. She planned to wear her own stockings—which was probably the biggest clue that underneath all the questioning, she wanted this to be a date.

Grace sat at her dressing table, her robe draped over her peachy silk slip, arguing with her reflection about the pros and cons as she brushed her hair. She pinned it up off her collar as per regulations—all the while wishing she could let it hang down around her shoulders. Next, she made a start on her makeup. When she opened the drawer to take out her compact and lipstick, she caught sight of a bundle of letters accusing her from their position at the front of the drawer. That was the purpose of her stashing them there, after all. To accuse her.

They were love letters, but she didn't think of them like that anymore. Now they were relics of her dead affair with The Artist. She looked at the red ribbon and the red letter *A* on an old Christmas tag hanging from the spot where the ribbon tied. She'd marked them with a scarlet letter to remind her not to be that silly girl again. She'd gotten the idea from a book, and twisted though perhaps it was, it had its intended effect.

She sighed, clenching her fist in hesitation before reaching into the drawer and pulling them out. She didn't need to undo the red ribbon to know what each letter said. The drawing folded up between the letters brought a blush of shame to her cheeks without her having to look at it. More so after Andrew's revelation at Sotheby's.

She was most definitely not the same girl she'd been back then, and Jack was not The Artist. He wasn't all fire and tempest, for one. He cared about propriety in a way that Alexander most definitely did not. Jack went to church and said he'd seen a sign from God about his wife. And that look of longing when he'd mistaken Grace for his wife still did funny things to her heart when she thought about it. This date—or whatever this was—might be the beginning of something so much better than what she'd had with Alexander.

She dropped the packet back into the drawer like a hot potato and instead grabbed her lipstick. A fortifying shade of deep red. She outlined her lips and pressed them together, telling herself she had carried on long enough worrying about that affair. Why should a man like that still have control over her after nearly three years? There were other, better fish in the sea. Jack Marsden, for one.

"Going on a date?" Her brother leaned on the doorframe, studying her reflection in the mirror.

If only she knew.

"Where have you been?"

"None of your business."

She spun on her chair to look directly at him. "Don't give me that! You've been gone all day, which seems rather a long time for someone who is meant to be in hiding. Where were you?"

"I went for a walk."

His casual attitude infuriated her. "A walk? Seriously? Did anyone see you?"

He rolled his eyes. "Spare me the questions, Gracie."

"Actually, I think I've been fairly good on the question front. I still don't know why you are here."

He pushed off the frame and turned to head back down the stairs.

She jumped up to follow him. "Don't you ignore me! We are having this out here and now."

She chased him down the stairs. "What if someone had seen you? Everyone in Lincolnshire knows our family! It only takes one person to make a phone call."

"I can't very well hole up inside this tiny cottage with you three the entire time."

"You're AWOL, Teddy! It's serious!"

Grace wasn't surprised he would want to go walking in the countryside to calm his nerves, but she was right about the risk.

"The house isn't exactly a safe haven with that Yank prowling around." Teddy spat the words.

Grace spat back. "Jack doesn't prowl! He's a good friend, and I am now having to lie to him."

His unexpected appearances meant she was constantly scrambling Teddy out of sight.

"If I'm interfering with your love life too much, Grace, I can go." Teddy looked like he might march out of the cottage then and there.

Grace assumed calm authority when she spoke again. "I'm just saying that we are all taking risks here. So in light of that, if you do need to get some air, could you do it at a time when you aren't likely to be spotted?"

Her fight with Teddy was only one of the things playing on her mind during the evening, making it difficult to focus on the film. On her right sat Maggie, her attention wrapped up in the magic of motion picture. On her left should sit a dashing US Army lieutenant. Not Nancy Filby, the butcher's daughter. Yet there she was.

Grace had planned to meet Maggie and Jack outside the cinema. She arrived first, greeting acquaintances with smiles and hullos as her nervousness grew. Her customary friendliness slipped when she saw Jack approach with a girl from the village, her arm hooked into his elbow. He made guilty introductions.

She forced herself not to frown. Years of training to be the polite hostess at Broughton meant she could smile serenely when everything under the surface wanted to scream for an answer.

"Grace, this is Nancy Filby. A friend of my landlady. Mrs. Johnston is sick and suggested I bring her along tonight. Nancy, perhaps you already know Grace?"

She heard his hidden explanation, but she could also read the other, more subtle clues in front of her. Clues that a man would be oblivious to.

Nancy's dress was old-style, inexpensive but recently updated with ribbon—something that would require fewer coupons than a whole new bolt of fabric. It was probably the very best thing she owned. Nancy's hair was nicely curled and flowed down her shoulders the way Grace wished she could wear hers, but her makeup was all beetroot and charcoal. None of that threatened Grace, who had enough lipstick and rouge to see her through the duration. But the nylons tripped her up.

The butcher's daughter was wearing new, shiny nylons that made the most of her skinny legs. The only place a girl like Nancy would get such a thing was from an American boyfriend. Like the one whose arm she held possessively in front of Grace's understanding eye.

Why would straitlaced, sensible Jack give a girl nylons if it didn't mean something?

Grace showed nothing but politeness when Maggie arrived, breathless from running the last few meters, but underneath the surface, confusion reigned. Especially when Jack produced tickets for himself and Nancy from his pocket.

"What is going on with you, Grace?" Maggie hissed as they walked into the auditorium behind Jack and Nancy.

"I just thought that he was unattached when I invited him along. I wanted to see what you thought of him. But there's obviously something going on there. Look at her legs."

Maggie looked at the nylons. She pulled her mouth to the side, doing the same calculations but coming up with a different conclusion. "I think she's more attached than him. He keeps looking back apologetically at you."

Grace shook her head, as much at herself as at her friend. "You're a good friend, Maggie. I just thought that . . . No, I'm just being silly. It wasn't a proper date. Just friends going to the cinema. It doesn't mean anything."

But the nylons might. She gritted her teeth and fought to keep a polite smile over her sulk.

They were forced to sit at the back of the stalls rather than six rows from the front, as she and Maggie usually did. Nancy asked if she could swap positions with Jack because of the tall man in front of her. The supercilious look Nancy shot Grace as she sat down infuriated Grace.

The newsreel began, showing aerial footage of a major offensive in Hamburg. A note of triumph echoed in the newsreader's voice as he described a great victory for the Allies.

"This was an Allied air assault without parallel in history!" the announcer exclaimed over footage of several Avro Lancasters taking off into the dusk sky. The film cut to an aerial view of the raid itself. The voice-over trumpeted statistics of the huge numbers of men and aircraft involved. Over one hundred thousand men, including the ground crews, had taken part in the assault.

Teddy's remorse became abundantly clear.

"Now we take up the story the next day, this time with the US Army Air Force, who proved that there are certain kinds of Hamburgers they don't like."

The script earned a titter from the audience, before the announcer reeled off a long list of military targets damaged in the raid. The accompanying footage showed proof of the raid's efficacy. Burned-out factories, shipyards, and ports "now as useful to the Nazis as last Sunday's newspaper." As the voice reinforced the scale of the Allied blitz, the crowd grew more enthusiastic.

Another newsreel picked up the story on the ground at a Bomber Command air station. The black-and-white footage of airmen jumping out of their bombers reminded Grace of her previous job.

She searched the screen, trying to recognize friends in the images. She knew the toll nightly operations took. She'd watched the faces of bright young men grow gaunt through the strain of their work. Even if they did put on a show, grinning and jostling to be included in the footage, at the pub they drank to forget. Like Teddy had.

These shots were carefully selected to boost morale among cinemagoers. No one wanted to see young men looking weary and frail—especially not when that young man could very well be your brother, son, or sweetheart. Her heart ached for the men ignored by the shot, the ones who couldn't bring themselves to ham things up for the camera.

The movie began with sweeping music and credits to introduce the stars. She tried to steal a surreptitious glance at Jack on the other side of Nancy. As she leaned forward, her eye caught on a face she recognized.

Two rows in front of her, across the aisle, Sergeant Millar sat with an empty seat next to him. After the dreamy sighs the girls in the library had endured this week, Grace expected it was intended for Charlotte. But just as the titles ended, Margot from Room Six came and sat next to Millar. If Grace hadn't sat through several conversations in the cafeteria where Margot had encouraged Charlotte to seize the day when it came to asking Millar out, Grace wouldn't have thought twice about seeing two people from Bartondale together. Now curiosity kept her eyes planted on the pair.

"What is Margot up to?"

Maggie was too engrossed in the film to hear her. With the auditorium only lit by the flickering light of the screen, Grace concentrated hard to see the pair properly.

Was Margot conveying a message to Millar from Charlotte? That she was unwell and couldn't join him perhaps? Or was Millar—and Margot for that matter—leading Charlotte up the garden path? Grace transferred all her irritation at Nancy Filby onto Margot. How dare she try to make a move on Sergeant Millar when she knew Charlotte was interested!

Grace couldn't keep her eyes from wandering back to the pair regularly, and each time she grew more agitated at the way Margot leaned into him, whispering in his ear. Grace was so intent on the micro-drama that she couldn't have recounted the story of the film if she'd been asked. But she supposed the date didn't go well—much like her own—because just before the interval screen displayed, Margot stood and scurried back up the aisle.

Grace couldn't help herself. She needed to give Margot a piece of her mind. For Charlotte's sake.

"I'll be back," she whispered to Maggie and pushed past Nancy and Jack. "Excuse me." The cinema doors were still swinging closed as she slipped out to catch a glimpse of Margot in the foyer.

"Margot!" she called. "What are you doing with Millar? You know Charlotte is interested in him! How could you?"

The woman looked up at her with surprise bordering on panic, which resolved itself into Margot's customary vagueness. Margo gave a dismissive hand wave. "I was just passing him a message from Charlotte."

Margot walked backward toward the exit as she spoke.

Grace snorted. "What kind of message was that?"

"The kind that will work! You'll see. Charlotte will thank me!"

Margot turned to push open the heavy glass door and slipped into the night.

Grace huffed. Under the lights of the cinema foyer, she felt foolish. It wasn't her business what schemes Charlotte and Margot had devised to make Sergeant Millar finally ask Charlotte out. Grace half suspected she had invented a drama to distract herself from Nancy Filby's nylons.

She ignored Nancy's glare and Jack's questioning looks when they appeared among the flood of people ready for intermission.

Jack had seen plenty of movies during his time in England. The army screened them to remind their troops of home, and Jack often went to the movies alone. While the other guys used the cinema as an excuse to be alone in a dark room with a girl, Jack had gone to be alone with his memories of Dotty.

It felt strange to be thinking about another woman now.

Not just one other woman. Two.

He knew Grace well enough by now to know the perfect politeness she showed outside the theater belied her real thoughts. It would have been rude to tell her in front of Nancy he had been ambushed by Mrs. Johnston.

"You look very nice, Lieutenant! What are your plans for this evening?" Mrs. Johnston had sprung the question on him when he came down clean shaven and ready to spend the evening with Grace and her friend. "Don't tell me you have a date?"

Was it a date? That question had hung in the air between them at Bartondale. He'd pondered on the way home, before deciding that it wasn't.

"Not exactly. I'm off to the movies with a friend."

"Just a friend?"

He didn't want to have this discussion with his landlady, so he changed the subject. "What about you, Mrs. Johnston?"

"Well, I was going to go to the cinema myself with Nancy. I bought the tickets earlier today, but I'm afraid I've come down with something." She coughed for dramatic effect. "I'm feeling so poorly that I had better stay home. Would you consider going with Nancy this evening? You can have my tickets."

At that very moment there was a knock at the door, and Mrs. Johnston opened it to reveal Nancy Filby looking up at him expectantly, wearing what he had to assume was her best dress with the pair of nylons that he had given her.

Boy, he was in trouble now.

He couldn't say no without being rude. He suspected even if he'd declared tonight to be a date when she'd asked, there was no way he could have stood against Mrs. Johnston's conniving. He'd set about being attentive to Nancy, all the while hoping to catch Grace alone for a moment so he could explain.

He lingered in the foyer during intermission while Nancy was in the powder room, and spotted Grace talking seriously with her friend near the ticket counter, their heads bent together. He hated interrupting what was obviously a conversation they were trying to keep quiet, but he needed to explain.

When she saw him approach, she sprang into hostess mode. "Jack, would you mind keeping Maggie company while I go and powder my nose?"

She flitted off before he had a chance to explain.

"It's so lovely to meet you, Lieutenant. I've heard so much

about you from Grace."

"All good things, I hope."

"Mostly." She narrowed her eyes. "Although, you really do need to come up with a good explanation for why that girl is wearing nylons."

He opened his mouth to speak, but he could think of nothing to say that didn't make him sound like a jerk. So as he'd done with Mrs. Johnston, he changed the subject. "You were recently married, Grace tells me."

"Yes, just in April. My husband is a pilot. He's at Scampton and I'm here, but we didn't want to wait until after the war in case . . . Well, you know."

"I understand." He supplied a brief explanation of his relationship with Dotty. "I would have married her after a week but had to court her for five years instead."

"You must miss her dreadfully."

"Every day, but lately a little less. Your friend has that effect."

Maggie raised her eyebrows and bit back a smile. "Grace has a wide heart, Lieutenant. She opens it to everyone. But if you really want to get close to her, you are going to have to do a little better."

"What do you mean?" Could this woman see right through him?

They glanced up to see Grace and Nancy returning from the powder room. Grace looked smug and Nancy bewildered.

Just before the pair were in earshot, Maggie leaned in. "Start by asking her out on a proper date. One where there aren't any extra people to get in the way."

CHAPTER SIXTEEN

9 August 1943

Teddy had banished himself to the large greenhouse in the farthest corner of the garden after too many close calls hiding from Jack when he walked her home in the evening. He insisted on sleeping out here, on a mattress that he had dragged in and crammed into a corner, legs extending under the potting bench. She told him he'd catch his death from the damp.

"Close to nature. More calming than an airfield barracks. And the roof doesn't even leak!"

His quip didn't have much energy behind it, leaving her to wonder if his remark was really a joke. "You can't be serious."

Perhaps her little brother had been driven mad by what he'd seen in the sky over Germany. His sleep on the sofa had been fitful, and he'd often called out or woke in tears and sweats. Was he trying to hide that by concealing himself in the greenhouse?

She'd read the regulations for the WAAF and RAF—both had been clear that she needed to encourage him to get back to his station as soon as she could. Within thirty days would be best, before more serious consequences for his actions kicked in. So she moved one of the wicker seats from the outdoor setting into the greenhouse and sat down to signal she wasn't moving until they were done.

"You need to tell me what's going on."

He flopped onto the makeshift bed, shaking his head.

She insisted. "I used to work at a bomber station, you know. I saw what they did night after night. I know it takes a toll."

Teddy swallowed, his Adam's apple bobbing, his jaw visibly tight. He stretched out on his back, elbows sticking out so his hands could cradle his head. But this wasn't a peaceful posture. Not with that vacant expression he wore.

"Whatever you think you've seen, Grace, you didn't see what we did to Hamburg."

Once he started, he couldn't stop.

"That first night, everything went right. We were spot on target. The window jammed their radars like we were told it would. The bombs did their job."

She'd seen men like this when she worked at Bottesford—remorseful and determined to drink away their time until they had to get back in an aircraft and do it all again. But she'd never seen it so closely, never in someone who didn't try to cover their emotions with bravado.

"There was more fire than I have ever seen on a raid. It was well alight when we got there, and we just added more. And we just kept going night after night."

She reached out and covered his hand with hers, causing him to look up and meet her eye. "I saw the newsreels."

He nodded. "Newsreels don't tell you what it smells like to fly through air thick with smoke from a burning city. Not just factories and oil refineries, Grace. Houses. Houses with people sleeping quietly in their beds. Children even." He paused, pained by his own words. "The top brass always told us to think about what happened to the sleeping women and children in London, Liverpool, and Coventry. But they were innocent people too."

Grace stayed silent, not wanting to move in case she broke the spell that had opened him up and pulled the story from him.

"We gathered around the wireless to hear the BBC report on the operation the following day. Some people cheered and clapped. I left the room, vomited into a latrine.

"When we'd landed and slipped into our beds, the people of Hamburg were still burning in theirs." Sobs shook his body.

Now she moved, sitting herself next to him on the mattress. He rolled over onto his side, drawing his long limbs up and wrapping his arms round them.

 She'd made him talk, but she had no words to respond. Nothing that didn't sound hollow or trite. She simply laid her hand on him and let him cry, praying that God would help her know what to do.

∞

Another envelope was on her desk when she arrived at work the next morning, placed on top of a blue manila file like another accusation. She was alone, but she still glanced around to see who might be watching.

Of course, there was no one. She'd arrived at work absurdly early because she'd been up since 2:00 a.m. worrying about Teddy. She'd given up any pretense of trying to sleep at four and had drained two teapots by six, so she figured she'd make a start on her work to distract herself.

Her eyes dropped to the envelope on the desk again, and she reached out to run her fingers across the heavyweight paper. Neat but otherwise indistinct copperplate writing with no postmark. Just like the one she'd received last week with the newspaper clipping.

Frowning, she grabbed up the envelope, inserted her finger into the gap of the fold, and ran it under the flap, separating the glue. She used more force than she needed to, and the envelope tore open, dropping its contents onto her desk.

She unfolded another newspaper article. Not *The Times*. This was from the *Evening Standard* and dated last week: "Mystery Girl Meets Dirty Duke!"

The salacious headline screamed up from the page.

Andrew Hastings, otherwise known as the Duke of Clarence, showed up in Mayfair last night with a mystery woman on his arm. The eligible duke and his mysterious mistress were seen whooping it up across some of London's most exclusive night spots, before being caught by our cameras in an amorous embrace.

The article continued, giving background on Andrew and speculating about the woman's identity. The accompanying photograph was small but scandalous, showing the Duke of Clarence in a compromising situation with an elegantly dressed blonde. They were obviously kissing much more passionately than was appropriate for a public place, judging by the position of his hands when the flashlight of the camera caught them. The duke was easily identifiable, but the woman's face was obscured.

She almost choked when she read the caption.

The Duke of Clarence caught in a compromising embrace with sultry socialite Grace Deroy.

Laughter bubbled up inside her at the absurdity of it. The woman's face couldn't be seen, but her hand raking through his hair was clearly visible. Around her wrist were several gold bracelets—almost identical to the ones she'd worn to dinner with her parents at The Savoy.

A cold hand gripped her heart when she examined the small photograph more carefully. The black-and-white newsprint couldn't show the color of the dress. Her eyes swept up to scan the article for more details about the woman's clothing. She usually drank up that information from the society pages. This time it was poison.

The article described the woman wearing an elegant jade-green gown, *simple but Grecian in design, with honey-colored hair falling in loose waves fastened only with a gold comb.*

The cold hand tightened.

Dress. Hair. Jewelry. All exactly the same as she'd worn to her mother's birthday dinner. Only this wasn't her. This was an im-poster doing a very good job of looking like her, and the paper appeared to have bought it hook, line, and sinker.

She sank into her seat, a thousand thoughts swirling through her mind. When Charlotte and Betsy came chattering down the hallway, she folded the clipping and slipped it into her pocket.

"Morning, Grace," her colleagues chimed as they walked into the library.

"You're here early," Betsy said.

Grace swallowed, her mind swirling. "Yes, I couldn't sleep."

"You look like you've seen a ghost, Grace! Are you sure you're not coming down with something else?" Charlotte paused in front of Grace's desk and gave her a curious look. Her eyes dropped to the envelope that lay forgotten where Grace had dropped it on the desk.

Grace snatched it up. "Yes, I'm fine. Thank you." But she wasn't. She'd simply perfected the art of giving a polite response to thoroughly shut down further inquiry.

Charlotte sniffed and turned away, making a face at Betsy.

Rioting thoughts refused to let Grace get on with her work. The article felt like a lead weight in her pocket. "You know, I have been up since very early. Had too many cups of tea. Excuse me while I use the ladies'."

Eyes followed her out of the room from under raised eyebrows, but she didn't care. She made her exit but headed for the rose gar-den instead. Surely the scent of the flowers in the dew of the morn-ing would help calm her. Seated on the stone bench, she pulled the article out of her pocket and read it through again, trying to put herself in the position of an objective *Evening Standard* reader following the society pages.

No one would doubt this was her.

Not with her name under the photo and the woman wearing the same clothing as had been written up in *The Times*. But she'd been tucked up in bed reading Agatha Christie, with her eyes and nose streaming from a cold on the night this was meant to have happened.

Grace had a good mind to call the offices of the *Evening Standard* and give them a piece of her mind. But the cold hand gripping ever tighter stopped her.

This didn't feel like a simple error. It felt deliberate.

It was obviously Andrew in the picture, and there were hundreds of other women in London with Grace's shade of honey blond. But how did they get her dress? It was a custom-designed gown from one of the best tailors in London. And how on earth did they replicate the bracelets that were French antiques passed down through six generations of her mother's family?

She couldn't stop the breaths that came in too-quick succession. Andrew must be behind this. The paper wouldn't dare publish something like this otherwise. Hadn't he practically told her he'd use the newspapers against her? But why would he do such a thing when she hadn't said a word about the painting? Was it a threat? Maybe he was simply showing off, demonstrating his power to make her life miserable if she said anything about the painting.

She hated the power he held over her, to make her burn with shame for something she hadn't done. She wouldn't let herself cry, no matter how tight the lump in her throat became. Wouldn't give in to this feeling of powerlessness, the weight of being so alone with it. Last time she'd felt this way, when that horrid painting had gone to auction only a few weeks after Alexander's death, she'd had Peter to help her bear it.

Who could she go to now?

Peter was at Debden. Teddy had his own problems.

She couldn't go to Jack. She liked him. What if he believed the worst and decided Nancy Filby was more his kind of girl after all?

Maggie had always been a stalwart friend, but Grace still hadn't told her about Alexander. Although her friend had experienced romantic scrapes of her own, she had grown up sheltered, a vicar's daughter. They'd only met when Grace had joined the WAAF and since that seed of faith, planted in Grace at Oxford, had blossomed. Maggie looked up to Grace. Could their friendship, one of the things she held most dear, survive her confession? She couldn't risk it.

Suddenly she knew why people enjoyed speaking to priests in the secrecy of the confessional. But she wasn't Catholic, so she couldn't just rock up, could she? And Oscar Williams, the vicar at her church, was too chummy with Maggie and likely to be just as scandalized.

No, she was on her own with this one. So alone that she ached.

———◦◦◦◦◦—◦(∞)

"She's resourceful, I'll give her that," Wilson said, forgoing the polite greeting and getting straight to business.

Jack sat down before responding. He'd schlepped all the way to Grantham to have this meeting. The pub hummed around them, the smell of hops strong in the air.

"What do you mean *resourceful?*" Jack asked.

Wilson slapped one of the preceding week's editions of the *Evening Standard* on the table and told him to turn to the society pages. Jack did and couldn't miss the headline about the Duke of Clarence. He shook his head at the picture of the duke in some kind of amorous embrace. As he did, his eye caught on the caption.

"That can't be right . . ." He checked the date on the newspaper.

He peered more closely at the picture. He couldn't deny that those were her bracelets, and the gown was similar to the one she'd worn at The Savoy, but without being able to see more of the woman's face or figure, it was impossible to tell if this really was Grace.

"You don't think it's her?"

"He's hardly her favorite person. Anyway, that's the weekend she was in bed with a cold."

Wilson's look told Jack he didn't believe "in bed with a cold" was a good enough alibi.

"I saw her with my own eyes. I'd be very surprised if she took a trip to London just for a smooch with the duke."

"You said yourself she was hiding something, and our agent tells us another important exchange was made sometime that week. She might have traveled to London for that and used the rest of her time to catch up with her old friend."

"Except I don't think they are friends," Jack said. "Whatever they were once, she's not still stuck on him."

"You aren't moving fast enough, Jack. We need answers now. Ask her on a date this weekend."

"I tried. She's away this weekend." He had actually made an idiot of himself blurting out the invitation in front of everyone in the library. She'd looked very sorry to have to turn him down and suggested that she was free the following week. All of which he told Wilson.

"Make that date happen, Jack. And tell me when it's confirmed."

Wilson's parting words rang in his ears the next day when he saw Grace in the rose garden. He asked to join her for lunch. Her indifferent nod told him she was preoccupied.

"Are you well and truly over your cold?"

"Hmm?"

After meeting with Wilson, her vague reply caused suspicion to flare.

"Oh yes. It's amazing what being tucked up in bed for a couple of days with Mrs. Christie does for a summertime sniffle!"

He remembered how she'd had a pile of the paperbacks on her bedside. But then another memory tugged at him. The sound downstairs, the heightened tension around him afterward, the begging in her eyes that he not ask questions. What was she hiding?

"I'm sorry but I'd be poor company today, Jack. I have a lot on my mind."

"Is there anything I can help you with?" Wilson would want him to dig deeper, though he was asking a genuine question.

She sighed. "I don't think so. My brother's in a little bit of trouble. I'm not really able to say anything more about it."

"Peter?"

"No, my brother Teddy. You haven't met him."

"I could be a listening ear."

For a moment he thought she would spill her troubles out to him, but she shook her head instead, closing off the subject with effortless politeness. "I need to keep my family's confidence. I hope you understand? Actually, I think I'm finished here. You enjoy the roses." She stood abruptly and marched off before he had a chance to ask more.

CHAPTER SEVENTEEN

10 August 1943

"What is taking you so long?" Worthington called from across the room. "You are normally fast at this!"

Despite trying to give his full attention to his mapmaking work that afternoon, Jack kept turning over yesterday's conversation with Grace. He dragged his attention back to his task each time it strayed, but what would usually take him minutes had taken over an hour.

He was working with the stereoscope, comparing reconnaissance imagery of Turin with the maps that Bartondale had produced. Jack usually took to his task of checking the details of factories and industrial plants with conscientious diligence. As the last person to touch the map before it went off to Bomber Command HQ, he figured if he made sure the simplistic line drawing of the city matched the aerial photographs precisely, then Allied bombs had more chance of hitting those targets—and only those targets. Not houses. Not the centuries-old buildings that housed innumerable cultural treasures.

"Earth to Jack!" Worthington did his best to steal Jack's his attention.

Jack decided not to break his already shredded focus with an answer. Through the stereoscope he identified the Fiat factory and cross-checked its coordinates with documentation from the researchers. Then he transferred his attention to the Bartondale map, making sure the size, scale, and position of the factory was accurately, if simplistically, represented. Everything seemed to line up. But was seeming enough? He had to be sure.

"We need to get these ones out this afternoon," Worthington insisted.

"I'm just finishing up." It would be easy to just stop there. No one would know if his work was sloppy. But he'd know. He'd never be able to think about Italy without a guilty conscience if he didn't do everything within his power to make sure this was accurate. He went back to the stereoscope to double-check the reconnaissance photos and check the topographical details.

"Finally!" Worthington, who never seemed to have the same compunctions about accuracy that Jack did, took the complete map and documentation from Jack. "I'll take these all up to the group captain for sign-off, then I'm heading to the pub with Margot. Coming?"

"So how long's that been going on?" Jack asked.

After a meeting earlier in the day, Jack had arrived back to his office to find Worthington talking with Margot. From their flushed and disheveled appearances, he'd suspected he'd thwarted a less-than-professional workplace interaction. Again.

"At least I'm a man of action!" Worthington avoided his question with an accusation.

Jack held up his hands, playfully defensive.

"You're always trailing after Deroy with puppy dog eyes! I notice things you know. And you are playing a losing game there, my friend. Deroy has her claws into the Duke of Clarence, poor man."

"What do you mean?" Jack's jaw tightened.

"Didn't you see the *Standard* last week? Caught on camera with him. I always knew there was something incredibly naughty lurking underneath the goody-two-shoes persona that she puts on. Anyway, are you coming for a drink or not?"

"I've got some things to finish off here." That wasn't exactly true, but he had no desire to be at the pub with Worthington and Margot, and a huge desire to address the jumble of thoughts in his mind more methodically.

"Suit yourself." Worthington rushed out.

Jack sat at his desk and drew out a blank sheet of paper. His pencil flew across the paper, and in no time he produced a reasonable likeness of Grace. He was a passable artist, especially when he'd spent so long considering her features he could easily draw them in his mind's eye. Still, his skill wasn't good enough to capture the preoccupied look she wore recently.

His mind wandered back to their encounter in the rose garden yesterday. He bit the end of his pencil and, pushing his chair back, stretched out his legs to rest his heels on the desk. She'd said her brother was in trouble. He'd watched her weigh the merits of telling more, but she'd obviously decided that would not help matters. So it wasn't medical trouble, then, or Jack might have been useful. He'd had to check against his notes when he got home, but Jack thought he recalled Teddy was with Bomber Command, a navigator. One of the end users of Bartondale's maps. Life on a bomber station was an incredible seesaw between life-endangering missions over Europe and trips to the pub to give you the Dutch courage to do it again the next night. There was ample room for trouble within that.

His pencil danced back to her nose, trying to draw it as having the sniffles. There was no doubt in his doctorly mind that she'd been genuinely sick that day. If she was fooling him, it was a disguise worthy of Mrs. Christie herself. But how sick? Maybe she'd been playing it up and using the time off from work for a secret assignation.

He shook his head over the drawing. All Wilson's knowledge of Grace was theoretical. His own came from close, personal study.

She held the honor and good name of her family as paramount. It seemed entirely out of character for someone who took propriety so seriously to be caught in the kind of embrace he saw splashed across the society pages.

Jack folded the piece of paper and slipped it into his breast pocket. At least he'd finally asked her out on a proper date. Maybe then he'd get Wilson his answers.

"This is the perfect spot!"

Maggie stared at Grace as though she had gone mad. Grace knew very well the middle of a potato field wasn't an ideal place for a picnic, but she wasn't thinking about atmosphere. She had secrecy in mind. There were no trees here, no way for anyone to overhear what she was about to ask Maggie.

"Perfect for what?" Maggie looked about for a place to set the picnic basket she had lugged into the field.

"Maggie, I have to ask you something." Grace didn't wait for permission. "Does Alec ever talk to you about his work these days?"

Alec and Maggie had worked closely together at Bottesford. Grace thought it was a fair bet that now that they were married, their pillow talk still involved the air force.

"Sometimes." Maggie didn't quite meet her friend's eye.

She was right to be cautious. They'd both seen the posters about loose lips sinking ships plastered about the place.

"I wouldn't ask you if I had any other choice. Did he fly over Hamburg?" Grace asked, her voice almost a whisper.

Maggie obviously knew exactly which operation Grace meant. She shook her head, then bit her lip. "But I was working in the control tower that week. It was a big raid, Grace. Almost every station in the Northeast was involved in some way. Seven hundred aircraft, maybe. They called it Operation Gomorrah."

Maggie worked as a radio operator for one of the huge number of RAF Bomber Command air stations now dotted around this part of the country. Hers was the last voice the aircrews heard before they left for their raid and the first voice they heard when they flew in. She sat in the control room during the operation, listening to the communications, so she had a unique perspective of an entire operation. Even though Maggie had already said more than she ought, Grace's eyes pleaded for more.

"Coming home on the first night, the Bottesford crews were triumphant. There were no losses, and the news reports hadn't come through yet. The next few nights were . . . much more sober. And by the end of the week, they all looked . . . empty." Maggie had to search for the right word to describe the men she worked with. "Why are you asking, Grace?"

She was treading on very dangerous ground, but she had to be straight with her dearest friend. "Do you remember Teddy, from Christmas? He's based at Skellingthorpe."

"Was he part of it too?"

Grace nodded. *In for a penny, in for a pound.*

"He's . . . AWOL. He can't face returning to his station because he can't face doing it again." Grace whispered even though there was no way they could have been overheard.

Maggie pursed her lips, as though thinking about the least seditious thing to say next.

"Alec flew in the dams raid." Maggie matched Grace's soft tone, although what she was saying was common knowledge. The crews in that operation had been widely celebrated by the press. They'd dropped bouncing bombs that had breached dams and flooded the Ruhr Valley just before summer. Alec had even been featured in a newsreel trumpeting it as another morale-boosting win. "He hasn't slept well since he saw the newsreel footage of . . . the outcome. He keeps waking up worried he is drowning."

Grace nodded. Tears prickled behind her eyes.

"What do you say to him?" Grace begged for any scrap of advice to help Teddy.

"I just hold him when he cries." Maggie's glistening eyes told Grace she had no idea what she was doing either. "And pray that the war will be over soon."

Maggie's words traced through her mind as Grace made her way back to the cottage, slow steps dragging. She'd get Sarah to draw her another hot bath so she could sort through her problems one by one. What to do with the fugitive resident of her greenhouse. How to get to the bottom of the stories in the *Evening Standard*. Her niggling worries about Olive. Whether or not Jack was really interested in romance or still had Nancy Filby on his mind. The last one was the least of her problems, but it still added to the scramble inside her head. A jumble that only intensified the moment she stepped into her cottage and met Sarah's fretful eyes.

"What's happened?"

"Olive pleaded for an extra slice of bacon when she was at the butcher's," Sarah explained. "She told them what we'd been given wouldn't easily be shared around four."

Mr. Filby, the butcher, was a jolly man with the plump, round physique of someone who never wanted for meat. His cheeks glowed red when he laughed, which he did often. His vigor ran counterpoint to his wife and daughter, who also helped in the shop but had skinny frames and mouths that only opened to give the most sparing of comments.

"Did the butcher say anything?" Grace asked.

Sarah shook her head. "I covered by saying that Lieutenant Marsden often comes to call on you. I know it was giving away too much information for the butcher shop queue, but I couldn't think of anything else that would point the gossips away from Teddy."

Grace didn't bother to suppress her fleeting satisfaction at the thought of Nancy Filby's face when Sarah had said that, no matter how uncharitable and nasty it was.

"Nancy didn't happen to be there, did she?"

Sarah frowned. "That's beneath you, Miss Grace. But she didn't look happy when her father told Olive that he'd find her an extra scrap 'because the way to a man's heart was through his stomach, after all.'"

"Let's go talk to her about it, shall we? You go and get the biscuits."

Olive looked thoroughly penitent and horrified at herself for being so thoughtless. She stood in front of where Grace sat on the sofa, her head down. "Will Teddy be in very big trouble if people find him here?"

The child deserved truth, no matter how hard it was. "I'm afraid so. He might go to jail—or worse. That's why you can't say anything to anyone."

Olive bit her lip. "What if I already have?"

Ice ran down Grace's spine. "What did you say?" She tried to sound calm, hoping to invite the child to give the whole truth.

"When Captain Jack was here the other day, he asked about Grace's brothers. I told him what fun Teddy was and how he would love Jack's pirate stories."

"Did you tell him Teddy was here?"

"Not *exactly*."

Grace made herself smile, even though she wanted to shake Olive. "Think very hard, and try to tell me the exact words you said."

"Here. A gingersnap might help." Sarah handed a biscuit over.

Olive didn't eat with her usual gusto. Instead, she nibbled nervously while she tried to think back to her conversation with Jack. "I told him all about Teddy and how fun he used to be to play with. I told him that lately he wasn't very cheerful and that Jack's stories might be able to cheer him up."

"Did you say when you'd last seen Teddy? Or anything about where he is now?"

Olive stopped eating to think, then finally said no with enough certainty that Grace let out the breath she'd been holding. Sarah reached out and pulled the child to her chest and surrounded her with a hug. It was too big a burden for such a little girl.

"I think you are out of the woods. But don't mention him to

the lieutenant again, you hear."

Olive smiled and pulled away from Sarah. "Do you think he is in love with you, Grace?"

"How old are you?" Grace exclaimed, amused by the sudden turn in conversation. "Nine going on nineteen?" Grace maneuvered the conversation again. "There's something else we need to talk about, Olive."

Olive looked like the biscuit had stuck in her throat. "I haven't done anything. I promise!"

Sarah shook her head at the girl's guilty conscience.

Grace suppressed a giggle. "I never said you had."

Olive relaxed.

"We are going to London next weekend. We are going to try to find your family."

Sarah's eyebrows almost hit the ceiling at Grace's declaration. But Grace was suddenly certain this was the right course of action. Olive, however, settled herself silently on the sofa next to Grace, looking down at her hands in sober reflection. Which had to be a first.

"What's the matter, Olive? You've been asking about them for weeks."

Olive's mother used to write frequently when Grace's family had lived at the big house. Sarah and Grace both assumed that the sudden stop to the letters meant they'd been among the victims of the bombs that fell on London. So, Grace suspected, did Olive.

"It's one thing to wonder, but it's another thing to know."

How could one little girl be so insightful? It melted Grace's heart. "It's probably time to find out for sure, don't you think?"

Olive worried her lip with her teeth, brow creased, then brightened. "Do I get to stay at The Savoy?"

Grace grinned back at her. "I would never dream of staying anywhere else."

CHAPTER EIGHTEEN

14 August 1943

The Savoy restaurant tinkled merrily around her, but she couldn't take her usual pleasure in it. Not when she was lying in wait for a scoundrel like Andrew. She just knew he was here. When she'd booked the room at The Savoy, she'd made discreet inquiries into him. This was, after all, one of his favorite haunts too.

She'd been caught off guard when she last saw him at Sotheby's, but now she was on the offensive, steeled against anything he could say. She wore her WAAF uniform on purpose. It gave her courage. Besides, if there were any photographers about today, pictures of her in a uniform would at least show she wasn't just a bright young thing gadding about town. Then she simply ordered a table and waited until he walked in with his date.

When the waiter led them past her table, she stood up and hissed in his face. "What exactly are you playing at?"

"Gracie! What a delight!" Andrew looked excited despite her obvious inclination to go for his jugular. "Have you met Martha?"

"I'm not interested in meeting any of your ingenues, Andrew. I want to know why you are dressing one of them up as me!"

He raised an eyebrow at her, then looked across at his date. "Why don't you meet me back at the room, darling? This might take a bit of time."

The woman nodded meekly and slipped away. Grace looked after her, immediately regretful she had used that word.

"Let's take this conversation somewhere private, Gracie."

"What, so you can have it reported that we had a clandestine catch up? I don't think so. And don't call me Gracie."

A waiter approached and held out the chair for him. She had booked a table for two, after all, and the waiter seemed anxious not to keep someone as important as a duke waiting. Grace remained silent while the waiter fussed with napkins, handed out menus, and filled their crystal glasses with water.

She eyed Andrew, the tension between them like an elastic band stretched to breaking. As soon as the waiter stepped away, Grace let fly, as quietly as she could. "I don't know why you are targeting me now, but it stops tonight."

"Targeting you? I can't imagine what you mean."

She clamped her hand to the table to stop it from slapping the self-satisfied look off his face. "I saw the story in the *Evening Standard*, Andrew."

The flicker of amusement in his eyes told her he knew very well what she was talking about. He glanced down at his menu as though everything on it displeased him. "Most unfortunate they made such an error with your name, I suppose, but not my problem. Take it up with them."

Her practiced politeness threatened to slip. "What are you playing at? She was dressed exactly like me. There's no way those stories would be in the newspaper if you didn't want them in there." She took a few breaths to keep herself on an even keel, even though hysteria clutched at her. "Why are you doing this? I haven't said a word to anyone about Sotheby's."

He gave her cold consideration that sent a shiver down her spine. "This is bigger than you, Gracie."

"Maybe I should tell someone what I know then."

"You don't have it in you. You might be a picture of virtue these days. But those sketches, Gracie. They tell a very different story."

No matter how prepared she thought she was to meet this accusation again, she still felt the heat rising to her face. His lip curled into a smile. Every fiber in her wanted to abandon the restaurant and flee the city, but she refused to let him muddle her thoughts by evoking her shame. She needed to be bold—even if it might have been easier to avoid saying anything else.

"I'm not that person anymore."

The look of disdain he swept over her was palpable. "Oh, Gracie. Still going on about that rubbish? Those university pals of yours really did a number on you, didn't they? I heard it all from Alexander."

"It changed everything. Besides, it's very clear now that Alexander was using me."

"Don't even say it. He was in love with you! It shattered him when you left, you know. I was the one who picked up his pieces. I told him not to drive out to you that day with that wretched painting, but he wouldn't listen. Your change of heart cost him his life!"

The careful mask of affability and unapproachable contempt he'd been wearing at the beginning of the conversation slipped when he spoke about Alexander. Underneath, she saw glimpses of pain, real and raw. He blamed her for the death of his friend.

"Don't put that on me. He was responsible for getting in that car and driving it too fast." The flush in her cheeks, the feeling of holding back tears, annoyed her, but she couldn't stop it. "Is that what this is about? Revenge for Alexander's death?"

She forced herself to meet the eyes studying her across the table. In his cold consideration, she felt so small.

"It's not, but it's a very satisfying side effect."

"Then why are you doing this?" She didn't want to sound desperate, but knew she did. The diners at the table next to them glanced her way.

A thin smile tightened his face. "As pleasant as this has been, Gracie, I think we're done here."

He signaled for the waiter.

"We certainly are not—" She cut herself off when the waiter appeared.

"Miss Deroy will be eating alone today." Andrew stood and threw his napkin down on his vacated chair. "I have business to attend to upstairs."

Grace felt the murmurs of the patrons around her resonate across her skin as she sat in the restaurant, more confused than ever.

———•◄(∞)

"Is this it, Olive?"

Grace, Sarah, and Olive stood in front of the building that was the last known address of Roger and Ann Brook, Olive's parents. However, the place was a ruin, like most of the suburb around them. The German bombs had certainly done their job on Hackney.

Olive looked around her and shrugged. "I don't really recognize much."

Grace patted the girl's shoulder with a sympathetic smile. Of course she didn't recognize much—she'd barely been into school when she'd left London to live with them at Broughton.

Sarah took the initiative to knock on one of the still-standing doors and made inquiries about the Brooks, but came back to them with nothing except direction to the nearest Red Cross center.

Grace didn't miss the look Sarah sent her way. She'd been telling Grace for months now that she needed to write to the Red Cross with the Brooks' particulars. A letter might have been more efficient than the three of them trooping here, but the visit gave Grace a reason to be in London aside from confronting Andrew. Convenient cover when she didn't want to admit her ulterior motive.

She was still unsettled by yesterday's meeting. She'd forced herself to go over the conversation several times, each time trying to

162

understand what Andrew was playing at. But she found herself more perplexed. He was still deeply grieving Alexander's death, that was certain, but he wasn't out for revenge. Instead that was a "satisfying side effect" for him. What on earth could his main game be?

She pushed the thrum of worry aside to focus on the immediate problem and looked around, grateful that her own home—though overrun by the military—was still standing.

"Come on. We'll go and find the Red Cross office, then have tea and cake to cheer us up."

Olive's lost little face brightened, and she walked ahead, with Sarah following the directions the neighbor had given her. Grace hung back, so preoccupied with the problems of the last few days that she managed to knock shoulders with another young woman, causing the woman's shopping to topple from her hands.

"I'm so sorry." Grace bent to retrieve the paper-wrapped packages. "Completely my fault."

As she handed back the packages, she looked the woman in the face for the first time. A jolt of recognition shot through her. "Katie! Katie Baines?"

Grace glanced down at the woman's belly, seeing for the first time how it swelled out, confirming the woman in front of her was indeed a friend from her last posting.

"Oh, Grace! Hello. But it's Katie Ables now."

"Of course!" How could she forget? Katie had been one of the prettiest girls in the WAAF when Grace had met her in her previous job, with blond hair, full lips, and the kind of smile that melted hearts. She'd practically thrown herself at Alec, but since he'd only had eyes for Maggie, she'd settled for one of his less scrupulous crew mates. The belly was the result.

They stood awkwardly for a moment. Katie hadn't been the kind of close friend Grace would immediately embrace, like Maggie, but Grace was no less happy to see her. She tried to keep her questions at a polite pace rather than raining them all down on Katie at once.

"When are you due? You look so well!" Pregnancy, as well as the compliment, gave Katie a glow. Though her belly was visible, it didn't look as big as Grace might have expected.

"Next month. I had to leave the WAAF when I started to show. I live with my parents again, while Jonty's at Scampton."

"And how is Jonty?" Grace grinned, allowing her soft spot for Katie's husband to show. He was one of the best and kindest men she had ever known, who had puppylike energy even though he bore terrible scars over his face. He wasn't the father of Katie's baby, but he had asked her to marry him because the real father wouldn't.

"He's very well." A genuine smile broke across Katie's face, giving Grace the impression that even though her marriage had been born out of convenience, it wasn't an unhappy one. "But what are you doing here anyway? This is not your usual haunt."

Grace gave a quick explanation about Olive and how they'd come to track down her parents. "We're on our way to the Red Cross now."

"Can I walk with you?"

"Of course. And if you tell us where the best place is for tea and cake, you can come. My shout."

Katie hesitated. "I have to make sure I get these back by three for my dad." She indicated the parcels that Grace had sent tumbling moments before, then glanced at the watch on her wrist. "But I think we've got enough time."

Grace and Katie chatted companionably about common acquaintances as they entered the Red Cross's Hackney branch, then waited in line for an interview.

A letter would have been quicker.

Grace quashed the thought. Every single person in the queue was looking for someone they loved. She covered her doubts under friendly chatter with Katie until they took their place at the front of the queue. A dark-haired woman sported a blue armband inscribed with a badge that labeled her a Searcher for the Wounded Missing and Relatives Department of the British Red Cross and Order of St. John.

"Let's start with the form, shall we?" She plucked a blank form from the top of the pile on the desk that sat between them and attached it to a clipboard. "Name of the person you are looking for?"

Between them, Grace, Sarah, and Olive gave enough information for the woman to fill out the form in its entirety.

"What happens now?" Olive piped up when they were done.

"Now, you wait." The searcher was kind but firm. "We always do our best, but it takes time." She moved her eyes back to Grace. "And our best doesn't always provide the answer people want."

Grace nodded at the code in the woman's words—she might not be able to reunite Olive and her parents.

"I understand. Thank you." Grace took Olive's hand and led her out toward the restaurant.

"Oh, the time!" Grace turned when she heard Katie exclaim behind her. "I have to get these back to my dad or he'll be furious! Sorry I can't have tea with you." Katie turned away, then turned back just as quickly. "The name was Brook, right? I'll ask around too. A neighbor mentioned a family who've had rotten luck over the last few months. I'll keep an ear out for you, maybe do some digging. Are you still at the same place?"

"Yes. At least, you can write to me there and I'll get it. But I'm sure you'll have your hands too full shortly to do any detective work for us."

Katie glanced at Olive. Compassion washed over Katie's face, softening her features, revealing to Grace a more grounded version of the flighty girl she'd known when they'd worked together.

"I'll do what I can."

"Are you sure you can't stay?"

"I'd love to. But there'll be hell to pay from my dad if I don't get these to him."

"All right. Give my best to Jonty, will you?"

Katie nodded. "Good to see you, Grace. I hope you find the girl's family." Then she turned and sped off with more pace than a heavily pregnant woman ought to have.

A long walk was what the doctor ordered for himself. A full day of hiking through the countryside. Mrs. Johnston had made hints about bringing Nancy along with him as a guide when she'd handed him his packed lunch and his mail. But he'd insisted—firmly—he was happier to be alone.

He'd already marked out his route on the map in the satchel bouncing against his hip. His notebooks were in there too. He planned to sit down for lunch and read over them. That combination of fresh air, exercise, and a long stretch of time for thinking usually helped him come to conclusions. It helped his "little gray cells" do their job, as Hercule Poirot would say.

He threw himself to the ground and sat under a shady tree for lunch. After laying his notebooks on the ground in front of him, he took out his wax-paper-wrapped sandwich and too-tart apple. He felt a bit like he did in his college days when he would go out with his medical textbooks and study notes, trying not to think about Dotty while he settled into study. The irony here was that he was trying not to think about Grace at the same time as reviewing notebooks, sketches, and diagrams all filled with her.

A jaunty whistle broke his concentration. He cursed himself under his breath. He should have known that he wouldn't be entirely alone. He looked up to see a man walking toward him, too close for Jack to gather up all his papers without looking suspicious. He managed to conceal the sketches before a gust of wind swept one of his papers toward the approaching farm boy, who swooped it up and brought it over.

"This looks like yours." The young man handed it to him with a smile, which drooped when he looked Jack in the face, although Jack couldn't tell how the man recognized him. The fellow looked no more familiar than any other villager Jack had seen while he'd been living here. His hands left grubby marks on Jack's paper.

"Bit old for fairy tales, aren't you?"

Jack glanced down, hoping the paper that had blown away was not incriminating in any way. Thankfully, it was just his descriptions of "Goldilocks and the three bears"—which was how he had coded his meeting with Grace's family at The Savoy.

"Just doing some thinking." Jack shut off conversation.

The man took the hint, tipped his hat, and walked away. Jack's gaze followed him, and the man glanced back once over his shoulder. Jack couldn't quite pinpoint what was out of place, until he was on the road walking home.

The voice! The kid might have looked like a farmer, but he didn't have the rolling midlands accent Jack had found so hard to understand in his first days here. He spoke with a crisp, cut-glass sound.

The exact same accent as Grace.

CHAPTER NINETEEN

16 August 1943

"Why, you sneak, Grace!" Susie greeted Grace playfully when she arrived at the office.

"We all thought you were sweet on OAF!" Betsy cried.

"I beg your pardon." The flood of dread through her veins told her what they would say next.

"The newspapers!" Charlotte giggled.

"You weren't kidding when you said you knew the duke, were you?" Betsy teased.

"Grace, what's wrong? We're just joking." Susie, always the most insightful, must have seen Grace go pale and lean her hand on the desk to steady herself. Susie's inquiry was enough to make the other girls go silent.

"Newspapers?" Grace's voice dropped low with dread.

Charlotte handed her a copy of the *Evening Standard*, folded back on itself to show the society pages. It was only a paragraph, but it was by far the most lurid story that had been printed.

Under the headline "Daring Deroy and the Dirty Duke," the newspaper told another fabricated story about a public encounter between her and the duke in the foyer of The Savoy. The newspaper claimed it had to take into account rules around public decency, then described an invented incident where Grace and the duke flouted those same rules. In the foyer of The Savoy, no less! She blushed at the idea before going pale with the horror of it.

She thought she'd heard titterings behind her back on the way in but had dismissed them, but now . . .

"It wasn't me." Her protest felt weak even to her. She didn't even know why she bothered, because she could tell her friends didn't believe her.

"What do you mean it wasn't you?" Charlotte asked. "You told us yourself you were going to visit him."

"I did, but we didn't . . ." She waved her hand over the newspaper because she couldn't find polite words.

She felt hot and cold and dizzy, like she was going to throw up.

Betsy and Charlotte both gave her dubious looks and returned to their work, but Susie put her hand on Grace's arm. "Grace, you really look like you are going to faint! Take a seat."

"You know, you're right. I don't feel well. I think I'll go . . ." She didn't finish the sentence before she sped out the door.

She almost made it out of the entryway, when more teasing assaulted her. Not the gentle, good-natured kind the girls had used, either.

"Gracie Deroy! Haven't you been a naughty girl?"

Worthington's voice sent a chill through her, stopping her in her tracks with his taunt. "You know, if that's how you wanted to spend the weekend, you didn't have to go all the way to London. I would have obliged."

She fought the nausea and spun around to give him a piece of her mind, but Jack got there first.

"Drop it, Worthington!" His voice was calm and commanding. One hand held the newspaper, but the other was balled in a fist, like he was going to lash out at any second.

"Don't give him the time of day, Jack. He's not worth it."

She grabbed Jack by the arm and pulled him out the front door and along the path that wrapped around the house, ending at the rose garden.

He kept pace with her, and when they stopped, he turned his face to scan hers. "Are you going to tell me what's going on?"

"It's not me." She pleaded her innocence, indicating the newspaper he still had in his hand. She was grateful he didn't open it to the story again. "It's not the first story that they have published."

It felt good to tell someone. Even if it came at a cost. She felt certain Jack would cancel their planned date now. After holding them back from him for so long, words seemed to tumble out of her now.

"The first one was after we were at The Savoy. Well, that *was* me that time but . . . you were there—you know what really happened. Then the *Standard* published another with a picture! My name in the caption, my clothing, but the face obscured. But it wasn't me. I was sick at the time. It looked like me—it was my clothing—but it wasn't . . ." She slapped her hand over her mouth to stop the sob threatening to escape.

"Slow down, Grace."

Her mouth and brain raced each other to piece everything together. The rest of her body helped by pacing around the garden.

"I did see him in London, but not like this. We didn't—" She didn't want to dignify the newspaper's report by repeating it.

She stopped pacing as realization dawned. Andrew had known this would be the weekend to put something compromising in the newspaper. He knew it would be almost impossible to deny having an encounter like this at The Savoy, when she had truly been with him there.

"What do you mean? You saw him on the weekend?" His voice was cold.

But her brain was racing so fast, she didn't have time to think about his disapproval. "I confronted him . . ." Her sentence drifted off as her mouth failed to keep pace with the thoughts swirling through her head. He'd been planning this even as she'd been confronting him about the other reports.

Jack waited silently for her to finish filing through her thoughts, which had now taken a different turn.

"I know what this must look like to you, but I swear there's nothing between us." She should give him a way out, a chance to reconsider being associated with her. "If you'd prefer to reconsider our date now, I understand."

"Absolutely not! I've been looking forward to it all week. I'm not going to let hearsay like this put me off."

"Thank you." A tiny bit of the stress and worry from the past few weeks slipped off her shoulders as she smiled. "At least I've got you."

Grace had been dreading this telephone call.

Her mother had left more than half a dozen messages with Sarah since the newspaper article appeared, and Grace's excuses for not returning the calls were wearing thin.

"She said that she thought she might want to come and visit you."

Grace translated the threat in her mind: "Call me back or I will come and find you."

She had better get this out of the way now, or she would be stewing over it during her date with Jack, when all she really wanted to do was drown herself in the delicious feelings inspired by his smile.

She flopped down onto the sofa as the operator connected her to the exchange. "Hello, Mama." She forced brightness into her voice.

"Are you determined to bring embarrassment down on your family? What do you think you are doing being photographed gallivanting around with that man?"

"Just to be clear, your main objection isn't the—what did you call it?—*gallivanting* itself. It's the fact you think I was photographed doing it!"

"You told me three years ago that I should forget any aspirations I had for my daughter to marry a duke. Yet here you are, going about with him as though you are already married."

"I'm not going about with him, Mother!"

"Really? Because the newspaper says otherwise, young lady."

Young lady. That title always stung. Her mother used it to conjure up every bit of her disappointment in Grace. She took a deep breath before she gave her explanation of what she thought had happened. That someone was trying very hard to make it look like she was engaged in an affair with the duke.

"Really, Grace. That is too farfetched, even for you."

Hearing her mother scoff had the same sting as being slapped in the face. If she couldn't get her family to believe her, who else would?

Her mother berated her without taking a breath for a good three minutes.

"I must fly, Mama. There's someone at the door." She dropped the telephone back into its cradle with more force than was necessary.

"Was that Mother?" Teddy's gentle voice carried to her from the kitchen door.

Grace nodded. "How much did you hear?"

"Enough to know that you are most definitely not keeping company with Andrew Hastings again. I thought you'd go blue in the face with your denials."

"Not that Mother believes them." She bit her lip while she debated showing him the newspaper clippings. She went to her writing desk and opened the drawer where she had stashed them. "Look at this."

She handed the three all-too-well-read newspaper clippings to him and waited while he read.

He let out a low whistle when he finished. "Eye-catching pictures in those first two, Grace."

"Yes, and someone has gone to an awful lot of trouble to make that second one look like me. But I was at home with a cold when it was taken. You can bet there's a third picture somewhere that is too indecent to print."

"Who would do that, Grace?" Teddy handed back the news clippings.

"Andrew's involved somehow, but the question is *why?*" That worried her the most. She couldn't work out why.

"I don't suppose this is a good time to tell you that someone came looking for you while you were gone. I let her into your room because she said you were lending her a dress. I thought it was that friend of yours who came over at Christmas. What was her name?"

"Maggie?" *Please let it be Maggie.*

"I thought so. Pretty, with dark hair."

"Half the girls in England could fit that description, Teddy."

He shrugged. "Was anything missing when you got back?"

She hadn't noticed anything, but she also hadn't thought to check.

"Don't let this get to you. Go out and enjoy your American. We'll figure it out when you get home."

If only it were that easy.

CHAPTER TWENTY

20 August 1943

Wilson had arranged every detail. He'd organized a car for Jack to "borrow from a friend" to get them to the restaurant in Grantham, which Wilson had chosen. He'd even arranged for a corsage for Jack to pin onto the collar of Grace's uniform when he picked her up from the cottage.

"This is a proper date, after all."

Jack tried to ignore the irony of his words and enjoy Grace's responding smile as he pinned the flower in place. This was only a proper date if your idea of courting involved inviting others to listen in to your entire conversation while you quizzed a woman on her history with a man who clearly made her anxious. Which Jack's did not.

"I'm just sorry I can't dress like it's a proper date. WAAF uniform at all times unless I'm on home leave, I'm afraid." Her mouth pulled to the side in apology. He'd heard her moan before having to wear the scratchy blue wool suit, pale-blue undershirt and tie, and awful stockings every day of her life.

"I think you look fine."

Fine wasn't the right word, but he knew she understood the feeling behind it, because her smile broadened and her eyes brightened.

At least Wilson had chosen the restaurant well. The quiet atmosphere and low light were nothing like the bustling British restaurant a block away. The waitstaff here were prompt without being intrusive, and everything happened to the music of a violinist in the far corner of the room. The intimacy the little corner table provided sure made dinner feel like a real date, until Jack considered that Wilson had probably opted for a location that would make it easier for him to eavesdrop.

Grace glowed all evening. She practically lit the dim room with her own luminescence. He basked in it through the entire meal as they talked easily about books and film and travel and their hopes for after the war. She pressed him on whether he would consider taking up medicine again. Guilt compelled him to answer her honestly.

"I don't know. Dotty's still dead. I can't change that."

"You must know that wasn't your fault. And who knows—maybe in time someone will come along who will help you restore your faith in your profession."

"I suppose stranger things have happened."

His voice almost caught in his throat as he moved the conversation on, unwilling to ask her if she wanted to be the one to help mend what was broken inside him. Not with others listening in. Still, heart flowed effortlessly into heart as they talked. If only that corsage didn't stare accusingly at him through the whole meal, eventually drawing him back to his real purpose.

His left hand and her right stretched toward each other on the table, not quite touching. The heat of her fingers made his own tingle.

"Thank you for this evening, Jack." Neither seemed to be in a rush to leave. "This has been such a wonderful night. It has cheered me up no end."

"I'm glad. I know this hasn't been a great week for you. You've seemed preoccupied for a while now."

He wished he could give her a night off from thinking about the Duke of Clarence. But every word was being weighed by other people listening somewhere else. The sooner they got to the truth of the matter, the better.

"Grace, what happened between you and Clarence?"

He fought every instinct to squirm under the long, hard look she gave him as she wrestled with what to say. When she decided he was worthy of her confidence, he tried not to appear relieved.

"I had such a crush on him when I was seventeen. But I think most girls did. He has every advantage in life—wealth, position, good looks—and knows exactly how to wield it to get what he wants. My mother was very keen that I pursue him. After all, who doesn't want their daughter to be a duchess one day?"

"It didn't come to anything?"

"No. He's got a cruel streak that I can't abide. To this day Andrew sets my teeth on edge."

That tracked with what he'd seen in London, her visceral response to the duke's presence when she had been dancing with him.

"But I did spend some time with him at Oxford, because I was head over heels in love with one of his friends."

Boy, did he want to ask about that friend, but he needed to keep the conversation on track. "So why did you go and see him last weekend?"

She skidded her hand forward to clasp his. "Please, Jack, do we have to talk about him?"

They would want him to press her more. Wilson had specifically ordered him to get that information. But when it came down to it, he couldn't. Not with her hand warming his, her eyes so wide and pleading. When it came to the crunch, he had no talent for deception. And whether he wanted to admit it or not, he was simply too in love with this woman to cause her more pain.

"Of course not."

He shifted his hand to take her fingers in his, then raised her hand to his lips and gave her knuckles a reassuring kiss. "In fact, let's get out of here. It's time I drove you home."

He knew he shouldn't linger long after he drove her back to her cottage. But there was still light in the day and enough heat that Grace took off her jacket and rolled up her sleeves. All he had ahead of him this evening was a difficult conversation with Wilson, not to mention Mrs. Johnston. He couldn't seem to make himself leave.

Their goodbye stretched on for an hour as they wandered around the back of the cottage to sit on the wicker sofa and kept talking about . . . nothing really. The stars, the garden, the next movie Grace was keen to see. Anything to delay. Just them, with no one listening in to what they were saying. In the creeping darkness of the garden, he wasn't a spy. He was just a man enjoying the company of a beautiful, fascinating woman who made his heart do wonderful leaps in his chest.

After they exhausted conversation topics, Grace rested her head on his shoulder. The smell of violets—sweet and powdery—tickled his nose and filled him with longing. Longing like he'd never felt before, not even for Dotty. Surely she could hear the way his heart hammered as he draped his arm across the back of the wicker sofa and let her settle under it as though it was the most natural thing in the world.

"I should probably go." His mouth spoke the opposite of what his brain thought. With her so close, his head was as light as a giddy teenager's. He knew he was acting like a boy, dragging himself away from his sweetheart to meet his parents' curfew, not the fully grown, once-married man he was.

"Good night then." She turned up her face so it was inches from his, overwhelmingly close.

All he had to do was lean forward slightly.

He pressed his lips onto hers, featherlight. She leaned in and reached her hand up to the back of his neck. That was all the encouragement he needed. He reached his other arm around her waist, pulled her into him, and deepened the kiss, completely lost in the feeling of her in his arms.

He couldn't know how long they were like that—it could never be long enough—before he heard a clatter at the kitchen door.

Sarah.

Light spilled from the kitchen in flagrant violation of the black-out restrictions. Jack sprang away from Grace. He laughed at being caught out like a schoolkid, before he saw the disapproving glower on Sarah's face.

"Relax, Sarah." Grace giggled, obviously on the same high as him. "It was a just good kiss." She giggled like she was thirteen again. "I mean, a good-night kiss."

Grace, at least, saw the humor in the situation. She turned back to Jack. "Good night." She sighed as she stood, leaving the seat beside him cold and empty. Was her every nerve ending suddenly alive and craving more? His sure was.

"Good night." He pushed aside the impulse to grab her hand and pull her back to the seat when he saw how Sarah's doorway disapproval deepened. Sarah's eyes didn't leave Jack as Grace walked past him into the house, her steps light with happiness.

Jack stood to leave, but Sarah stopped him.

"With all the other Deroys away, I'm the one who needs to step in here and say I hope your intentions are honorable, Lieutenant Marsden."

Did the guilt twisting his stomach show on his face?

It must have.

"I thought so. What? Do you have a wife back home?"

Tell the truth when you can, he reminded himself. "No wife. I'm a widower."

"Just mind you don't hurt her, all right? She deserves better." Sarah turned to leave.

"I'm not going to hurt her."

If only the very next moment didn't show him up for the liar that he was.

CHAPTER TWENTY-ONE

Grace didn't go too far into the house while Sarah spoke with Jack, no doubt giving him a stern talking to about his intentions toward her. Instead she sat at the kitchen table, tingling from head to toe and reliving every moment of that kiss. The brush of his lips on hers, tentative and soft until she gave him a little encouragement. She flushed afresh at the memory of how he'd held her tighter, parted her lips with his. The spicy notes of his cologne still lingered as a knock sounded.

"I'll get it!" she called to Sarah and made her way to the front door with dancing steps.

Expecting Martin or one of the staff at the big house, she didn't bother to peek through the window first. If she had, she might not have opened the door.

Two civilian men with grim expressions met her on the stoop. "Grace Deroy, you are coming with us."

Her heart, still dancing from Jack's kiss, seized in her chest as one man grabbed hold of her arm. "What are you doing? Let me go!"

She raised her voice, hoping to alert Sarah and Jack, if he was still here. The second man grabbed her other arm and yanked her from the cozy cottage and into the front garden.

"Don't manhandle me! What is going on?"

Volume was her only weapon against them, but her suddenly dry throat couldn't make the right sound. The men didn't respond. Not with words and certainly not by loosening their grip. She struggled against it, but their hold only tightened. They propelled her down the path, her feet barely touching the pebbles. She shrieked at the sight of two more men waiting by a car on the other side of the gate.

Fear clutched at her heart. She was being kidnapped. Terror and adrenaline made her strong. But the men were stronger. They forced her up the path toward the roadway. She struggled more in her panic, lunging to hold on to the front gate when the men tried to bustle her through it.

"What's happening? Who are you? What are you doing? Let go of me!"

Whoever these people were, she wouldn't be ripped from her home like this without a fight. Kicking and wrestling as best she could, she tried to use the gate as leverage. Another set of hands joined the others, easily dislodging her clasp on the gate.

"Let me go!" The scream tore out of her throat. "Get off me! Do you know who I am? Let me go!"

Her frantic eyes adjusted to the dark and registered the scene outside her home. Cars. More men, moving like shadows in the night, into her house.

"Put her down! Explain what's going on!"

The fear and fury in Sarah's voice mirrored Grace's own when she saw a black car parked on the road outside the gate, its door open and ready to receive her.

They were taking her away.

Another scream tore through her throat.

Her eyes ricocheted around the scene until they landed on a familiar face. Someone who might save her from this incomprehensible fate.

"Jack! Jack!"

Even in the dark, she saw how he hesitated. For one dreadful moment she thought that he would let them take her. But he moved, blocking the path with his body so they couldn't force her into the car.

"Give her some dignity!"

His voice carried some authority, enough that the men loosened their grip. She struggled free and stumbled toward him.

He caught her, but instead of reaching around her protectively, making her feel safe, he held her at arm's length. His hands rested gentle and firm on her upper arms. It might as well have been a caress compared to the clench of the stranger's hold. But she couldn't take any comfort in it when she saw the way he looked at her.

"Here."

He pressed her uniform jacket into her hands, the corsage he'd pinned to her lapel earlier now a crumpled mockery. Taut confusion replaced his earlier tenderness.

"What's happening?" She searched his face and found guilt in his eyes. The fear that pooled inside her wasn't the panicked kind. It was deeper and harder to fight.

He knew. He knew what was happening.

"Jack? Please, what's happening?"

"Answer their questions, Grace." He stepped away, avoiding her eyes.

Her own eyes widened in disbelief. Then the other men were at her elbows again, forcing her into the car.

Hopelessly overpowered, she screamed, hoping someone at Bartondale might hear. In a final vain attempt to avoid being shoved into the car, she struggled like a mad cat being forced into a bath, complete with hissing and scratching. One of the men had to shut the door on her fingers to finally get her in, but as soon as he did, the driver hit the accelerator.

"It's no use screaming now, Miss Deroy."

One of her captors pressed his hand against a satisfying pair of red gouges on his cheek. When his hand dropped away, he appeared much more sinister than he had a few moments ago. She shrank back.

She screamed again, knelt up on the seat, and slapped her hands against the rear window of the vehicle. The screams turned to sobs as she watched her cottage and Broughton and Jack and Sarah and everything she loved disappear into the inky night.

———————◦⊷∞⊶◦———————

"You blew it, Jack." Wilson eyed him with unmistakable contempt. "I tried to do this gently. But you didn't even try to ask her questions, Jack. Now time has run out. We have to get our answers the old-fashioned way."

"What does that mean?"

A civilian with the stern face of a police officer approached and handed Wilson one of the manila folders they used at Bartondale. Wilson flipped it open, using a flashlight to check the contents.

Jack saw the aerial photographs as Wilson flicked through them.

"What's DZ-95401?" Wilson asked.

Jack hesitated as he tried to place why he knew that number. "It's in France, I think? Grace has been trying to find those photographs for weeks."

"Has she? Funny they turned up under her bed, then."

"We also found a bunch of letters from the Duke of Clarence among her things. She lied to you last night, Jack."

"I don't think—"

"That's the problem. You didn't think. Not with your head anyway!"

He wanted to mount his defense by biting back that Wilson should have chosen a professional spy if he wanted the job done properly. But the way Grace had screeched his name still rang in his ears. He'd never be able to erase the look of terror and betrayal that had come over her face when she'd pieced together what had happened.

He'd wanted to tackle the men holding her and lay punches

into them. But the fire within him didn't overrule the pure mathematics of the situation. There were far more of them. He couldn't have stopped her from being taken, even if he'd tried.

"I'll be in touch with further instructions." Wilson slipped into one of the other cars and drove off too.

Jack stood in the empty laneway, stunned.

"Who are you?"

Sarah's voice stirred him to turn toward the house. He took a few steps toward her terrified eyes, but she scrambled into the house and barricaded herself behind the cottage door.

He had no choice but to return to his accommodation. Mrs. Johnston met him at the door, but he had no time for her disapproving interrogation.

Jack spent the night pacing. This was all wrong. Not just the entire situation nor the way Grace had screamed his name. Not the insults Wilson had spat out at him, but something he couldn't place. Something to do with the file.

As soon as he thought his commanding officers would be awake, he ran to the phone booth in the village. After a few phone calls, he managed to get through to Lieutenant Colonel Lewis. The conversation wasn't pretty.

"Fell in love with the girl, did you?" Lieutenant Colonel Lewis smirked down the line.

Too true, but he wasn't going to admit it. "Sir, something's not right. My mission was to work out whether or not Grace Deroy was somehow colluding with the enemy. I've spent weeks here and found nothing except a woman who's worried about her reputation."

"Wilson told me you were blinded by emotion and missed vital clues."

"I didn't miss anything." Ice edged his voice. He might be in love with her, but he was sure of this. "There was nothing to miss. She isn't guilty. The king of England is more of a fascist than her!" He barreled on, spilling out the words he had practiced during the night. "Sir, if they have arrested the wrong person, and I think they have, then there is still someone inside Bartondale leaking information."

Lewis grunted. Jack knew a military man needed a military kind of reasoning.

"With respect, sir, I was dragged into this in the first place because leaks from Bartondale were going to impact our men. I am concerned if they've mistakenly arrested Grace Deroy, then the job isn't done. Our men are still at risk, sir. You have to keep me in play."

The lieutenant colonel was silent for a long time before replying. Jack held his breath until his superior spoke.

"I'll talk to Wilson." He didn't sound happy about it.

CHAPTER TWENTY-TWO

Grace sat in a cellar.

It was a windowless room with a single bare bulb hanging from the ceiling, but the place smelled the same as the cellar at Broughton—like vinegar and clove, aging ham and drying herbs.

This was probably some kind of pantry.

Or it was once. Before the door was reinforced.

Until they—whoever *they* were . . . she still didn't know—had taken down the shelves and moved a table and two simple wooden chairs in here.

Yes. She couldn't be sure but, from the flashes of her surroundings she had seen on the way in, she'd deduced this was a basement, probably of an old house like Broughton, that had been converted into . . . what? That was the question.

A prison?

Her skin crawled with fear. If her own home had been requisitioned and turned into a mapmaking facility, perhaps others had been seized and given over to uses that were far worse.

After the long, circuitous car journey here—a route designed, she was sure, to confuse her in the night—she'd lost all sense of where she was. She didn't know how long she had been waiting in this room, but the longer she did, the more she became certain the delay was meant to intimidate her. But why?

She sank down on one of the hard chairs as weariness invaded her bones. A sudden muffled cry, coming through the thick wall of the room, sent a chill down her spine and made her jump to her feet again.

"Hello? Is anybody there?" Her voice shook with fear.

No response. She called again. "Hello?"

She listened for more cries. When none came, she was left wondering if she had imagined it. As she sat back down at the table, more warily this time, she knew she hadn't. The ragged, pained quality of the sound was not something that came from within her. But it turned her blood to ice.

Grace had never felt more alone.

She became aware that her fingers were throbbing, probably from when the car door had slammed on them. That sensation made her aware of the bruises created by the rough hands that had dragged her from her home. Weariness and confusion engulfed her, dragging her eyelids down.

But there was no time to pray. Two men, different ones this time, flung open the heavy door. They wore plain clothes. One looked distinctly thuggish, while the other sported a finely tailored suit.

Fear made every hair stand on end, like she was a cornered cat ready to strike out. Would they grab her again and drag her somewhere else?

"Take a seat, Miss Deroy," the suited man said. "The more you cooperate, the sooner this will be over."

Sooner what would be over?

Grace stared at him, trying to work out where she had seen him before. When he sat down in the chair on the opposite side of the table, placing a manila folder like the ones they had at Bartondale in front of him, the recognition clicked in her head.

He was at Sotheby's. With Jack. But he'd had an American accent then, not the Oxbridge one he used now. What name had he given? Bitman? Butler? Did it matter? It probably wasn't his real name anyway. Glancing at the other man, who assumed a position in the corner of the room near the open door—in case she tried to make a break?—she sat opposite him

"What's your name?"

"You know that already. Grace Deroy. Corporal in the Women's Auxiliary Air Force." She didn't recognize the small voice going out of her, so she cleared her throat and summoned the best defense she had in these circumstances. "My father is Sir Henry Deroy. I don't know what he's going to make of this."

She thought she saw the faintest twitch of a smile on the man's face, before he continued. "Where do you work?"

Was this a test? She wasn't meant to mention the work that she did. But surely the existence of Bartondale was not a secret from whoever these people questioning her now were.

"I think you know that too. In the library at Bartondale."

"You asked for the posting. Why?"

She blinked. "Because, it's . . . it was my home. It's been in my family for generations, and I wanted to make sure it wasn't harmed by Air Ministry thugs."

"You consider the Air Ministry to be thugs. How so?"

She snorted. "They certainly have no respect for three-hundred-year-old furnishings!" But as she spoke, understanding that he might have a deeper meaning dawned. "I don't mean their war work. I'm in the WAAF!"

"What's the significance of DZ-95401?"

She recognized the number. She had spent a great deal of time over the last few weeks looking for that file. It was the one she had left on Worthington's desk and then been blamed for losing.

"I can't talk about my work." She didn't mean to clam up, but she didn't know who these people were. She could be contravening the Official Secrets Act if she gave details about the work at Bartondale.

"We know you took the file, Corporal. We want to know why."

Grace frowned. "Is this a trick? You know very well I signed the Official Secrets Act like anyone else and can't talk about my work."

The man persisted, leaning in and knitting his fingers together over the folder on the table. "Why did you steal the file?"

"Steal it? I didn't."

But the photographs were missing, weren't they? And now she was being interrogated about the file. She had to defend herself. "It was a careless error."

"Do you expect us to believe that? We found the photos under the floorboards of your bedroom."

She'd had a hiding place there for her jewelry, but she'd never put any photographs or files there.

"You're lying."

Then she heard that terrible cry again, clearer this time, without the door to muffle it. Someone—a man, perhaps? It was difficult to tell—was letting out a deep, tortured moan. She glanced toward the door. The brute guarding it didn't flinch or react to the heartrending sound. Neither did the man opposite her. He simply pressed on, as though there wasn't someone in pain just outside the room. Ice ran down her spine at their lack of reaction.

"Why did you take the file, Miss Deroy? Who are you working with?"

They clearly suspected her of something far more sinister than carelessness, or why would she be in a place like this? The truth was her only defense.

"I put the file on his desk."

"Whose desk?"

"Lieutenant Worthington's."

"You went to London straight after that, didn't you?"

"Yes."

"You met with the Duke of Clarence in London?"

Deeper fear prickled inside her. They were asking questions that they already knew the answers to, which scared her more than anything else.

"I met with him by accident."

"He's your lover, isn't he?"

"Lover? No!"

"That's not what the newspapers are saying. The picture they paint is clear. The *Evening Standard* even has a picture of you! You can't deny it!"

Another cry from beyond the room pierced the air. The chilling lack of compassion on the faces of the men in the room compelled her to her feet. Andrew Hastings became irrelevant to her.

"What is happening? Where am I? I won't answer any more questions until you tell me what's going on."

∞

Back in his room, Jack dropped to his knees, ignoring the pain as they hit the hard wooden floorboards, barely softened by the rag rug Mrs. Johnston put next to his bed.

How could he let them take her?

And why did seeing Grace ripped away from her home make the memory of Dotty resonate through him this way? Was it because Dotty was wrenched away from him? Not in the same tangible way as Grace, of course, but the feeling of one loss echoed the other.

His chest tightened, and he willed his too-shallow breathing to calm down. A sob escaped anyway. Even to his own ears it was a horrible, soul-wrenching sound.

He didn't want the memories to come flooding back to him. Watching Dotty labor for two full days. Knowing something wasn't quite right but being unable to separate the personal and professional when it was his own wife crying out in pain. Watching the increasingly serious faces of his colleagues as things didn't progress the way they should have. When they'd suggested they might have to operate, he didn't hesitate for a second. Of course they should, if it would help her. But finally the labor progressed, before they even had a chance to prepare the operating theater.

Her cries as she pushed now rang in his ears, the way Grace's did this morning. But the silence that followed was worse than the screams.

No baby wailing into life. No wife crying with joy.

As midwives worked feverishly to revive the little girl, Dotty hemorrhaged. His colleagues pulled him from the room as he screamed at them to help her.

All he could do in that moment was fall to his knees and pray. Not with words but with great soul-filled groans.

For nothing.

He knew from the look on the approaching doctor's face it was all in vain. Dotty was gone. The baby was dead.

None of his medical training prepared him to enter the room where the doctors and midwives laid them both together, the baby in her mother's arms. There was no point in praying for them then. That night the room he and Dotty had been preparing for a babe, with powder-yellow paint, sat as empty as the bed next to him. As empty as he was.

All these feelings were meant to be buried and done away with. Despite being years and continents away from that moment, the grief assaulted him as real and raw as it had been then.

He sobbed, not caring if Mrs. Johnston heard.

After the blank weeks that followed their deaths, joining the army had felt like a logical choice. He'd reinvented himself as an army officer, drawing on his knowledge of maps and surveys from his early days in his father's shop. The days before Dotty.

He hadn't exactly lied about his experience, but he'd played down his medical training. The recruitment officer was a friend of his father's, and he either took pity on Jack in his grief or simply assumed that as Bill Marsden's son, he had wanted nothing more than to follow his father into the mapmaking business. In the brew of war, they didn't check his medical credentials thoroughly enough to insist that he become part of the medical corps.

But that had ultimately led him here.

To Grace.

Who was now gone too.

She wasn't dead, but he'd seen the look on her face. She was lost to him.

She'd never trust him again.

———◄∞)———

"Miss Deroy, tell us what your relationship is with Andrew Hastings."

Scared though she was, Grace wouldn't be drawn on any topic—Duke of Clarence or otherwise—until she had more of a grasp on what kind of trouble her words could get her into.

"Not until you tell me why I'm here and what this place is."

The man across from her sighed, flipping open the manila folder in front of him. "You started an affair with him at university, didn't you?"

"No." Perhaps she should shore her story up with more detail, but then she'd have to tell them the truth about Alexander. She couldn't bring herself to, not when she recalled this man's reaction to that dreadful painting at Sotheby's. "I never—"

"There's no point in denying it. Your affair is all over the papers. Tell me, do you whisper the names of target locations to him over dinner or wait until you're in the throes of passion?"

"Stop it!" She almost retched at his blunt insinuation.

He began to read from this file in front of him. "'He has every advantage in life—wealth, position, good looks—and knows exactly how to wield it to get what he wants.' Is that what he did to you? Use his natural advantages on you?"

She stared back at her questioner. Those words. Weren't they her very own? She'd said almost the same thing to Jack in the restaurant last night. At least, she thought it was last night. He glanced up to gauge her reaction before continuing to read from the paper in front of him.

"'I had such a crush on him when I was seventeen. My mother

was very keen that I pursue him. After all, who doesn't want their daughter to be a duchess one day? I did try for a time.'"

"No." She couldn't be sure whether she was responding to their question or to the heartbreaking reality that someone had been listening in to her conversation with Jack. The thought poisoned every memory she had of him, making his kiss taste bitter on her lips.

"It's all here in black and white."

He pushed the single piece of paper he was reading from toward her, turning it so she could read clearly. The neatly typed page was a direct transcript of her entire conversation with Jack. But their date had only ended a couple of hours ago. To have the conversation transcribed, typed, and filed in such a short amount of time indicated that many more people were working behind the scenes than she saw in front of her here.

Her stomach plunged as she remembered that sob that had rung through the open door. Wretched and agonizing. She lifted her eyes to the man opposite, then glanced over in horror at the man by the door. They were military intelligence—they had to be. She'd heard rumors about places that interrogated people, of course, but the gravity of being inside one slapped her in the face.

"I am not having an affair with him. I think he is a beast!" Her voice fought through her muddled thoughts.

"You better start telling us what you know, Miss Deroy."

"I don't know anything about stolen files." The words were barely out of her mouth, when she realized they might be false. Of course, she didn't know any details about leaks from Bartondale or the file that had been missing. But she did know something about Andrew.

Her interrogator must have seen her expression change. "What do you know, Miss Deroy?"

"Nothing that relates to Bartondale."

"Go on."

She rummaged through her memories until she found two that fit together, like the first two pieces in a jigsaw puzzle.

"You were there. The painting he auctioned off at Sotheby's was a fake. I-I'm very familiar with that artist's work."

The man across the table remained inscrutable. Perhaps he already knew about the painting? She hesitated to say more, deciding against mentioning Alexander, hoping to avoid the truth about that particular matter being laid bare on the table between them.

"Why were you at the auction?"

Words she had been holding back came tumbling out now, as she sorted through all her thoughts. "I read about it in the newspaper and knew something wasn't right. It was only after I confronted him about it that these stories started to appear in the newspapers. The first was based on a photograph that was taken at my mother's birthday. But the second is definitely not me."

"But you did go to London to meet him again? Why?"

"Yes. I went to London to confront him again, and he published a third."

"He published?" Her interrogator leaned on the pronoun, with no small measure of contempt in his voice. "The last I heard, the Duke of Clarence was influential in the art world. You expect us to believe he has power over the London press too?"

"His father was friends with the Duke of Windsor, and I've seen Andrew in newsreels with the King. A story so scandalous could never appear unless he wanted it to. I went to London to confront him about it."

"What did he say?"

She thought back to Andrew's exact words at The Savoy. She'd asked him directly what he was playing at, and he hadn't given a good reason.

"That hurting me was a 'satisfying side effect,' I think he said. I think he's trying to discredit me somehow." That was the only conclusion she could come to about the stories. And considering she was the one being interrogated, he seemed to have succeeded.

"Why would he do that, Miss Deroy?" The man across the table closed the gap between them slightly, leaning in as though it would help her put her thoughts into order.

"I think he's happy to hurt me as revenge over the death of an old acquaintance."

"Who?"

She didn't want to mention The Artist's name. Not here, not like this. "Alexander Blakey."

For the first time in their conversation, the man in front of her looked surprised. "The artist who painted *The Blue Lady*?"

She nodded. "But if you want to know anything more, haul Andrew in for questioning!"

Her interrogator glanced at the man by the door, who turned and hurried out of the room. Then the suited fellow slipped all his papers back into his file and went to follow him. At the door he turned to ask one last question.

"And how do you know the painting sold at Sotheby's is a forgery?"

She hesitated, but her heart affirmed again that the truth was her only defense.

"Because it's a painting of me."

Her shame was now laid out for everyone to see.

CHAPTER TWENTY-THREE

21 August 1943

"I'm sorry about the last twenty-four hours."

In the front passenger seat of the same Bentley that had stolen her from her home, a man sat with his body twisted at a strange angle so he could look at her.

Grace turned her face away from the man in the front seat to look out the car window at the passing countryside. She couldn't be too far away from home, since the rolling farmlands still felt familiar.

"You understand—we had to be sure."

"There is very little about what has just happened that I understand." She looked back at him, hoping to see some remorse to go with the words of apology. Moments after her confession about the painting, she had been escorted from the room, with much less haste than when she had been escorted in.

"Except that you stole me from my home and kept me in a cellar for . . . for I don't know how long."

"My sincere apologies. And it's only Sunday, Miss Deroy—"

"Corporal Deroy." For some reason she needed to cling to her rank today.

"Corporal Deroy." His concession felt hard won. "I'm Wilson Weathers." He looked like he might offer her his hand to shake, then thought the better of it.

"Not Brad Butler, antique dealer at large?"

"No." His brow creased. "I know you are angry, but the bottom line is information from Bartondale is falling into the hands of our enemies. Not all the time, but often enough for us to be worried. We have suspicions Clarence is part of it, but we don't know how. Your family connections, your history with the Duke of Clarence, and your animosity about having your home requisitioned made you a natural suspect."

Grace huffed.

"We've had people getting close to you, observing you for weeks to rule you out. But that didn't work."

That sick feeling washed over her again.

"So you were spying on me?"

"Not very effectively, as it turned out. The newspapers kept confirming that our methods weren't working. So I had to step in."

"I thought only the Nazis spied on their own citizens."

The man in front of her wasn't interested in justifying his means or defending his methodology. He was only interested in outcomes.

"Now you know, Miss Deroy."

"And the place we've just been?" She recalled the cries she'd heard from outside the room. "What was that place? I heard . . ." What did she hear? Someone crying out? Someone in pain? Some being tortured?

"That, I'm happy to say, was theatrics for your benefit."

"Is it always just theatrics?"

Steel crept into Wilson's gaze. "Ask yourself if you really want to know the lengths we go to to keep this country safe."

He spoke with such cold resolve that she suddenly thought it was better that she didn't know what the country's military intelligence service was capable of.

Wilson continued. "This is war—our enemy is cunning, and we have to be, too, if we are to prevail. In this case secrets are being leaked. You had means, motive, and opportunity, so we had to be sure. After this weekend, we've ruled you out."

His words sank in as the car zipped through the countryside in a blur of green. She couldn't be sure, but she suspected the driver was taking another repetitive and circuitous route—probably to keep her confused.

"Are you going to tell me who it is? Who's been spying on me?" She already knew, but she wanted him to say it.

"I think you know who."

Jack.

She tasted bile in her throat. "He was reporting everything to you." A statement, not a question, but Wilson confirmed it with a nod.

She swallowed down the sick feeling as the landscape turned familiar outside the car window. These were the lanes she had traveled all her life. She should feel comforted by the familiarity, but the revelation about Jack made her numb. Apart from the tears she tried to will away.

Wilson was wise enough to leave her alone with her thoughts for the rest of the drive. Like a camera lens coming into focus, Grace saw all her interactions with Jack clearly, as if for the first time. She thought back through every conversation, recasting him with ulterior motives and her as the stupid girl who was duped. When the vehicle pulled up outside her cottage, she felt so heavy she could barely move. Wilson held the door open for her.

"You understand that you can't speak about this to anyone," Wilson murmured as she stood. "Not your father, not your brothers, not your friends."

The door of the cottage swung open. Sarah, Peter, and Olive tumbled out of the front door and up the path. Relief at seeing them surged through her, but she kept her look steady and her voice sarcastic. "Don't worry—as you know after this weekend, I am the trustworthy sort."

Gravel barely crunched under Peter's feet as he flew up the path and grabbed Wilson by his lapels, shoving him up against the car.

"What did you do to my sister?" Peter's spit hit Wilson's face as he growled out the words.

Grace stilled Peter with her arm on his. "I'm all right, Peter. And he was just doing his job."

Peter let go of Wilson and grabbed Grace up into a ferocious embrace. She sank against him. Sarah came close to pat her back, and Olive clung around her waist. Face buried in Peter's neck, she heard the car door click and the motor rev before the wheels of the vehicle crunched on the lane and the car sped off.

Her brother ushered her into the cottage. Only then, in her own home surrounded by the people who loved her best, did she let herself sob like a child.

———◦⦿⦿◦———

Wilson was in Jack's room when he arrived home from church on Sunday, casually flipping through the papers on his desk. Jack fought the urge to grab Wilson by his lapels, shove him up against the wall, and make him talk. The fact he had been praying through the entire church service for God to help him help Grace was the only thing stopping him.

"What have you done with Grace?"

He held himself in check, framed in the doorway, trying to look casual, when every hair on his body stood alert.

"Mrs. Johnston let me wait in here while she slipped out to the butcher. She's nice."

Jack bristled. "Stop playing games, Wilson. Where's Grace?" He wanted his voice to sound menacing, but the desperate sound that came out worked too.

Wilson raised an eyebrow, not giving anything away. He held up Jack's notebook and gave it a little shake as he talked. "You're very methodical, aren't you?"

"Note taking. Comes from being a doctor, I guess." He spoke through gritted teeth. To find that notebook, Wilson would have had to search Jack's room thoroughly.

"And pictures too?" Wilson flipped open to where Jack had tried to capture Grace's likeness on one of his first days here.

Jack's restraint snapped. He strode across the room and ripped the notebook from Wilson. "Where is she? Just tell me that she's okay."

Whatever Wilson saw in Jack's stare made him relent. "She's back in her own home. Her housekeeper and brother are with her."

Jack sank onto his bed with relief. "Did you hurt her?"

"No! Who do you think we are! The Gestapo!?"

That was what terrified him. He didn't actually know what lengths MI5 would go to if they were interrogating her.

"You were right about her."

"But you had to arrest her to find that out?" Jack scoffed. "You couldn't have just believed me? Trusted in the job you put me here to do?"

"Well, you have to admit, Marsden, your judgment was a little clouded by Goldilocks here." He held up the notebook again, using her code name to let Jack know that he'd read the whole thing.

"You know, I don't even want to know what you are doing here. Just get out, okay?"

Wilson didn't move. "It's not that simple. Grace Deroy might not be the leak, but someone is going to a lot of effort to make us think she is. Don't you want to find out who?"

Jack stiffened. That was what he'd been saying all along, wasn't it? Wilson's single-minded pursuit of Grace had led him to neglect other leads. Worthington, for example, or even one of the higher-ups.

"I thought you planted me here especially to rat on Grace. Didn't you say I was the only one who had that special mix of skills to get close to her?" Jack spat the words, disgusted he had gone along with this.

"But now that you are here, you are useful. You have everyone's trust. I don't want to have to send in someone else to start from scratch."

"I don't have Grace's trust anymore."

How quickly things had changed from Friday night, when she'd practically dissolved into his arms as they'd kissed.

"Well, you have to get it back, don't you? Because she might not be the leak, but she's the key to catching the person who is."

Jack shook his head.

"This is ridiculous. Just arrest the duke if you think he's behind it. Don't toy with good people who are just trying to do their jobs." He might as well have included himself in this.

"We need more evidence, and for that we need to identify the leak at Bartondale."

Jack noted Wilson's professional calm. He was used to this game.

"She can help us."

"Why would she want to after this weekend?"

"Because you were right. She's just trying to do her best for the war effort." Wilson quoted Jack's own words back to him as he headed for the door. "Your job now is to make her see this is what she needs to do."

"What if I refuse?" He should have asked that question months ago, back in Lewis's office.

"There are courts-martial and a variety of proceedings I can look into."

Jack felt the threat hit him in the chest.

"But I won't need them. Because at the end of the day, you're the same as her. You don't want to see any more US flyboys getting shot down unnecessarily."

Had his CO already spoken to Wilson? It didn't matter. Wilson was right.

"She'll never trust me again. Not as far as she can throw me."

Wilson nodded. "I'll be in touch." He turned to leave. "Don't forget what the real game is, Marsden. You're here to prevent military secrets getting to the enemy, not to fall in love."

Too late for that.

CHAPTER TWENTY-FOUR

24 August 1943

Jack raised his hand to knock at the front door. He didn't need any transatlantic etiquette book to know the permission he'd had to simply wander around to the back garden was now revoked.

Besides, he had another visitor with him.

Wilson.

Jack demanded that, if Wilson wanted Grace's help, he come and ask her for it.

Sarah answered the door, but he barely looked at her when he caught sight of Grace, her long legs folded under her as she leaned on the arm of the sofa talking to someone, though he couldn't see who. She wasn't in her uniform, but her rose-colored day dress was almost as breathtaking as her green gown. Something he couldn't think about right now.

"Lieutenant Marsden." Confusion passed over Sarah's face when she saw Wilson. She must have recognized him from the night Grace was arrested.

Jack swallowed, but he didn't take his eyes from Grace. "Sarah, this is Mr. Wilson Weathers. We need to talk to Grace."

Sarah looked to Grace for her permission, then opened the door wider to admit them.

"All right then. No doubt we'll need tea. I'll put a pot on." She hurried to the kitchen.

Whatever Grace was thinking was concealed behind a careful mask. Her hazel eyes transformed to steel as they followed Jack into the room.

"You remember my brother, don't you?"

Jack spun around and was greeted by Peter staring daggers of big-brother contempt at him.

"Grace, I know that what I am about to say will sound . . ."

When he'd first met Grace, he'd thought it unfair to have to conceal the truth from her. Relationships that began with lies never ended well. But now, just when he was at the point of having to tell her the whole truth, he felt his throat seize up and words desert him. Again.

"This is . . ."

"Mr. Weathers." Grace cut him off, looking beyond him with that flint-filled gaze. "How could I forget when I had the pleasure of being hosted by you last weekend?"

He knew from the stillness of her countenance that she was not going to make this easy.

"Can we speak with you privately, Miss Deroy?" Wilson wasn't intimidated by her sharp sarcasm.

"You're in my house now, Mr. Weathers, and this is as private as we get. Anything you have to say you can say in front of my brother."

"Who exactly are you, Mr. Weathers?" Peter spoke up. "Who do you work for?"

Wilson must have been doing the calculations behind that blank facade of a face—and coming to the same conclusion Jack had. Tell the truth where possible.

"Military intelligence. Generally my role is to weed out Nazi sympathizers who have infiltrated our domestic operations and stop them from doing any further damage."

"What? And you think she's one, so you sent a handsome man to charm her secrets out of her?"

Jack shouldn't feel so justified at the scoff in Peter's voice, but since it was also Jack's first reaction to the harebrained scheme, part of him was glad someone else thought the whole scenario was ridiculous.

"Let me explain as simply as I can." How did Wilson always seem like he had control over a conversation, like he was masterminding it, even when his audience was so hostile? "Despite dealing with highly classified information, Bartondale has always been as leaky as a sieve. My job was to determine why. We found a connection between the leaks and the Duke of Clarence, who has considerable connections to royalty. Every target that has had advance knowledge of our raid is also one where Clarence has considerable business connections. We didn't have to look very far for a link between Miss Deroy and the duke."

Jack watched the muscles in Grace's throat tighten.

"You were our prime suspect for some time, Miss Deroy. Your centrality to the facility gave you critical access to information. You had means and opportunity. But we were unsure about motive."

"Motive? What motive could Grace possibly have to leak information?" Peter demanded.

"We suspected a clandestine relationship."

Peter snorted. "Is this a joke?"

"We also believed that she must resent the presence of the Air Ministry in her home." Wilson continued as though that assumption was entirely rational.

"Of course she does, you idiot." Peter's rage had to be directed at someone, and Jack was happy for Wilson to bear the brunt of it. "We all resent it. Everyone in England resents this war. It doesn't mean that we aren't doing our best with whatever cards we are dealt."

Peter ran his hands through his hair, then turned the guns of his frustration on Jack. "And you! How did you sleep at night, wheedling your way into our family just to inform on her?"

"I told them she was innocent every chance I could." Jack's soft words barely cut through Peter's indignation.

"If anything, Jack had too many scruples for his own good. Couldn't bring himself to ask hard questions."

Somehow Jack didn't feel like this was going to be the best course of defense, not when he saw Grace's face.

———•◁∞)———

"Was any of it real?" The kiss ran through Grace's mind, now devoid of its magic. "Was anything you told me true?" Tears welled in her eyes, and her throat tightened to match, strangling her words.

"Grace, I . . ."

Jack glanced around at the other faces in the room. Perhaps he wanted to have this conversation in private, but this was about as private as she was going to get with him from now on. She enjoyed watching him squirm.

"Everything I told you about myself was true. I'm a widower and trained as a doctor."

"How could you let them listen to us? I thought it was a real date."

He swallowed hard, and she knew him well enough to see he was weighing his words, struggling for the right ones.

"I was following orders."

Peter snorted. "I bet you were. A dream assignment, I'd say."

"Not for me." He went to take her hand, but she snatched it away from him. She didn't want him to touch her now.

"I told you about my wife, Grace. I—"

"For the sake of time, I'll fill in some details, shall I?" Wilson's dispassionate voice cut him off. "His experience at Medmenham meant he could be useful to Bartondale. But his job was to work out the connection between you and Clarence. He seemed to be the kind of man you would easily fall for. It was a relatively simple task—that he managed to botch entirely."

"C'mon. I didn't botch anything." Jack's eyes flared at Wilson. "I told you at every point that she was innocent. You kept saying that I needed to get closer, find out more."

"I arranged a date for you so that you could jolly well do that, but you couldn't bring yourself to ask her anything directly! I had to step in."

She saw the truth of everything Wilson said in Jack's eyes. Wilson had arranged the date.

"And you held back information, Jack!" Wilson threw down a tightly tied bundle of paper onto the table.

She must be numb, because she barely flinched at the stack of letters from Alexander that she kept in her dressing table drawer, tied tightly with red ribbon and marked with a scarlet letter.

"I told you everything! There's nothing incriminating in those."

Her stomach turned over. Jack had already read the letters. To do that he would have had to search through her most personal belongings without her knowing.

"A stack of letters marked out with Andrew Clarence's initial and you didn't think that was significant enough to tell me about? C'mon, Jack!"

"You all think you're so clever, don't you?" Her hurt was rapidly transforming into anger. "But you've been watching me and studying me and reading my personal correspondence for weeks, and you still don't know the real story."

"Grace, you don't need to tell them." Peter spoke up in warning, moving to sit next to her on the sofa and offering her his handkerchief.

"I don't care anymore, Peter!"

She looked directly at Wilson to spit out her words. "The letters aren't even from Clarence. They're from Alexander Blakey."

She took her satisfaction from watching her words land on the surprised MI5 man who thought he was so on top of all her secrets.

"The artist?" Jack asked.

"Yes, Jack. The artist." She laughed at his shocked face, but the anger coursing through her was like a fire in dry tinder. She wanted to hurt and shock him. "He was my lover! So sorry if that shocks you, Mr. Courted-My-First-Sweetheart-for-Five-Years."

He flinched when she evoked the memory of his wife with such viciousness. Good.

"It's not even an initial! It's an accusation! Haven't you read the American classics, Jack? Shame on you!" Her eyes burned into him. "It's a scarlet letter! It's my own accusation of myself. It might be childish, but I look at this pile in my dressing table drawer every day to remind myself that I am not that person anymore."

Peter rested his hand on her shoulder. She knew he meant it as a caution, to quell her cruelty. She glanced at her brother.

"You don't have to tell them, Gracie."

His words stole the heat from her, like water on still-hot embers.

"I went to university ready for adventure and romance. Andrew Hastings had some delusion of grandeur he could make a name for himself in the art world by being a patron of aspiring artists, like the Medicis or something, so he plucked Alexander Blakey from obscurity in Paris and helped him woo the intellectuals in Oxford. He introduced us."

The words hurt, but now that she had started her story she wanted to finish it. Still, she didn't know what details to give to the gaping faces confronting her.

"From the moment I met Alexander Blakey, I would have done anything for him. He could inspire that in people. I was young, desperate to experience the world, and he was all too willing to teach me what he knew about it. You both have enough imagination to guess how things happened. It's not even an original story."

She wanted to defend herself by telling them how the light inside him, fueled by some kind of fire in his soul, shone so brightly it outshone everything else with its mesmerizing glow. How persuasive he could be, especially with someone so willing to be persuaded. How expertly he took a naive girl and transformed her into his plaything to serve the cause of his art.

"It only lasted a few months. We kept it secret. He openly courted others—men and women—and I told my mother I was going about with the Duke of Clarence's son to give myself cover on the home front. I don't think even Andrew suspected anything. Until recently."

Peter knew everything. But the other two men stood riveted to the spot by her story. She bit down hard on her lip. The pain steadied her for the next part.

"I'm the model in most of his artworks from that time. His muse, he called me. He was gaining acclaim in the art world when I wanted to break it off. It was messy. He felt betrayed. Said we were creative partners. So I agreed to let him paint me one more time."

Her face didn't even flame under the tears rolling down it. She recalled the conversation like she'd only just had it. She'd told him that their affair was over. His betrayed look had pierced her from under that stubborn lock of blond hair that always fell over his eye when he painted. She'd said she was ashamed to be his model and wouldn't do it anymore.

She tried to be clear, but how could he understand what she meant about Christ and repentance and the new faith gripping her heart, when she didn't fully understand it herself? Alexander had used her confusion against her and begged her for one last night.

"That night he painted *The Blue Lady*, but I left for good. He crashed his car driving out to Broughton to give it to me."

Just like that the fire that fueled his art had burned out.

"I'm ashamed of that time. I thought it was forgotten. But Andrew must have found drawings of me. Alexander's sketches are so much more realistic than his paintings." She turned to Wilson. "You were there when *The Blue Lady* sold at Sotheby's, but I knew it was a fake. Andrew threatened to tell the world about my affair if I said anything. He says he has sketches of me. So I didn't say a word. I don't know why it's so important to him now, but I think the stories in the newspaper are his way of reinforcing to me how much power he has in case I tell anyone."

Telling them was a catharsis. The truth wasn't what set her free from her shame—the Lord had done that—but it still felt good to speak it.

"Miss Deroy," Wilson said, "Clarence has overplayed his hand. While you were with us last weekend, he tried to slip another story into the society pages."

She shrugged. What did it matter now?

"It verifies your story in more ways than one. Which gave us an idea."

Wilson paused, to make sure he had her full attention. He did. "We'd like you to sue the *Evening Standard* for defamation."

CHAPTER TWENTY-FIVE

27 August 1943

Edward Bacon, King's Counsel and Deroy family lawyer, had been the keeper of her family's secrets for as long as she had been alive. More than a mere lawyer, he was her family's trusted friend, as zealous to protect their interests as if they were his own. He did his job so well, their parents had named Teddy after him. Grace rarely used his full title. She called him Ed to his face and Old Ed to her brothers.

"It's a big risk." Old Ed eyed Grace carefully as he spoke.

From where he sat ensconced in a leather wingback chair, hands steepled under his chin, the lawyer looked older than his fifty years. His hair was as white as the first snow of winter. But that also made him look distinguished and at home among the floor-to-ceiling bookshelves and mahogany furniture.

They'd wasted no time on tea or sherry or cake or any of the other things they were offered at 10:00 a.m. after they were waved into a large office that smelled like leather and cigars. Instead, Peter had outlined Wilson's suggestion. Old Ed had looked bored at first, his finger absentmindedly outlining a seam on his seat as Peter and

Grace had sat stiffly in their chairs, spilling all the details. By the end of the story, he'd been rapt. The intrigue brought life to Old Ed's creased face, like he smelled a challenge.

"So these stories, they're really all made up? They say that they have photographic proof."

Grace explained about meeting the duke at her mother's birthday but confirmed she knew nothing about the others.

"The photo in the second story is small. It shows someone who looks like me, but you can't see her face. I'm sure the other one they claim to have will be similar."

"We have to do this without mentioning anything to do with Grace's work or even what happens at Broughton—or Bartondale—these days," Peter said.

Wilson had reluctantly granted them leave to mention to Old Ed the MI5 connection. When Peter did, the lawyer's eyes, which didn't flinch at the mention of art scandals or bribery, widened. "It has to appear as though she is simply suing the newspaper, not digging about trying to get Clarence to reveal his hand. But in the end, our game is to find out who the mole at Bartondale is."

"I know it's a risk." Grace stared down at her hands as she spoke. "But isn't it the right thing to do? If our targets are leaked, the Germans put up stronger defenses. Antiaircraft guns and night fighters. I used to work on an airfield, Ed. I know what it's like when a whole crew doesn't come home . . ."

How could she look Maggie in the face again if Alec's plane got shot down and she could have done something to stop it? Where would Katie and her baby be if Jonty got shot down? Grace had already lost enough friends in this war. "I just can't bear the thought that doing nothing might mean more people die."

"Clarence obviously has some big Fleet Street players in his pocket. There's nothing to indicate he can't pay off judges too." Old Ed thought aloud. "Even if he doesn't, he'll claim that the woman in the pictures is you. You'll claim it's not, and the whole thing will hinge on who the judge believes more. The word of a duke is a powerful thing, Grace. Are you prepared to lose the case to expose the traitor?"

She had asked herself the same question last night, but even as she was praying God wouldn't let it come to that, she knew she had to trust Him even if it did. "If I have to."

"Then I will have to advise your parents to stay uninvolved," Old Ed said gently. "They'll need to distance themselves from you. If this goes wrong, they can't be tarnished by association with you. You must look like their wayward daughter."

Grace nodded, like a child agreeing to something she didn't want to do.

"There's also the matter of the painting. Does Clarence know about it? If he does, it will surely come up in the newspaper's defense. They'll use it against you."

"He knows."

"And you're still sure you want to go through with it?"

She nodded again, trying to keep the tears in. Old Ed was one of the few people who knew how closely she guarded that secret. He'd helped her cover up her shame when *The Blue Lady* had come up for auction after Alexander's death.

"Lately, I suppose I've got used to admitting the connection, even though I'm not proud of it." She fought away the memory of confessing everything in front of Wilson. And Jack. Although she didn't care a whit what he thought about her, now that she knew about his lies.

"There's something else you should know about," Peter said. "It's about Teddy."

"He's AWOL." Grace explained what she'd learned from him about flying over Hamburg, as well as how he'd been missing since the day military intelligence arrested her. "He must have thought they were coming for him. Please don't think poorly of him."

Old Ed, who'd flown with their father in the first war, appeared more businesslike than sympathetic. "Well, that's one thing in our control. If we can find him and get him back to his airfield, then it will be better for him as well as for you. We don't want them to somehow use a traitor in the family against you."

"I think he's probably still in Lincolnshire, around home. I didn't want to involve anyone else, but I suppose there are a few trusted people who might help us look for him."

"Yes. Limit the number of people but have them actively look."

He stood, letting them know their appointment was over, and shook both their hands before ushering them from the room. "Leave it with me. I'll call when I know more. Are you staying at The Savoy?"

In the hall outside the office, Peter put his arm around her shoulders and squeezed her in a side-on hug. "Old Ed's in. He's a whizz at these things, so let's just wait to see what he comes up with. In the meantime, I'm treating you to lunch."

———◦⋈◦———

Jack wrapped his knuckles on the door of his own office as a warning to Worthington and Margot. When he opened the door, Worthington was sitting at his desk and Margot was casually leaning against it with one hip. He doubted they had been in that position a few moments earlier.

"Afternoon, Margot."

Margot slipped out past him with an apologetic smile—or at least it would be apologetic if she didn't beam with a just-kissed flush to her cheeks.

Jack shook his head at his colleague as he placed the two manilla folders of photographs from the library on his desk. Susie, rather than Grace, had handed them over, informing him that Grace was on indefinite personal leave. This surprised him, since when Wilson had left her cottage after getting her to agree to sue the *Evening Standard*, he'd practically ordered them both to work together.

"Well, naturally, Mr. Weathers," she'd said, sarcastic politeness dripping from every word. "We should keep our friends close."

The way she'd looked at Jack had told him he could finish that sentence for himself.

And our enemies closer.

Without the mandate to get close to Grace, Bartondale was a lonely place. Despite his politeness, he regarded each of his colleagues with suspicion. Every conversation became an opportunity to find out who else at Bartondale might have a connection to the duke. But so far he'd come up empty.

He shook his head as he flipped open the file and took out the photographs, preparing a pair to line up under the stereoscope so that the churches, hospitals, factories, and markets of the German village would jump out at him. For the first time since he joined the army, he felt a pang of longing for the work he had trained for at medical school all those years. He'd been top of his class back then and on track for a plum position as a surgeon one day. Until Dotty had died. Then he'd taken refuge in maps and photos because they couldn't die under your hands.

"Jack?" Worthington broke into his thoughts. He must have been staring into space. "Are you all right?"

"Fine." He stood and took his two photographs over to the stereoscope. "Say, Worthington, what will you do when the war is over?"

"Assuming we win, you mean?"

"Of course."

Worthington leaned back in his chair, arms crossed, and pondered the question like it was brand new to him. "Pick up where I left off, I suppose. University. I was studying architecture at Oxford."

"Oxford?" The mention of the same university Grace had been to snagged his attention. "Did you know Grace back then? I heard she'd studied there once."

"No. The Deroys have always been too high and mighty for me. We do have some common acquaintances though."

Even with his eyes glued to the stereoscope, Jack was blind to the details in the photographs, his whole attention captured by Worthington's words. He had to press Worthington on this. It could be a connection. He kept his tone casual.

"Say, did you know that artist guy who was at university at the same time? Blakey?"

"Can't say I did. Although judging from some of his paintings, I wish I had mixed in the same circles. Naked women everywhere, it would seem."

Hidden by the stereoscope, Jack rolled his eyes. Worthington really did have a one-track mind. What had Grace called Worthington on his first day? That's right. A beast that she wouldn't touch with a ten-foot pole. How apt. Poor Margot. She seemed sweet, if a little vague sometimes. How had she found herself mixed up with Worthington?

Jack dismissed the connection and refocused on his photograph, giving the stereoscope his entire attention for the rest of the afternoon.

"Ladies. After you." Jack later stood back and extended his arm for Margot and the girls from the library, indicating they should pass ahead of him. He'd been preparing himself to face a pang of guilt and longing as he passed the turnoff to Grace's cottage, but the women's conversation distracted him.

Snippets of conversation drifted back to him, and eavesdropping had become a prerogative.

"I wonder what we can expect in the newspapers this weekend, what with Grace off in London in the arms of her duke," Margot said.

He had the distinct impression she wanted to release a cat among pigeons.

"Don't be so unkind, Margot!" Susie defended Grace. "It's all nonsense. Grace was so upset by those newspaper reports. She's probably in London trying to get to the bottom of it."

"I heard that she's gone to London to deal with a very *particular* problem," Betsy said.

Charlotte, the most impressionable of all the girls, took the bait. "Really?" Shock colored her voice. "But she always seemed so prim and proper all the time!"

"Charlotte! You know Grace," Susie said. "She would never do half the things that newspaper is claiming, and in public! And, Betsy, wash your mouth out for repeating such rumors."

"Excuse me, ladies." Jack couldn't help himself. He tried to push past them as away to stop their gossip.

"Lieutenant." Margot's voice was sickly sweet as it flowed after him. "You and she are close. Do you know what Grace is doing in London?"

"She's not really pregnant, is she?" Charlotte worried aloud.

He should walk away, but he had to do what he could to correct the lies being circulated about Grace. "C'mon, Charlotte. This is Grace we are talking about. Have a little faith in her."

"Are you sure you aren't blinded by your own love for our lady of the manor?" Margot was sure keen to upset the applecart today.

"My vision is twenty-twenty, thanks, Margot. From what I hear, she's gone to London to take the newspaper and their lies on. You'll be reading retractions before you know it. Good night, ladies."

He'd probably said too much, so he made a hasty escape down the drive. Every time he approached the turn to Grace's cottage, he gave himself a good talking to about not looking longingly toward where she lived. But today his attention was forced that way by Sarah, who raced up the path toward him.

"Lieutenant, I need your help."

⌁∞)

Jack accepted her invitation—surly as it was—to come in, trying not to appear wistful as he looked around, searching for traces of Grace. Sarah left him with Olive while Sarah made tea and arranged a plate of biscuits, returning just as he was finishing a pirate story.

"Is that it?" Olive complained. "I thought at least there'd be a few more dead bodies before the end."

"You aren't impressed at their decision to all live in harmony on a tropical island?"

"It's not very realistic is it? They're *pirates*."

"Perhaps I'll write a sequel."

Olive grinned at him, then scampered outside to act out some of her ideas in the garden.

While pouring tea, Sarah gave Jack a brief account of Teddy's situation. As Jack reached for a cookie, he thought he heard Sarah mutter "Pft! Men! Always motivated by food."

He ignored it. "So he was staying here for how long?"

"He turned up just when Grace got sick."

"That explains how strangely you all acted when I called in unexpectedly." A pang of guilt racked him. After protesting Grace's innocence to Wilson, seeing them act so guilty had made him change his tune and tell Wilson Grace had something to hide.

Sarah gave him a stern look. "Yes. He ended up staying in the greenhouse. When Grace was arrested, he must have thought they were coming for him, and we haven't seen him since. We think he's still around here somewhere."

"You don't think he'd leave Lincolnshire entirely? It would be safer."

She shook her head and moved to Grace's writing desk, removing a frame containing a picture of Teddy in his RAF uniform. "We hid all the photos of Teddy while he was here just in case you made a connection. He's not a coward, you understand, but he's a sensitive soul. Running from his own conscience, I think."

Sarah passed the frame to Jack. He studied the photo, concentrating on that youthful face, smiling proudly. "I've seen him before. Not in uniform but along the riverbank one day."

"I'll show you the greenhouse. We might find something that can help us." When she led him out to the back of the garden, she surveyed the greenhouse through its open door. "Nothing's changed here as far as I can see. The mattress, the books, the spilled teacup. Everything was as it was the day Grace was arrested. So he hasn't come back for anything."

"I'm not a detective, Sarah. Just like I'm no spy. But I'll do what I can to find him. For Grace."

Sarah nodded. He sensed her hardening her heart against his earnestness.

"I have made some delicate inquiries, but there is still one place I need to try. We need to start by talking with Nancy Filby."

His stomach sank. That was why she had asked him to help her right now. She thought she'd get further with Nancy if he was with her.

Sarah couldn't hide her satisfaction at his look of dread.

CHAPTER TWENTY-SIX

28 August 1943

"Why didn't you tell me any of this before now, Grace?" Dear, faithful Maggie. She only had two days of leave to enjoy what they could of London with her husband, but she'd just spent the whole afternoon hearing Grace's woes. They sat facing each other with their legs tucked up underneath them on the plush sofa in Grace's room at The Savoy.

Grace shrugged. "I suppose I didn't want you to think badly of me. You only met me after I joined the WAAF, and by then I could feel how the Lord had changed me. And I suppose I didn't want to open old wounds."

"Nothing could make me think badly about you, my dear friend."

When Maggie embraced her, Grace could feel the tears that she had held back all afternoon spill down her face. "I'm crying so much lately—it's really quite ridiculous!"

Maggie pulled away. "My mother used to say that no one really knows what they believe until that faith is tested. This will be the making of you."

Grace wanted to take comfort in her friend's words, but they gnawed at her. Wasn't the private breakup with Alexander enough? Why did God have to drag it all up again and put it in the public spotlight? It felt cruel.

"What does Jack say about it all?"

Grace hesitated. "It turns out Jack isn't the man for me."

"He didn't bring that girl on another date, did he?"

"No." She longed to tell Maggie everything, unpacking the details of her date with Jack one by one. The dinner, the lingering conversation, the good-night kiss. But official secrets were tricky things when it came to her friendship with Maggie. Since she couldn't tell her friend how the night had ended, and how that had irrevocably changed her opinion of Jack, she switched topics.

"Say, you didn't happen to come by and borrow a dress, did you? About two weeks ago?"

Maggie shook her head. "No I didn't. But don't think I didn't notice how quickly you changed the subject just then! If Jack Marsden holds your past against you, he's simply not worthy of you. I'm so sorry you have to endure the papers making up all this nonsense. I never believed a word they said. Alec and I will never buy another edition of the *Evening Standard*. Oh blast!"

"What is it?"

"I have to go. I promised Alec I wouldn't be late, and as it is I'll be running all the way to Leicester Square." Maggie kissed her friend in a whirlwind goodbye and made for the door at such speed that she careened into Peter as he came through it.

"So it turns out that in addition to being a lawyer, Old Ed is a miracle worker." Peter flopped down in Maggie's place on the sofa. "He's managed to get us an expedited hearing and a closed courtroom. No press allowed on account that military secrets might be divulged. Since it's a judge-only trial, we might manage to avoid the worst of the scandal as well, but his powers don't stretch that far." Peter paused, clearly assessing her reaction to his news before continuing. "I also spoke to Father."

She stood and walked to the window, leaning against the frame and looking out onto The Strand.

"Is Father going to come?" She dreaded knowing the answer. She couldn't bear facing him, but she was also devastated to think he would doubt her.

"You know Old Ed told him to stay away." Peter didn't look like he agreed with the lawyer. "Father's also trying to keep this from Mother. Doesn't want her to cause a fuss. It might do more harm than good."

She could see the logic in that. Mother was capable of impressive histrionics. Wouldn't the press just love that?

"And Teddy?"

"Sarah and Jack are working on it, but they haven't had any luck yet." Peter took her elbow and led her back to the sofa. "Come on—let's go through this again."

"Do you remember what Old Ed said about the basics of a libel trial like this? We are claiming they have damaged your reputation with lies. They have to prove they didn't lie. They'll have witnesses, and so will we. There's examining and cross-examining. Then the judge decides by himself, with no jury for this kind of thing. Since they really are lying, we should have the upper hand. But it's not that simple. All our witnesses will be pitted against Andrew and his testimony."

"So who are our witnesses?"

"We've dealt with a lot of them through sworn statements that say you were nowhere near the duke at the time the newspaper alleges. So Sarah and Jack, to say you were sick, and staff at The Savoy, who all confirm you never left your room that night. In the witness stand there'll be you. Then we have the reporter herself and . . ."

"Andrew."

"Yes. We can't avoid his testimony."

The tea she'd had with Maggie turned over in her stomach, like it wanted to climb back up her throat. "Old Ed thinks we can do this. It will be a hard slog, but if Andrew lies in court, that carries its own penalty."

She must not have looked convinced.

"Remember the real reason you're doing this, Gracie."

How could she forget?

———◦⟪∞⟫———

Nancy swept the entryway to the butcher shop, humming a happy tune after the store's half day of Saturday trade. Her face clouded over when she looked up and saw Jack approach with Sarah.

Not a promising start.

She paused a few beats before resuming her sweeping. But not her hum.

"Hi, Nancy. We need your help."

Another pause in the sweeping, probably when Nancy registered that he wasn't here for her. She cast an annoyed glance over his shoulder at Sarah.

"The lady of the manor is off in London, isn't she? With a duke, I hear."

Okay, so she was still annoyed about the night at the cinema. He might as well address the elephant in the butcher shop. "Nancy, I know that . . . I didn't mean to . . . I'm sorry that I didn't get to explain things properly."

She shrugged, not missing a stroke of the broom.

"I don't have time to explain everything now, but one day maybe we can—"

"Jack!"

Sarah's voice cut him off. Jack was glad. He'd almost promised to take Nancy out to dinner to make it up to her, which would no doubt have dug a deeper hole. Sarah's look told him to get over himself and focus on the task at hand.

"We need to find Teddy Deroy. He's gone AWOL."

She met his eye properly for the first time, offering a glint of recognition, but resumed sweeping. This time she seemed a little too focused on the black-and-white tiled floor. "I don't know what you are talking about." But she did. That was clear from the conflicted expression dancing across her face.

"We know he's around here somewhere. Have you heard any chatter in the shop? Anything about an airman in hiding?" Sarah said.

Nancy pressed her lips together over her crooked teeth. Sarah was probably reconsidering her decision to ask Jack along. Nancy was clearly more inclined to speak with Sarah than with him. He took a step back and let Sarah take over the conversation.

"If he goes back to his station by himself, there'll be less of a penalty."

Nancy shifted her weight from foot to foot, her sweeping forgotten. "I told him I wouldn't tell anyone."

"Well, you haven't told us anything, have you? He's safe with us, Nancy, but he just got spooked."

Nancy's thinking played across her face as she weighed everything Sarah said. For one long moment, Nancy looked like she would send them packing. Finally she said, "I can tell him you're looking for him. Then it's his choice if he wants to see you."

"Thank you, Nancy." Sarah almost gushed in her relief. "Jack will be at the pub at half past six tonight. Will you tell him?"

Nancy nodded. She stepped back into the butcher shop, shut the door abruptly, and hung the *Closed* sign in the window. As she disappeared into the back room, Jack briefly wondered whether Teddy was hiding in that back.

"We should follow her!"

"I don't think that's the right thing to do." Sarah bit her lip in thought. "What if she spots us and warns him off? Then we'll never find him—not quickly, at least."

"And what if he doesn't show? Then we are back to square one."

"Not exactly. We know for sure he's around here now, and we know Nancy can get a message to him. That's more than we had this morning."

His beer sat untouched on the table in front of him.

Jack had met Wilson at The Crown a time or two, but he'd never felt so out of place as he did now. Most of the patrons looked like they had well-worn places on their seats, whereas he must look like an interloper. The levity of the pub's atmosphere around him reinforced the feeling.

What if Teddy didn't trust him?

He wished he wasn't alone. But it couldn't be helped. Sarah was off to London to help Grace. He'd already waited more than two hours, until well after eight thirty, glancing up hopefully as each new patron entered. Close to nine, after fending off female attention three times by saying he was waiting to meet someone, Nancy Filby walked through the door.

Alone.

She took the seat opposite Jack, ready for some kind of reckoning. He got the dreadful feeling she'd spent the entire afternoon planning to confront him rather than trying to find Teddy.

"I couldn't find him."

"Did you try?"

"I said I would, didn't I?"

"Sorry, Nancy. It's just really important that—"

"I'm not stupid, Jack. I know what the rules for desertion are."

"There's more than that. His sister's defamation case will be heard tomorrow. The newspaper's lawyers might use the fact that he is absent without leave to prejudice the judge against her."

"So this is all about her?" She narrowed her eyes.

Mentioning Grace was clearly a mistake. He couldn't lose Nancy as an ally. "Look, Nancy. I know I've been an idiot. My behavior must have confused you, but this is so much more than what it looks like. There's a lot at stake here."

Although not entirely placated, Nancy was curious enough not to leave. She sat silent, unreadable, for the longest time. "I did look for him, but I couldn't find him. I do know he's been hiding in the Tookleys' barn. I've taken him bread a few times."

"Can you take me there?"

"Now?" She was right to look unimpressed by the idea of sneaking into a barn at night with him, if all the stories US GIs told about where they ended up with local girls were true.

"No!" Jack corrected quickly. "I don't mean that! But we really need to find him."

She gave him a long stare before she made her decision. "I won't go anywhere with you, Lieutenant Marsden. But if I see him again, I'll tell him you're looking for him."

She stood up so quickly her chair toppled over behind her, hitting the floor with a clatter that hushed the pub's murmur.

Without warning, and as the whole pub looked on, she picked up the full beer glass and threw the contents down the front of his shirt. "That's for leading me on with the nylons."

No one in Lincolnshire could miss her triumphant smile as she flounced out of the pub.

CHAPTER TWENTY-SEVEN

2 September 1943

The hard bench, behind Old Ed and his solicitor, pressed into her back as she sat.

After a night of tossing and turning, Grace felt ready to be called as the first witness. She didn't mind public speaking. At school she had excelled at it, relishing her every opportunity to match wits with the team of boys from St. Antony's. She took no joy in having the attention on her in a real courtroom. The weight of the air around her felt heavy with history. The judge still sat in dour grandeur as he presided, fully wigged and robed, on a velvet-lined chair behind a dark-paneled bench. Despite looking objectively silly, something about the traditional garb reassured her. This kind of justice stood the test of time.

"We will prove the stories published about Corporal Deroy in the *Evening Standard* on both the second and sixteenth of August are categorically false and libelous in nature. They have caused her grievous reputational harm, and as such, the newspaper should be made to pay damages."

As Old Ed spoke, his assistant wrote notes as copiously as the courtroom stenographer, whose rapid-fire fingers recorded a transcript of everything Old Ed said. To their right, the newspaper had a whole army of lawyers, all men in wigs and gowns who listened, brows furrowed, in silence to Old Ed's address. There might not be a jury, but it still felt like an alarming number of people to convince, most of whom were being paid by the other side.

His argument was simple: They would prove Grace was nowhere near London when the first story was written. And with the other, because she'd been staying at The Savoy when the paper claimed she was cavorting with the duke in the foyer, they would prove that such behavior was entirely out of character for Grace.

She didn't miss the irony. They were literally putting her character, not his, on trial.

She could barely swallow with her dry throat as she made her way up to the witness box under the gaze of every single eye in the room.

Old Ed led her through the questions. They had practiced her answers several times over the weekend under the watchful eye of Wilson Weathers. She had resented the way his presence reminded her of Jack's deception. But it also reinforced the real purpose of the trial—to draw the duke out and discover the identity of his contact at Bartondale.

Despite the weekend of practice, Grace didn't sound nearly as confident on the witness stand as she did during those debates at school.

Old Ed nodded at the judge to indicate he had no further questions. As he sat, he gave Grace a fleeting smile, meant to reassure her before the more hostile questions began.

"Miss Deroy." Sir Ernest Chester QC, barrister for the newspaper, began his questioning. Swamped under his horsehair wig, his fine features looked out at her with spindly cunning. "You contend that this story printed in the *Evening Standard* on the second of August is a complete fabrication. Is that right?"

"Yes, I wasn't even in London on the night referred to in the story. I was at my home in Lincolnshire."

"How can you expect the court to believe that when we have

photographic proof in front of our very eyes?"

"I believe these photos show the duke with someone who looks very much like me—with the same stature and the same hair—but who isn't me. You can't see the face clearly in the photographs."

"But this isn't the first time you've been featured in the newspaper with the duke, is it? I'd like to draw the court's attention to this edition of *The Times* from the twenty-sixth of July."

He held up the folded newspaper with a flourish, which made the fold in the center dramatically open, revealing the picture of her and Andrew dancing at her mother's birthday. The photo where his hand was on her backside.

"This is you in this photograph, isn't it?"

"Yes, that photo is of me." She heard a titter undulate through the courtroom. "The duke showed up intoxicated and uninvited to my mother's birthday dinner and insisted on dancing with me—which I did so as not to cause a scene."

"In this picture in *The Times*, you are wearing a one-of-a-kind gown made for you by Burton and Co., are you not?"

"Yes, but—"

"The same gown appears in this *Evening Standard* picture, correct?"

"It is a very similar gown, but it's not mine."

"You expect the court to believe that despite the fact the woman in this photo has your hair, your stature, and is even wearing your bespoke gown, this woman isn't you?"

"Yes." It sounded as weak and flimsy as she felt. "It's not me. I was in bed at home with a dreadful cold."

"Supposing we go along with your story for a moment." He postured, taking a long look at each of the photos, as though trying to compare them. "You know the Duke of Clarence, don't you?"

"Yes. I met him through my brother when I was seventeen." She silently willed the lawyer not to ask anything more about that.

"And you knew him at university. Is that correct?"

"Yes." Her hands clasped in her lap tightened around each other.

"In both these pictures you appear to be very close. Are you seriously trying to tell the court that the Duke of Clarence has you mistaken for someone else in this second picture?"

She had practiced this part with Wilson, who'd instructed her to be very careful about her words. "I'm saying someone has gone to a great deal of effort to make this look like a photo of me and the duke. I can't say what the duke himself knew or didn't know about that. All I know is that I was at home in bed with a cold."

"Can anyone verify that, Miss Deroy?"

"Corporal Deroy. Yes, my housekeeper and a colleague, a trained doctor actually, who came to visit me during that time."

"So the only people who saw you were a woman you already pay and a man you've been seen on several dates with? That's quite convenient."

How did he know about that? She opened her mouth to speak, but the lawyer plowed on.

"Let's turn our attention to this second story. Were you also tucked up in bed at home on the night of the sixteenth?" The barrister dropped the first two newspapers on the desk in front of him, then picked up a different edition of the *Evening Standard*.

"I wasn't at my cottage that night. I was staying in London at The Savoy."

"So you don't deny meeting His Grace there?"

"I don't deny meeting him. But I most definitely did not stumble from a car into the hotel foyer at eleven p.m. as the article suggests." She edged her voice with ice. Every man in the courtroom leaned in simultaneously to hear better. "I had some business to discuss with him. And did so in the restaurant at lunchtime."

"Just the restaurant at The Savoy."

"Yes. At lunchtime."

He read from the *Evening Standard*. "'Scandalous socialite Grace Deroy continues her pursuit of the Duke of Clarence in the most outrageous way. The couple were seen in amorous embrace in several darkened night spots last night. Several witnesses saw the couple flouting every rule of public decency in the foyer of The Savoy, a hotel famous for its discretion.' This story is backed by five witnesses, Miss Deroy. Are you telling the court they are all making things up?"

"I'm saying that those witnesses are mistaken. The Duke of Clarence may have been 'cavorting' with someone, but it wasn't me."

"Five witnesses—six if you include the duke himself—saw you on this night, Miss Deroy. I'm afraid your argument is as flimsy as the chiffon in that dress of yours. That is all, Your Honor."

She almost suffered whiplash from the sudden conclusion to his questioning.

Her legs felt like jelly when she finally stood and left the witness box, still under the scrutiny of the frowning men in the room.

———◁∞▷

Jack wanted to wish Grace well before the proceeding began, but the trains wouldn't cooperate. He had to get an update about Grace's testimony from Peter while the judge took a break.

"How did it go?"

"Old Ed says it's hard to tell. Grace held her own, and so far there haven't been any surprises. But it's early days. I'm fairly sure Old Ed will tear the reporter to shreds, but Andrew comes after that, and he's the real wild card."

Peter sat ramrod straight on a bench in the public foyer of the court. Jack took a seat next to him but bent over, elbows on knees, to spin his cap in his hands. Despite their halting conversation, onlookers would probably think they waited for two entirely separate matters.

"Has Wilson made an appearance?" Jack glanced around, half expecting to see the man hiding in the shadows.

"No, but he met with Grace and Ed yesterday."

The speed at which Wilson had gone from seeing Grace as a

threat to seeing her as an ally took Jack's breath away. "How is she?"

"Defiant." Peter grimaced.

"Isn't that good a thing?"

"I don't know. Depends on what the judge is expecting, I suppose. I'm glad you weren't here. Seeing you would have shaken her."

Jack nodded despite the gut punch in Peter's words.

Commotion in the foyer caught their attention. A throng of people swarmed in, displacing the pensive quiet of the building. It was mostly reporters, who Jack had come to regard as their own kind of bottom-dwelling scum. A tall, raffish fellow stood in the center of the ruckus—Andrew Hasting, the tenth Duke of Clarence. He was courting the media.

Even with the space between them, Jack felt Peter tense at the duke's crisp voice carrying across the foyer.

"What will you say in court today, Your Grace?"

"Just the truth. Really, I can't say more than that because it's all got to go in front of the judge. But"—he lowered his voice, like he was about to give them a scoop—"Gracie Deroy and I have known each other for years. Oh look, there's her brother."

He expertly deflected attention toward Jack and Peter. The pack swung about as one, enfolding them both in a sea of notepad-wielding reporters and bright flashbulbs.

"How can your sister deny the truth of the photographs?"

"Do you have any comment on the court proceedings this morning?"

"What do you think about your sister's affair with the Duke of Clarence?"

While the attention of the pack was focused on Jack and Peter, Jack spotted the duke and his valet slipping away, likely to find privacy.

Peter held his obvious desire to shout at them in check with his clenched jaw. "The salacious lies the *Evening Standard* has printed cannot be ignored. We are confident the judge will see the truth of the matter and this will be dealt with swiftly."

Peter grabbed Jack's arm and hauled him away from the pack.

"Bunch of gutter-dwelling wolves . . ." Peter muttered as they hurried away and took shelter in a side room. "Of all the sensationalist rubbish . . ."

The words died on his lips when they walked straight into Clarence.

"Peter, old chum! Can't say that it's a surprise to see you here! And you brought the American with you again. Charming."

Sleazy, slimy, and all too cool, Jack didn't like the sober version of this guy any more than he liked the inebriated one.

"You won't get away with this, Clarence." Peter's voice was dangerously strained, and his hands were curled into such tight fists, as if at any moment he might snap and punch the duke in the nose.

Jack understood the desire completely.

"Me? What have I done? It's the newspaper she's suing."

"Fed by your lies!"

Jack put his hand on Peter's arm, hoping to calm him.

"Shows how much you really know about your sister, Deroy."

"You think her past with Blakey gives you the right to feed these stories to the scandal sheets?"

Clarence's lip curled. "It certainly gives me ammunition."

Peter didn't even have to move a muscle. Jack was the one who took a swing at him.

CHAPTER TWENTY-EIGHT

Old Ed made mincemeat of Edwina Morrow, the *Evening Standard* reporter. He used skillful, sardonic questioning to get her to admit that she had only been on the job for a few months when an anonymous tip came through. She thought writing up the scandalous story would help make her career. Grace almost felt sorry for the woman as she faced Old Ed.

Almost.

The woman kept fiddling with her hair, hanging in an elegant coil over one shoulder, perhaps hoping she seemed charming to the legal fraternity populating the room. In fact, it made her seem fidgety. Confusion drove across her face when her eyes settled on Grace.

Of course she's confused. She's never seen me before.

After establishing all the preliminary details of the reporter's life and work—including how she never thought she'd have the chance to write for a newspaper, much less have her byline featured on such high-profile stories until the war changed her prospects—Old Ed started with questions about where she acquired her information for the stories.

"I can't reveal my sources." She had a smug confidence in the line that Grace detested. "It's against my professional ethics."

"You write a gossip column. Surely ethics don't come into it."

"Even if I wanted to divulge my source, in this case I don't know who they are. A woman called the paper and told me the Duke of Clarence was going to be at some art auction. He's always got something happening around him, and in my line of work, you don't look a gift horse like that in the mouth. The first time it happened, I went alone, just to see if the information was credible. Missed out on a terrific scoop, so the next time she rang, I went with a photographer."

"That's when your photographer took this photo?" Old Ed held up the edition of the *Evening Standard* with the captioned photo of the duke supposedly with Grace.

"Yes," Morrow said. "We didn't break any rules. They were in public. It didn't seem like the proper place for such, shall we say, enthusiasm for the task at hand."

Grace's stomach turned over at the thought.

Several lawyers sniggered. "They scarpered, of course, once the flash went off."

"How did you identify this was Grace Deroy? After all, you can't clearly see her face amid all that . . . 'enthusiasm.'"

"The dress. I recognized it from another story about her and the duke in *The Times*."

"You recognized the dress?" Old Ed pressed her.

"It's a distinctive dress."

"But you never saw her face?"

"It's the same dress, same height, same hair, same, shall we say, level of comfort with the duke she had that night at The Savoy."

Grace fought the urge to stand up and yell "objection" at the top of her lungs.

"She might be having a change of heart now, but it is definitely her in the photograph."

Doubt flickered across the reporter's face. She added, "I wasn't going to add a caption with her name in it just in case, but my editor put it in to make the story more juicy."

"Let the record show we have submitted statements from Corporal Deroy's housekeeper, as well as a US Army officer, to show she was definitely at home in bed on this night. Just as we have statements from staff at The Savoy, who declare Miss Deroy was in her hotel suite all evening the night you reported that she was, how did you put it, 'flouting laws of public decency' in the foyer."

"Look, I had five witnesses who saw them! All respectable people, patrons of The Savoy," the reporter exclaimed.

"How were they so sure the duke was with Miss Deroy?"

"One of the women recognized her. All of them described her distinctive green dress and jewelry."

Grace almost scoffed at how much authority the woman gave to the testimony of her dress and jewelry. But then, the young woman was a society reporter, and Grace guessed that was her stock and trade.

"I hope you took down that woman's name, Miss Morrow!"

Grace deduced from her stricken face that she was a little lax in her journalistic duty to collect the names and addresses of her witnesses.

"She wouldn't give it! Anyway, my editor will back me up on everything. Besides, the duke himself doesn't deny the story."

"And just why exactly were you at The Savoy that night?"

"I got another tip, but the photographer and I got waylaid, so we didn't get there in time to see it."

After the newspaper's lawyer finished questioning Morrow, giving her the chance to spread even more slander, the judge dismissed her from the witness box and called on the next witness. The Duke of Clarence.

Grace's heartbeat thundered in her head as he entered the court, his stride smug and self-assured as he approached the stand.

He always was as cunning as a fox.

His testimony, delivered with the superiority of high rank,

thoroughly condemned her. The worst part of it was that the bare facts of their relationship, as he outlined them, were true. They'd known each other for years. She did spend time with him at university. But, blast him, it wasn't the cozy relationship he made it out to be.

"I ran into her and her family at The Savoy a few months back. We reconnected, shall we say, on the dance floor."

Liar.

"That must have given her ideas. I was surprised when she suggested we meet. But she is a beautiful woman and, well, the pictures sort of tell the story about what a great time we had."

He played to the basest instincts of the other men in the room. Grace squeezed her hands together so they wouldn't fight to slap that smirk off his face.

"How can that possibly be, Your Grace? My client was tucked up in bed with a cold on that night. Several witnesses can confirm this."

"I don't know what they saw, but I'm telling you Grace Deroy was with me that night. And she appeared to enjoy herself immensely."

Old Ed ignored his innuendo. "We also have staff at The Savoy who can testify she was alone in her hotel room on the night of the sixteenth when you claim she was with you."

"I suppose the judge will just have to decide who is more credible—a duke backed up by several eyewitnesses or service staff who are used to being paid to keep the secrets of the rich and famous. I have no hesitation about saying Grace Deroy was up close and very personal with me on both occasions."

"Let the record show my client categorically denies this."

Old Ed pressed the duke for more details about the two nights. She knew he was fishing for small details in Andrew's story that might trip him up, but the judge was quickly irritated by lines of questioning that weren't about the photos. A sick feeling stole into her heart. What if Andrew had the judge in his pocket as well as the editor of the *Evening Standard*? Old Ed certainly didn't look satisfied when he resumed his seat.

Sir Ernest Chester QC was almost as good as Old Ed in the courtroom. Grace still had chills thinking back to the way he'd questioned her. However, he seemed a bit too chummy with Andrew for her liking.

"A large part of Miss Deroy's case against the *Evening Standard* relies on her supposed 'good character.' She would have us believe that she was tucked up in bed on each of the occasions in question because she isn't the 'type of girl' who would do this. In fact, her counsel has furnished us with statement after statement attesting to her good moral character. What do you say about this?"

She would have scoffed at the question if she wasn't so sickened by it.

Andrew looked directly at her when he answered. "As you know, I have many connections in the art world. In thirty-eight I was patron for an up-and-coming artist called Alexander Blakey. He wanted a classical education to go with the substantial experience he'd already gained in the salons of Paris, so I agreed to send him to Oxford."

"What is the nature of Mr. Blakey's art?"

"Objection, Your Honor. How can this possibly be relevant?"

The judge dismissed Old Ed. "Answer the question, Your Grace."

Grace had the distinct feeling the judge already knew the nature of Blakey's art.

"It's fairly modern in style, but the subject matter is more suitable for the boudoir than a polite drawing room."

Two of the newspaper's lawyers tittered. Another one leered.

Grace knew exactly what he was going to say before he said it. He was going to reveal her most closely guarded secret in a courtroom where it would be a matter of public record, reported for years to come. How had she been talked into bringing this case against the newspaper?

"Grace Deroy was also at Oxford at that time, was she not?"

241

"Oh yes. She knew Alexander quite well. In fact, she was one of his models." The courtroom drew in a collective breath. "I would go so far as to say that she was his favorite. He certainly liked to draw her without a stitch on."

The judge gave Andrew free rein to speak on for several minutes, and he made the most of them, painting a lurid picture of her relationship with Blakey. Grace thought she would self-combust from shame as she sat listening to her secrets spill from his mouth.

Heat rose in her face, and she bit back tears. She didn't hear all of the story he spun, because her blood pounded in her ears, deafening her. But she knew enough of what he was saying to know how damning his testimony was.

"These are bold claims, Your Grace. Can you substantiate them?"

Grace knew he could. He'd told her as much at Sotheby's. He had drawings of her.

"Oh yes. As executor of Blakey's estate, I'm in possession of several original sketches where Miss Deroy is clearly identifiable. Her face and every other part of her."

"Objection!" Old Ed leapt to his feet. "Accepting such drawings as evidence would be gratuitous and unnecessary. Miss Deroy does not deny having an affair with Alexander Blakey. But her past behavior doesn't automatically mean she would engage in the outrageous public display the *Evening Standard* has falsely and maliciously reported!"

The lawyers exchanged legal arguments for a few more minutes, before the judge ruled that he didn't need to see the drawings after all. The way the men bickered back and forth about the sketches, as though they were children's finger paintings and not incredibly realistic charcoals, made her throat constrict with despair. Even with the drawings safely kept out of the public view, the damage was already done. She could ask every friend she had to testify about her good character, but it couldn't compete with the testimony of a duke in court.

Even forcing herself to think about the real reason she was here didn't comfort her. It was all very well to say you didn't mind a trial if it saved lives, but living the reality of that was entirely different.

She heard the judge's gavel slam down. He must have announced their adjournment for the day. Murmurs swelled into conversation around her as she crossed her arms on the bench in front of her and sank her head upon them.

"C'mon. They've finished. Let's go find them." Peter spoke up beside Jack.

Grace's brother seemed to have developed a newfound respect for Jack after the incident in the lobby. Jack's punch hadn't landed—the duke's valet had seen to that. But Peter apparently appreciated the gesture.

Grace sat with her lawyer in a side chamber of the courthouse. If Jack hadn't seen Wilson through the doorway, he might have waited outside to give the siblings privacy while they took their legal counsel. But this was business, not personal.

"All things considered, it was a good outcome," Wilson was saying as they entered.

"Excuse me?" Grace's voice rang with indignation from where she sat slumped at a large table. "How on earth could today be described as 'good'? My character was assassinated in public and on record."

"Well, yes." Wilson was forced to check his enthusiasm. "But remember why we are doing this, Grace. In his glee at dragging your name through the mud, he's neglecting details. Today we learned that his accomplice is likely a woman. That narrows the field at Bartondale down considerably."

"How on earth do you come to that conclusion?" Peter gave voice to what Jack was thinking.

"There was a woman phoning in tips to the newspaper. There

was another woman who conveniently 'recognized' you in the car—and was able to convince five other people and a reporter that they saw the same thing. There's certainly some smoke and mirrors involved, but we are closing in." Wilson looked very pleased with himself.

"Well, if it's a woman you're after, you've already got a man in place." Grace's angry sarcasm pierced Jack, as he was sure she intended. "Jack, old boy, looks like your services are needed after all."

"Go a little easy on him, Gracie," Peter said. "He took a swing at Clarence before. Missed him, but it's the thought that counts."

Did Jack see Grace's lips quirk up then, or was he imagining things? A half quirk maybe.

"Teddy did say that a woman came to borrow something from me while I was away in London. He let her go up to my room because he thought she was a friend of mine—but that could have been when the photographs were planted."

"It does narrow things down," Jack said. "But there are plenty of women working at Bartondale, and you told me at the beginning of all this that no one else has the same kind of connection to Clarence that Grace has." He eyed Wilson.

He shrugged "I suppose we might have overlooked something."

"You don't say," Jack replied.

"Worthington might. Have a connection, I mean." Grace frowned.

"Charles Worthington's not a woman." Peter snorted.

"I know. He's a beast of a man!" Jack couldn't agree with Grace more on that point. "He said something to me a few months ago that I didn't think twice about until today. He said he'd heard rumors about me. I dismissed it at the time because I didn't think anyone else could possibly know about Blakey and me."

Wilson looked thoughtful. "What do you think, Jack? You work with him."

Grace looked up at him expectantly. He didn't want to disappoint her, but his brain scrambled for some connection.

"He's a complete slob, not entirely incompetent, I suppose. I don't know what Margot sees in him, but—"

"Margot? From Room Six?" Grace asked. "What's she got to do with anything?"

"I have to knock every time I want to enter my own office so they can pretend they weren't just making out before I walked in."

Peter and Wilson both sniggered, but Grace looked deadly serious. Jack guessed her brain was whirring into action behind her hazel eyes.

"I wonder . . ."

Grace looked as though she was still wondering if she should speak the complicated thoughts running through her mind. "Could *The Blue Lady* painting have anything to do with the leaks?"

"It hasn't been something that we've investigated until now, but I can get my people going back over information for connections to Blakey."

"Yes, do that. In the meantime I want to get back in that witness box tomorrow." Whatever silent maneuverings her brain had been doing had obviously yielded results. It changed her whole bearing. The slump had gone, and her eyes now shone with the resolve of someone who wouldn't give up easily.

"Why?" Wilson asked, all too aware of her change in demeanor and slightly surprised at being ordered about.

"Because I have to defend my character. And if the connection has to do with Blakey, I know just the thing that will draw out the traitor."

CHAPTER TWENTY-NINE

3 September 1943

Grace felt ready for the *Evening Standard*'s lawyer. Sometime around 4:00 a.m. she had woken with rage bubbling through her. That was normally the time worry assaulted her mind, but today her righteous anger felt like an answer to prayer. As dawn squeezed its way through the crack in the curtains of her room, she knew she was ready to fight back.

Old Ed and Wilson had worked late into the night to help her devise a strategy that would expose Andrew as a less-than-scrupulous operator, as well as flush out the mole at Bartondale. They still weren't guaranteed a win in court, and their plan would take weeks to play out to its end. But it started now, with Old Ed asking her about her affair with Alexander Blakey while she was under oath, having sworn on the Bible to tell the truth, the whole truth, and nothing but the truth.

"I met Alexander Blakey at Oxford. He was a completely compelling man, and I think I was in love with him from the moment I set eyes on him. I'm sure he could see that. He had lived a very avant-garde life in Paris and persuaded me to throw aside some of my . . . principles. We had an affair."

The judge drilled a stern stare into her, but she focused on her story. If she had to say this so publicly, she would jolly well make it count.

"It was completely secret. I don't think anyone else knew at the time. I didn't even tell my own friends. As His Grace mentioned, I was the model for many of Alexander's works during those months. Alexander could be tumultuous. One minute you had his whole attention and basked in it. The next you were just another piece of furniture while he worked without regard for anything else. He would go into frenzies of painting and sometimes didn't sleep for days."

She sucked in a steadying breath. Even when she'd first confessed to Peter and asked for his help, she hadn't spoken this frankly. Now she was telling the entire world, with a stenographer taking down the details.

"When you've thrown yourself so completely at a man like that, it's hard to pull yourself away. But I used to walk home from his studio and past a chapel that held choir practice twice a week. I started to leave Alexander when I knew choir practice was on so that I could listen to the singing. It was like Alexander would deplete me and then the singing would restore me. Not just the singing, but the words of the songs. The idea that no matter what I did in secret, no matter how broken and confused I felt, the Lord was bigger than those feelings." She couldn't hear another sound and knew the entire courtroom hung on her every word. "It wasn't a sudden revelation, as some people have. It was a pull on my soul every time I heard that music until I became convinced that I needed to ask the Lord's forgiveness, and not just for the affair.."

She must have been silent for a long time, because Old Ed had to prompt her. "How did this change things for you?"

"I told Alexander I was leaving. He begged me to stay."

The moment came flooding back. Alexander's passion and despair, the fury with which he'd painted that final time she saw him.

Surely they would scoff at her if she tried to explain the super-natural power she felt had been given to her in that moment that allowed her to walk away. The words came to her in the form of the music she'd heard at one of the choir practices.

"Do you know the old hymn 'And Can It Be'?"

Blank stares met her question.

"There's a line in the verse at the end, right at the part where the soprano break into the descant." She heard the tune in her head as she recited the words. "'My chains fell off, my heart was free. I rose, went forth, and followed thee.' I feel like that's what happened to me."

Now Grace made her appeal to the judge. "Yesterday, the Duke of Clarence meant to use this information to disparage my charac-ter for his own ends. But I've told the whole truth to illuminate it." She appealed directly to the judge. "I am ashamed of my past, Your Honor. But that's just what it is. The past." What were the next lines of the song? No condemnation now I dread? Yes, they gave her strength now. "I'm simply not that person anymore."

As Old Ed sat, the judge looked just as he had done throughout this whole trial, stern and slightly bored. Grace couldn't be sure this tactic was working on him. However, as Wilson had reinforced over and over last night, there were bigger fish to fry than winning this lawsuit.

Sir Ernest Chester stood up with a gleam in his eye Grace would have found dangerous if she wasn't emboldened by telling the truth.

"Miss Deroy, can you tell the court what Alexander Blakey's most famous artwork is?"

"I believe it is *The Blue Lady*."

"For the benefit of the court, I will read from the Sotheby's catalog. 'The Blue Lady is an erotically charged portrait—thought to be Blakey's mistress—showing a nude woman reclining across a bed, her sad gaze directed toward the evening scene outside the window.' This is a painting of you, is it not?"

"Yes, it is."

The murmur from among the lawyers didn't cause mortification to spiral through her like she'd expected.

"Are you seriously asking the court to believe that a woman unashamed to admit to being the model for what is widely regarded as one of the most salacious artworks of the twentieth century so far *wouldn't* be the kind of woman brazen enough to conduct a semipublic affair?"

"I am ashamed of that painting." Grace tried to keep her voice calm. "In the past I have spent a great deal of money trying to make sure the painting remained out of public view. I bought it anonymously after his death."

Chester postured for the judge, but Grace had the impression he was buying time to think on his feet.

"Well, you made a tidy profit from it when it was auctioned at Sotheby's a matter of weeks ago, Miss Deroy." He shook the catalog he had just read from. "That doesn't speak of shame to me."

This was the turn in the conversation that she had been waiting for. "No, I didn't. In fact, the painting auctioned for that eye-watering amount was a forgery. I still have the original in my possession."

She wanted this scandalous revelation to ricochet around the courtroom as the previous one had. However, there were only a few who recognized the gravity of what she was saying. They shifted uncomfortably in their seats.

"Your Honor, this is entirely implausible! The painting was verified by Blakey's patron, the Duke of Clarence. It cannot be a fake."

"It's my job to decide what's implausible, Sir Ernest." The judge's stern demeanor hadn't shifted, but this was the first time he'd rebuked the newspaper's barrister. "If you have no further questions, please take a seat."

This was the opportunity Old Ed had been waiting for. He approached the witness stand. "Let us be entirely clear here, Miss Deroy. Are you saying that the painting verified by His Grace is a fake?"

"Yes. Yesterday, the newspaper strove to malign my character to defend itself against publishing lies. But they are relying on the word of a man who falsely verified that artwork, presumably for his own gain."

"How do you know that the auctioned artwork was a forgery?"

"As I said, I own the original. I was ashamed of its existence. So I bought it anonymously when his estate auctioned it after his death. I hid it away at my house. I never intended for it, or my involvement with it, to see the light of day ever again."

"Where did you hide it?"

"In a place no one will ever find it."

"No further questions." The older man gave her a kindly nod as she stepped down from the witness stand.

Grace couldn't help wishing for some kind of dramatic flurry after her revelation, but all she heard was the smack of the judge's gavel as he announced he was adjourning the court and reserving his judgment for another day.

⋯◄∞)

"Blue Lady Confesses All!"

The headline screamed at him from the afternoon newspaper, above an article that went into great detail about Grace's affair with Blakey but missed the whole point of her story. The Brits sure loved a scandal, and the murmurs around him on the train as he traveled back to Bartondale told him all he needed to know: in the court of public opinion, Grace's past actions made her irredeemable.

Hadn't they listened to the rest of her testimony? Tears pricked his eyes when he read how she'd quoted Wesley's hymn to explain the change in her life. Maybe it struck a chord in his heart because he knew what it cost her when she spoke.

By being fixated on the story of Grace's affair, the gossipmongers on the train had also missed the biggest revelation of the morning. Her admission she owned the original *The Blue Lady*. Old Ed had mentioned that the duke had paled during Grace's testimony. He'd obviously thought she would shrink into her shame. She'd sure showed him. They said that by the time she'd accused him of lying and confessed to owning the painting, he'd looked quite ill.

Although anyone catching a glimpse of his nonchalant face in the foyer probably wouldn't know anything was amiss. As Jack had left the building, Andrew had been holding court in front of a gaggle of reporters, protesting his innocence.

"Your Grace, were you aware that the painting sold at Sotheby's last July was a forgery?"

"That's utter nonsense spoken from the mouth of a harpy!"

"You didn't know the painting was a fake?"

"It's nonsense. She has a long history of hiding who she really is, and she is bitter that our affair exposed her. I'm now sorry I ever touched her."

Jack's fists tightened. Andrew was the one who would be sorry.

"Leave it, Jack." Wilson had pulled Jack by his elbow. "This is not where the game ends."

"It doesn't bother you that he gets away with saying whatever lies he likes?"

"Not really. What bothers me is that he's been leaking Bartondale's secrets to the Germans. That's why I'm here."

Jack looked at him in disgust.

"You really don't care about Grace at all, do you? She's just a means to an end."

Wilson had looked at him as though he were simply stating the obvious. His parting words to Jack resonated long after he was on the train. "I don't care what feelings you've developed for her while you've been at Bartondale, Jack. Your mission is still the same. And you need to get back there and carry it out to its end."

Get close to her.

That had been his mission, hadn't it?

He doubted she would ever let him close to her again.

CHAPTER THIRTY

7 September 1943

The idling of a car engine under his window woke Jack, but the steady knocking at the front door drew him to the top of the stairs, where he saw Mrs. Johnston answering it. He rubbed sleep from his eyes, slowly waking up to the urgency of the situation.

"Who is it?" Mrs. Johnston, rollers in her hair and night cream on her face, called through the door. "It's two a.m.!"

"Sarah Michaels. I need to speak to the lieutenant."

Sarah didn't stand on ceremony. She pushed the door, forcing Mrs. Johnston to open it fully for her, and glanced up the stairs. She looked like a woman on a mission.

"My apologies, Julia." She glanced at Mrs. Johnston, then focused her eyes on him. "We need your help, Lieutenant. Miss Deroy has a medical emergency. She says you'd know what to do."

Fear squeezed his heart. "Is she okay?"

Judging by the way Sarah's expression softened, his face must have drained of its color. She nodded, glancing at Mrs. Johnson again. "Yes. It's Olive."

"I'll be right down."

Less than two minutes and he was dressed and taking the stairs two at a time. Something he hadn't done since working as an intern.

In the car, Sarah admitted the truth in a hushed tone, even though Martin was long trusted by the family to keep quiet about what he heard. "It's not Olive. It's Teddy."

Frown lines cut into Jack's forehead as unasked questions danced through his mind, but he kept silent. Martin drove fast, despite the lack of light from the shielded headlights that pointed the beam to the ground instead of straight ahead. They were at the cottage in no time.

Sarah led Jack up the fragrant garden path. He ignored the summer smell of flowers he would usually drink in as Sarah fumbled for her key at the door. Once inside Jack started toward the stairs.

"Not up there." She led him through the kitchen, out the back door, and across the garden to the greenhouse. Through the glass he could see the slight glow of a kerosene lantern.

Sarah turned to Jack. "He's very ill, and we didn't know who else to call."

Jack had no idea what to expect as he pulled open the greenhouse door. He didn't anticipate the way his heart would leap when he saw Grace in her robe with her hair flowing loosely down her shoulders. But Nancy Filby also stood next to her, looking over a man sleeping fitfully on a mattress on the ground. Despite the warmth of the summer night, he was shivering.

"I'll go," Nancy murmured to Grace. "Will you let me know that he's all right?"

Grace nodded. "Yes. And thank you, Nancy. We are in your debt."

Jack stepped back so that Nancy could shuffle past him. There was barely room for three people among the plants now, casting grim shadows as the light from the lamp hit them.

"Thank you for coming, Jack."

Jack nodded with grim resolve, then squeezed past Grace, breathing in hints of her soap and perfume among the more earthy greenhouse scents. As he knelt to the mattress, something more sinister hit his nostrils.

Sweat and vomit tinged with the distinct, pungent odor of alcohol. Strong stuff, not the watered-down beer from the pub. The pieces of the puzzle fit together well enough.

"Alcohol poisoning. Has he been like this long?" Jack felt the patient's clammy forehead.

"I don't think so. Nancy said she found him in Tookley's barn like this around dinnertime. She waited until nightfall to drag him here. Apparently he's sometimes alert, but I haven't seen it. The publican sells moonshine out the back of the pub."

"If we take him to a hospital, we can—"

"We can't," she said firmly. "If we take him to a hospital, he'll be tried for desertion. He needs to go back of his own accord."

He gave another grim nod.

"Well then. We need to wait and see how the poison works its way out. But, Grace"—he searched her face—"I have seen this before. This can damage his brain if we don't treat it."

She nodded, looking back at him like a terrified child in front of a parent. "But he'll live, won't he?"

Jack sighed, wrenching his eyes away from her to look at the patient again. If he could get Teddy to a hospital, then he might be able to remove the poison. Without that avenue available to him, he couldn't be sure what might happen.

However, Teddy did have one advantage. He had someone to care for him and make sure he didn't choke if he vomited, to revive him if he turned blue. In that case he would make it through the night.

"Probably."

Grace heaved in breath.

"I can watch over him tonight, if you like. You look exhausted."

He wasn't sure where aiding a deserter fell in the long line of moral compromises he had made since being assigned this job. But he'd also made an oath once as a doctor to protect life. That was what mattered here.

"I'm so sorry to bring you into this." Her usually elegant posture sagged. "He flew over Hamburg, and it didn't sit right with him. He shouldn't have told me but . . . I think I'll stay."

"Then I'll stay with you."

———•⊶∞)

"Grace."

Someone said her name.

A man's voice, as sweet as warm caramel.

Her head fell heavily, jolting her eyes open.

She hadn't intended to fall asleep and leave Jack on watch. But sometime during the night, she'd removed her dirty slippers and pulled her feet up onto the chair, tucking them under her. She woke with her elbows folded across one of the wicker arms and her chin resting on her forearms.

Teddy slept calmly on the mattress, and Jack sat on the ground by his side, elbows on raised knees, his back leaning against the leg of the potting bench. His voice had stirred her.

"I'm sorry. I drifted off." She unfolded her limbs, which were sore and stiff from being doubled up in the too-small chair. "How's Teddy?"

"I think he'll pull through. Can Sarah stay with him today? Someone should be nearby."

Grace nodded, running a hand over her face before she stood. She extended her hand so she could help him to his feet, expecting him to be just as stiff and sore. She pulled him up so they were eye to eye, standing so close she could feel his heat on her skin.

"Thank you, Jack." Three words didn't seem like enough to contain her gratitude. She had barely exchanged a word with him—not a civil one, at any rate—since she'd been arrested. Yet he came in the middle of the night without asking questions and then stayed to make sure Teddy made it through.

"Any time you need me, I'll be here for you. Grace, I . . ."

His eyes, his whole expression, were soft in the light of the summer dawn. She wanted to lean into that softness, as well as run a mile from it. "Don't say anything, Jack. Right now, I can't . . . I just can't . . ."

She bit her lip as all the worry and exhaustion of the night caught up with her. Tears threatened, so she lowered her head, hoping he wouldn't notice.

Too late.

"Grace." He said her name with that impossibly gentle voice again, the one that spoke of his own vulnerability as well as turning her tired mind to mush.

"Please don't . . ." But she didn't even know how she wanted that sentence to end. *Don't touch me?* Oh, but how she wanted him to wrap his arms around her! *Don't be kind?* It made it hard to resent him the way she wanted to.

Just don't make me love you again.

"Hey." He closed the distance between them and wrapped his arms around her, drawing her into him.

She couldn't stop herself from melting against him. She wasn't so short that she could cry against his chest, but she made a good go of sobbing into his neck, her arms clinging around his waist. His hands ran up and down her back, soothing her. She felt every move through her thin nightgown and robe. They warmed her and made her shiver at the same time.

She should pull herself away, but it was like his every caress was especially designed to convince her to stay pressed against his solid chest. Anchored by his strong arms. One hand ran up her neck into her loosened hair. His touch lulled her, bewitched her. She sighed into the intimacy, craving more of the tingles he created across her skin.

Eyes closed, she let him distract her from everything. The inescapable fact she had confessed her darkest secrets in public. The uncertainty every day of knowing she worked with a traitor. Even her pallid, sweat-soaked brother lying on the greenhouse floor at their feet.

She turned her face and found his lips with hers, feeling the tiny moan he gave as he squeezed her in his arms, returning the kiss with a ferocity that spoke every feeling from the last few days.

But before she could get lost in the feeling, he stopped abruptly, stepping back, his face strained by a thousand types of guilt.

He cleared his throat. "I'll call back this afternoon after work. And you should keep Olive home from school for the next few days."

"Olive? Why?"

"She was the excuse Sarah gave for summoning me in the middle of the night. If Olive is running around like a mad thing the way she usually does, Mrs. Johnston's tongue will wag."

He left the greenhouse without a look back at her. He was long gone before she could breathe again.

CHAPTER THIRTY-ONE

8 September 1943

"I told you, Grace. I don't remember."

Jack saw the honesty in Teddy's eyes up close, because as Teddy protested, Jack was shining a flashlight in his eyes, checking the way his pupils responded.

"I can't remember anything about the last three days!"

"Yes, but this happened weeks ago, when I went to London with Sarah and Olive."

Teddy winced, as though his sister's voice caused him pain. "Do you have to shout, Grace?"

"I'm not shouting. You're hungover."

Teddy groaned and sank his head into his hands, elbows resting on the kitchen table. Sarah puttered around them, making tea. She'd hauled Teddy out of the greenhouse while Jack and Grace were at the big house and forced him to take a bath. While he was indisposed, she'd absconded with his foul-smelling clothes and left his uniform, clean, pressed and smelling like lemons and lavender on a stool outside the bathroom door. Something Teddy didn't seem happy about.

"You're lucky to be alive, son." Jack assumed his serious doctorly tone, hoping Teddy understood exactly how fortunate he had been.

Teddy lifted his head from his hands briefly. "Is that what you call it?"

Jack softened his voice so it didn't cause Teddy's head to throb. "I don't think there's permanent damage. But it's hard to say. The brain is a weird and wonderful thing. You might have memory problems, concentration issues. They might get better with time. Each case is different."

"In other words, you are an impossible fool for trying to drink yourself to death, Edward Deroy, but despite your idiocy, God has seen fit to pull you through this relatively unscathed." Grace did nothing to modulate her voice, letting it reverberate around Teddy's head.

Teddy scowled at her mention of God. It looked like it hurt.

"I've brought the best medicine I know for this kind of thing." Jack placed a metal tin in front of Teddy and flicked the lid open. Pungent, like just-burnt caramel, the aroma permeated the air.

"Coffee," Teddy muttered.

"I know you prefer tea here, but I'm afraid it just doesn't do the job in cases like this."

"Doctor knows best."

Sarah took the tin and brewed some coffee as best she could without a proper pot, a process involving a lot more clanking and rattling than Teddy thought was reasonable, judging by the winces he made.

She served the thick, black liquid in one of Grace's floral teacups. "Drink up, Teddy. And try to remember *something* about that woman!"

Teddy scowled and mumbled into his cup something about Grace's voice piercing bone. Jack left Teddy to his brew, standing up and taking his own teacup to where Grace stood near the back door. He hoped for a quiet word with her, to murmur an apology for kissing her. But she wouldn't give him the chance. She latched her attention on Teddy when he spoke.

"I know what you're doing. You've sobered me up and now you are sending me packing."

"Not quite. We have sobered you up, and we are taking you back to the aerodrome."

Teddy looked ready to bolt out the kitchen door. "Grace, I've told you. I can't."

She took the seat Jack had vacated moments earlier and took Teddy's hands. "Teddy, two weeks ago I would have told you that there was no way I could stand in court and confess my most humiliating secrets. But I found strength I never knew I had, and I know it came from the Lord."

Teddy scoffed, as bitter as the coffee he drank and deeply sarcastic. "You think 'the Lord' will give me strength to drop more bombs on innocent people while they sleep? That's some God you've got there, Gracie."

"Teddy," Jack chimed in behind him. "Assuming the Royal Air Force works like the US one, you're not going near an aircraft anytime soon. You'll be in prison, maybe even dishonorably discharged."

"But if we do it this way, there's less chance you'll be hanged, Teddy. You can thank Peter and Old Ed for that."

"You told them?"

Grace gave him the kind of look that big sisters the world over reserved for their baby brothers. "Of course I did. Both of them want to help you, Teddy. And we all, very much, want an end to the war that doesn't involve you being dead."

At her mention of Peter and Old Ed, tears brightened Teddy's eyes. "What about Mother and Father?"

"We'll tell them as soon as you are back at your station. But I am certain they care as much as the rest of us."

Teddy drank his coffee in silence, keeping his tears at bay, until Grace pressed him again about the woman who'd called while she was away. "Don't you remember anything else about her?"

Teddy shrugged, so Jack tried a different tack. "Just tell us what you remember."

"I thought she must be one of Grace's friends, so I introduced myself as the gardener, hoping she wouldn't catch on. She said you were loaning her a dress, which is something you do all the time, so I let her in. But since I was playing the gardener, I couldn't exactly follow her upstairs."

"Was she in uniform?"

Teddy shook his head, then seemed to regret it. "Civvies."

"What about her accent? Was she from around here?"

"It was hard to place, but she sounded educated."

Grace pulled an exasperated face, clearly frustrated he had nothing more to offer than "pretty," "brunette," and "educated." She let her voice pierce through his brain again.

"Well, drink up, little brother. Because on the way back to the aerodrome, you are going to thank Nancy Filby for bringing you here and saving your skin."

He mumbled his halfhearted protest into his coffee.

———•◦∞◦———

Grace's camaraderie with the girls at work had evaporated into suspicion. Although she tried to go through the motions of friendship, fear of them being traitors kept her constantly preoccupied. Any one of them could fit into Teddy's frustratingly vague description of the woman who had been in her room. In her worry, she was losing files and neglecting The System that had once been her pride and joy. She was even making careless spelling mistakes, which she hated more than anything else.

At least Teddy was safely deposited back to his station. That was one less worry to distract her from the task Wilson had given her. Revealing in court that she owned *The Blue Lady* was just the first step toward drawing out the mole, but the excitement that had zinged through her when they'd concocted the plan had now fizzled into doubt. After two weeks back on the job, they had no more leads. Grace began to doubt her gut instinct that the painting was somehow connected to the leaks.

"Just go about your job as usual. But keep your wits about you. You know the rhythms of the place, and you'll feel when something isn't right."

Did Wilson tell Jack that when he'd started work here? She suddenly felt some sympathy for the gormless, stricken look he'd worn during his first few weeks. She was almost certain she was giving her friends that exact same expression.

She quelled her sympathy. The wound of his betrayal still smarted, but he inspired a merry-go-round of other emotions too. Especially when she thought about that morning in the greenhouse. Something she did too often.

"Should I take these upstairs, Grace?" Susie asked. Group Captain Carter had put Susie in charge of the library while Grace had been away at court.

"No, I'll go." Grace went to take the files from Susie.

Instead of handing them over to her, Susie kept hold of them for a moment. Grace's eyes shot to Susie's, even though she had been avoiding them all day. Susie had dark hair, was reasonably attractive, and had worked in a real library before the war. She fit the bill for the person Teddy had seen.

"Are you sure?"

Grace nodded.

Susie gave her a quick smile that Grace thought was meant to be encouraging. "We all read the newspapers. Are you all right?"

Grace bristled. "Of course. I'm just taking a while to get back into the swing of things." Did Charlotte and Betsy just snigger behind her? She spun to check, but they were both hard at work at their desks. Perhaps she was simply paranoid. They both had dark hair too.

"Well, can you take these to Room Six on the way?" Susie asked.

"Happily."

At least no one in Room Six snickered behind her back. They didn't seem to bat an eyelid at the idea of her being the model for *The Blue Lady*. In fact most of them gave the impression that posing naked for a famous artist was so unremarkable as to be boring.

Margot even tried to identify with her. "I posed once for Picasso without a stitch on," she'd said the first time Grace saw her after confessing all in court.

"You know Picasso?"

Margot simply shrugged and flitted away. Grace took her time considering Margot's hair color. It wasn't that dark, compared to some of the others here, and she was much less attractive than Susie and Charlotte. Grace wished Teddy had paid more attention that day so she had something else to go on. After all, hair could be dyed, beauty was in the eye of the beholder, and accents could be changed.

"Come in," the group captain boomed when she knocked.

"Here are the files you requested from the library, sir."

He wasn't at his desk. He was in the far corner of the room, supervising his secretary, who was rooting around Grace's old wardrobe. The floor around them looked like a paper factory after an air raid. All the Air Ministry paperwork, including boxes and files, had been removed from the closet and spread over the rose-patterned carpet.

"Just over here, Deroy."

As she moved closer, she saw the women he supervised had removed all the file boxes from the wardrobe and arranged some kind of pile system across the floor.

"What on earth happened to my wardrobe?" She almost kicked herself for being the one to mention this was her former room. The group captain usually did that.

"There was a break-in last night. Made a right royal mess of all our documents, but we don't know why. We're trying to work out what was taken."

"Oh, how terrible!"

The doors of the wardrobe were flung open, giving her a clear view of the panel that made part of the secret compartment. Her fingers itched to be able to check whether or not what she had hidden in there was safe. But she couldn't do that now, not with all these people here.

"And they just made a mess of this wardrobe. Nowhere else?"

"Yes." The group captain looked at her thoughtfully. Then he addressed his secretary. "Daphne, would you mind? I need to have a private word with Corporal Deroy here."

The way he said it made her shiver. She tried to ignore the look Daphne cast her way as she left the room. His innuendo had been bad enough before her past had become public. Now he obviously thought that he had permission to give voice to his every wolfish thought.

"What do you say to staying late to help me fix up this mess tonight, Corporal Deroy?"

"I don't think that would be entirely appropriate, sir."

"Come on, Deroy. I know you aren't shy about these things. We could go to dinner first."

"I've told you before, sir, I . . ." Her voice trailed off as her gaze drifted to the wardrobe. Her brain made several leaps in logic and concocted a plan of attack before her mouth had even begun to speak. "I can't do dinner. But how about lunch?"

CHAPTER THIRTY-TWO

"Could you sign here, Lieutenant?"

Grace handed him a file. He offered a friendly smile as he took it, noting how her serious gaze flicked down to the note attached to the file.

Rose garden. 15 minutes.

Grace's elegant copperplate writing was reduced to an alarming scrawl. When he glanced back up, her eyes had become urgent.

He opened his mouth to ask more, but she gave an almost imperceptible shake of her head. On the other side of the room, Worthington sat at his desk, admiring Margot, who sat on it. Jack nodded slightly so Grace would know he'd seen the message.

Fifteen minutes later he arrived at the rose garden, slightly out of breath. "Are you okay?"

She pulled him down to sit next to her on the stone bench, where he'd once told her the whole story of his romance with Dotty.

"There was a burglary last night in the group captain's office." She whispered in such a low tone that he had to lean in close to hear. Anyone looking on would think the words they exchanged were much more intimate.

"What was stolen?"

"I don't know. But I know what they were after."

She paused for so long he wasn't sure she would continue. It was like she was assessing him for trustworthiness all over again.

"Well, are you going to tell me?"

"I hid *The Blue Lady* in a secret compartment at the back of the wardrobe in the group captain's office."

Wilson had tried to get the details of where she kept the original painting out of her since they'd made the connection between the painting and the leaks. She had been tight lipped, only saying that it was secure at Bartondale.

"How could they know it was there?"

"I don't know. Insider information, perhaps? Listening devices? Honestly, after everything that's happened to me recently, I'm inclined to believe anything. But, Jack, if it's gone, we've lost our best chance of luring them into the open."

"Okay, so what do we do?" Working with Grace instead of against her sent a thrill through him.

"First, we have to work out if it's actually gone. The compartment looked intact to me, but that could just mean they put the panel back when they were done. Right now is the perfect time to look. The files are all out while they try to sort out what's missing. I've arranged for the group captain to take me to lunch. All you have to do is—"

"What? Grace! You can't!"

Tales of Group Captain Carter's wandering hands and penchant for young women in uniform had reached him on his first day at Bartondale. Grace had even regaled him with stories about rebuffs. The group captain wasn't the kind of man to stop at lunch if he thought something else was on the menu.

"It's too late for that." She dismissed his concerns. "All you have to do is get into my room—I mean his office—while we're gone.

Everything is out of the wardrobe, so all you have to do is reach up to the panel at the top and feel for a latch on the left. Your fingers are bigger than mine, so you might have to jam them in, but once you get it, the panel will come off."

She rattled off her other instructions, speaking quickly to get it all out before she had to make her meeting time. They agreed that if the painting was there, he should remove it and bring it to her cottage after work.

Before she could leap off the bench and dash away, he grabbed her hand. "Please be careful, Grace. With Carter and . . . well, I don't know. Just don't—" Tongue-tie revisited him, reminding them both he was no mastermind of plots and intrigues.

"Of course, Jack."

Back in his office, he put on a show of working and made sure he spotted Carter's secretary eating in the cafeteria. He estimated he had about fifteen minutes to check for the painting before anyone either noticed he was gone or stumbled upon him.

In the group captain's office, everything was as Grace said it would be. He tiptoed through the papers on the floor, shuddering at a creaky floorboard even though he knew there was no way his steps could be heard amid the bustle of the work on the floor below.

Grace's instructions to open the secret compartment were clear enough. He slipped his fingers into a crevice in the top left corner of the closet, working them along to feel for the latch. It took a moment to work out if it lifted, pressed, or pulled, but eventually he heard a satisfying click, and what looked like the solid back of the closet came away.

Disappointment gripped him when he saw no painting in the narrow space exposed by removing the panel. The thief had found it before them.

Then his eye caught a flash of blue. Pinned to the back of the removable panel was *The Blue Lady*.

She took his breath away.

Perhaps it was the fact the painting at the auction had been a fake and the forger hadn't managed to recreate the genius of the original. Or maybe it was because he now knew the story behind the artwork and that Grace had inspired it. But he suddenly saw so much more in the bright blues of the painting than he had that day at Sotheby's.

Hurt.

Desire.

Beauty.

Yearning.

He'd never had a painting stir all these things inside him as he gazed at it.

The artist's brilliance drew him in so that he had to shake himself out of the feelings the brushstrokes evoked. Considering this was a painting of Grace naked, he really shouldn't be looking at it so carefully. Nor for so long.

He worked out each pin individually with his surgeon's hand, careful not to damage the canvas. He knew he should roll it up, but he had no way to conceal it other than to fold the canvas and slide it into one of the manilla files he'd brought with him up to the room.

He'd already lost critical time staring at the painting, so when he did leave the room, Carter's secretary was returning from her lunch.

"Sorry, ladies. I came up here to deliver a file, but silly me brought up the wrong one." He grinned his apology.

She seemed to buy it, but he didn't let out the breath he was holding until he was safely back in his office, the painting in his briefcase.

———————⊷⟨∞⟩

Grace took the precaution of warning Martin about the nature of the lunch. She instructed him that under no circumstances was he to take them anywhere else other than the restaurant in Grantham and then straight back to Bartondale. Carter was technically Martin's boss now, but she guessed he had enough loyalty for her family to count on him as an ally.

"And if possible, could you arrange for some emergency at Bartondale that forces us to have to go back there in about"—she looked at her wristwatch—"say forty-five minutes?"

"Should I be worried that you have switched sides and are now working for Gerry, miss?"

"You of all people must be used to my hijinks, Martin!" She hoped her grin belied the seriousness of what she had asked of him.

The lunch itself crawled along at an interminable pace. Getting Carter to talk about himself managed to spare her from most of his more oafish remarks. The others she deflected with her own brand of polite evasion. It wasn't scintillating conversation by any means. Not when her every fiber wondered if Jack could pull off their hastily planned heist.

She glanced at her watch again just as a waiter brought them boiled summer pudding to finish their meal. Martin should be in with news of a crisis any moment now.

"But enough about me. It must be tedious for you to hear my life story. Tell me about how you met Blakey."

Lord, help me get out of this line of questioning safely.

"I was at Oxford with him. He was very charismatic. Such a bright, compelling mind."

"I knew the whole Blakey family, you know. His father and I grew up together and dined at their house several times after I returned from the last war."

"You did?" She almost choked on her pudding.

The conversation suddenly became interesting. Alexander had never been forthcoming about his family, only mentioning they'd had a falling out before he went to Paris as a teenager.

"Yes. His parents weren't the most conventional people. Let their children run wild, which is probably why they became artists."

"He never told me much about his family. How many children were there?"

Hopefully, this came across as simple, polite chitchat and not the interrogation it was.

"Three. One of the boys, the older one, died in an accident. Terrible stuff. Alexander was devastated and never seemed to recover any kind of equilibrium. He would have dreadful rows with his parents and ran off to Paris as soon as he could."

Her mind raced like fingers through a filing cabinet, trying to remember bits of information from her conversations with Alexander. "I do remember him saying he wasn't on speaking terms with his family. Do you know what they fought about?"

"No. Though it was probably money. I suspect he was a prodigal who wanted to abscond to the literary salons of Paris with his inheritance. He probably talked them into handing it over. He could be very persuasive."

Didn't she know it.

"His sister is cut from the same cloth. That's how she got her job at Bartondale. Talked me into it."

"His sister works at Bartondale?"

"Yes. Margaret Blakey. Although she's styled herself as Margot Monteroy now. Didn't want her professional work overshadowed by her brother or something."

That would be how she knew Picasso. Thinking about her face now, Grace saw the resemblance to Alexander. She ticked off Margot's attributes against Teddy's list. It could very well be her.

"Anyway, I thought you would know all this considering how close you were."

"We didn't talk much about his family."

"I bet you didn't talk much at all!" He leered. The glint in his eye was dangerous, and the pudding was almost gone.

Where are you, Martin?

"How strange she never said anything to me?" She glanced at the doorway.

"Well, she's split with the parents too, I'm afraid, but it wasn't as lucrative for her as it was for Alexander. But enough about that.

I'm sure *The Blue Lady* herself has much more interesting tales to tell. Perhaps—"

"Excuse me, sir. I don't mean to bother you, but you are needed back at Bartondale."

Martin arrived not a moment too soon.

She let out her breath and stood to leave. "Well, I suppose we must get back."

"Yes. Well. Right, then."

His confusion almost made her snort with laughter.

"I'm terribly sorry," he said. "Such an enjoyable meal and ended too soon. We should do this again."

Absolutely not.

She opted for a tight smile instead of bellowing what she really thought and let herself be bustled into the car by Martin.

"Would you mind dropping me at the cottage, Martin?" She was desperate to telephone Wilson with what she knew, and Jack had promised to meet her here as soon as he could get away.

Carter placed a hand on her knee. "Shall I—"

"No!" She cut him off more loudly than was polite, causing Martin to look up at her sharply in the rearview mirror. She had to shut Carter down properly or work at Bartondale would become unbearable.

"Thank you for a lovely lunch, sir. But we can't do this again. It's not appropriate."

"But you are *The Blue Lady*! What do you care about what is appropriate?"

"That painting doesn't define me. And it certainly doesn't give you license to treat me like this. Don't make me have to tell my father!"

With that she flung open the car door and bounded out of it down the path to her cottage. She didn't realize anything was amiss until she opened the front door and saw Sarah slumped at the kitchen table.

CHAPTER THIRTY-THREE

Jack's mind worked faster than an aircraft engine during takeoff. Now that they had the painting, he and Grace would have to use it to lure out the traitor. They should speak to Wilson about how on earth they did that.

"Finishing early?"

Jack jumped halfway to Bartondale's high ceiling at Worthington's comment, getting a strange look from his colleague.

"Yep," he said shortly. "I, uh, need to get back to—I mean, I have a meeting . . . with a friend."

Worthington's look intensified, but then a light seemed to dawn in his mind. "Who's the girl, then? Not one of the pretty things from the library?"

Jack held back a groan. Of course, Worthington would think that was why he was sneaking off well before the end of the workday. It was exactly what Worthington would do.

Tell the truth where you can. He supposed that advice still stood.

"Actually, yes. Grace, if you must know."

"Deroy! You sly thing, Jack. You kept telling me you have no interest in *The Blue Lady*?"

"What?" Had Worthington really just mentioned the painting in Jack's briefcase?

"I'm not judging. Every man here is curious."

Someone had to put that man in his place.

"Shut it and stop being a pig, Worthington. Not every woman is here for your gratification. Grace deserves so much better!"

"What's got into you?" Worthington called out as Jack strode from the room.

His jitters continued. Every cheery greeting from a colleague was an accusation striking right at the heart of his conscience. He tried to smile in response. He even lingered to chat over weekend plans with a few of them, keeping a tight hold on the briefcase that seemed like it was screaming out his guilt.

Once out of the building, he picked up his step. Jogging would be suspicious, but he walked so fast he was puffed when he reached Grace's cottage.

The sight of the blue door slightly ajar made the hairs on his arms stand up straight. Neither Grace nor her diligent housekeeper ever kept this door open. The back door always, but never the front door.

"Grace?" He pushed on the door. It opened with a creak, revealing Sarah sagged at the kitchen table straight ahead of him. If he didn't know Sarah, he might wonder if she had simply fallen asleep with her head resting on her outstretched arm. But Sarah would never do such a thing in the middle of the day.

He heard voices from upstairs in Grace's room. His heart skipped a beat when he heard Grace protesting she didn't have the painting. He glanced around the room, expecting to see Olive slumped on the sofa, but no one else was near. With catlike steps, he crossed to Sarah and reached out two fingers to feel the pulse point on her neck. Sarah moaned.

She was alive. A cold teacup sat on the table in front of her.

He raised it to his nose and sniffed. Honey. Lots of it. Probably to mask a bitter poison.

"Sarah!" He whispered in her ear, trying to rouse her.

She moaned again, but this time she opened her eyes and met his with a glassy stare. She tried to sit up in her seat, but Jack could see she felt heavy. She looked around the room, confused.

The voices drifted down from upstairs.

"Just give it to me and you'll never have to hear from me again!" a woman's shrill voice demanded.

"Sarah, what happened?"

"I just sat down for a moment to drink my tea . . ." she replied in a vague and groggy voice.

"So you didn't see who is upstairs with Grace?"

She shook her head, then looked like she regretted doing so and rested it back down on her arm.

Content Sarah would be all right for now, Jack focused his attention on what was happening upstairs.

"Jack!" Grace's scream was a bullet to his heart.

A thousand possible causes for her scream raced through his mind in a split second—none of them good.

The sound of footsteps on the stairs meant someone was coming.

"Sarah, you need to stand now."

He grabbed her elbow and hauled her up to stand on groggy, unsteady legs.

"You need to go and get help. Grace is in danger."

The mention of Grace's name seemed to crank Sarah's mind into gear. She staggered to the open back door and stumbled through it.

Help her, Lord. Help us.

———◦∞◦———

Following the sound of someone rifling through her belongings instead of using the telephone to call Wilson immediately was a mistake. Grace saw that now. But she'd heard the clatters and smashes upstairs and had wanted to assess the situation first. She'd thought she could creep up quietly and scope things out before reporting back to Wilson.

Just when she was nearly at the top of the stairs, Margot Blakey flew out from behind the bedroom door, bellowing like Boudica and waving a knife at Grace's face.

Grace flung herself to one side with a shriek, narrowly avoiding the blade as it came toward her. Her shoulder slammed into the wall as Margot crashed into her. Burning pain shot through her upper arm.

Before she could recover her balance, Margot grabbed her by the hair and dragged her into the bedroom. When Margot let go, she stepped back and held the knife in front of her.

"Just give it to me and you'll never have to hear from me again!"

The frenzied glint in Margot's eyes terrified Grace more than the blade. She'd never seen Margot like this. She'd never seen anyone so crazed.

"Give me the painting!"

"I don't have it."

Margot screamed in frustration, a guttural, piercing screech.

"You do! You said so in court!"

"Here. I don't have it here!"

"It's not in your old room. It must be here." Margot shot desperate glances around the space, as though she expected to see the painting mounted on the wall.

Both of their eyes widened as they heard a man's voice resonate up from the kitchen.

Jack.

Grace shrieked out his name, causing Margot to lunge at her. She tried to move out of the way, but her feet wouldn't seem to move. Margot grabbed her arm, twisted it behind her back, and forced her down the stairs. She felt the end of the knife jammed up against her side, coercing her forward.

She stumbled on the first few steps. For some reason her feet just wouldn't work the way she wanted them to. At the bottom of the stairs, she noticed for the first time that her side was wet.

It wasn't until she saw the look on Jack's face she knew something was very, very wrong.

———————◦◦◦◦

Grace's sensible WAAF-issue shoes stumbled on the bottom step, followed by Grace herself. He glimpsed her tightly drawn face before his attention was drawn to the woman behind her.

Margot Monteroy.

She had twisted Grace's arm behind her and held one of Sarah's large carving knives to Grace's right side under her ribs. He didn't like the angle. One thrust and she could stab straight up into Grace's liver.

But that wasn't the biggest problem.

Grace had a fast-growing bloom of red blood extending from under her arm down her right side.

"What's he doing here?" Margot hissed into Grace's ear. Frantic spit flew out. "You should both be at work!"

He wasn't sure if Margot's words were meant for them or whether she was ranting to herself. Her wild eyes weren't focused on either him or Grace. He eyed the crimson down Grace's side. If he were a gambling man, he'd put money on a bet that Margot had managed to sever an artery somehow. In which case he had to act now or Grace would bleed to death.

Grace's face turned gray. She swayed backward against Margot. *Please don't let her fall against that knife, Lord.*

He might be able to stem the flow of the blood from an arm, but he couldn't do anything about a liver.

"You want the painting, don't you, Margot? I've got it. But you have to let me treat Grace first. See? She's bleeding."

Margot paled at the sight of that much blood. "She shouldn't even be here. I just want the painting."

Grace moaned. Jack could tell she was about to faint.

"Sure thing, Margot. Just let me help Grace and you can have it."

Grace slipped to the floor, avoiding the knife. Thank God! Jack darted forward, reaching her with enough time to ease her head down so she wouldn't hit it.

"Grace! Grace! I'm here. I need you to stay with me, okay?" His medical training surfaced right on cue. He identified the problem—a deep gash under her upper arm was spurting blood now that it was angled this way.

Definitely her brachial artery.

Grace moaned, weaker than before.

"Come on, Grace. Hang in there," he muttered.

Time was critical.

He'd have to improvise a tourniquet. His fingers worked at the tie around his neck, undoing it in record time and wrapping it around her arm as far above the gash as he could get it. He tied it tightly, but for an injury like this, a simple knot wasn't enough.

"The painting! I want the painting!" Margot screeched when she saw the bleeding had stayed.

His brain had no time for that question, no matter how loudly it was yelled. His singular focus was stopping the blood and saving Grace's life.

He raced to the kitchen, yanked open a drawer, and grabbed a butter knife, then slid back to the floor next to Grace. He slipped the knife under the loop his tie had made around her arm and twisted it to create a tighter clamp.

"The painting!" Margot screamed again. This time she looked like she might use the carving knife again.

"In the briefcase."

National security and priceless art be damned. All that mattered was Grace.

Margot lunged for Jack's briefcase, tore it open, and emptied it onto the kitchen floor. Her eyes went as wide as saucers when she saw the canvas, grabbing it up as her prize. She sucked in her breath like a rabid animal with manic eyes. For one dreadful moment, he thought she might slash at him, angry at the way he'd folded it. Instead she made a guttural sound—half growl, half scream—and ran for the front door.

Grace moaned again. Her eyes fluttered open.

"Margot. His sister." She managed to get the words out before her head lolled to the side again.

He had to find more help. Reluctantly, he strode away from her side to the sitting room. He lifted the phone receiver. "Ambulance," he told the operator, who immediately put him through to the depot in Grantham.

They dispatched a van. He hung up the receiver and immediately picked it up again. "Grantham Hospital."

Once connected he didn't give the nurse on the other end of the line time to speak before telling her to get the operating theater prepped for surgery, explaining the kind of injury about to arrive in the ambulance. "And she'll need blood." He glanced at the amount on her clothes and on the floor about her. "Three pints at least, but I don't know the type."

Grace moaned again. He hung up on the nurse at the hospital even though she was mid-question and returned to the floor next to Grace. "Please stay with me."

Lord, please keep her safe. His heart cried out his prayer. But praying brought no comfort.

After all, he'd prayed this prayer once before, watching Dotty give birth. He'd prayed it as doctors and nurses had surged into the room, rushing to save the hemorrhaging mother and her breathless child.

The Lord hadn't given him the answer he'd so desperately begged for then.

There were no guarantees for Grace now.

CHAPTER THIRTY-FOUR

Grace smelled antiseptic and dried blood. When her eyelids fluttered open, she saw Jack sleeping awkwardly on a wooden foldout seat next to the hospital bed she was lying in.

Her eyes blurred. She blinked to clear them.

When they opened fully, the room was dark and he was gone.

Next time she opened her eyes, light streamed in through a window behind her somewhere. She was conscious of an ache in her arm and looked down to see a thick bandage circling it.

A glass of water sat on a little table beside her bed. She tried to reach it for her parched throat.

"Oh, it's good to have you awake, Miss Deroy." A cheery nurse approached from an observation desk on the other side of the room. The nurse held the cup to Grace's lips. The water went some of the way to removing the furry, scratchy taste in her mouth.

"Your doctor will be in soon, I'm sure."

"What happened?"

"I'll let him tell you. You rest now."

She leaned back on the pillows, fighting to keep her eyelids open. She didn't want any more rest after being asleep for goodness knew how long. She wanted help to sort out the memories from the dreams.

Margot was Alexander's sister—she remembered finding that out at lunch with Group Captain Carter. Margot was the connection to Andrew at Bartondale. She wanted the painting. Grace remembered Margot screaming at her. But not a lot else made sense.

She shut her eyes against the strain of thinking, and when she awoke again, Jack was there, holding her hand.

Her doctor, like the nurse had said.

Peter sat at the foot of her bed too.

"Hello." Her croaky greeting received relieved smiles from them. "Is someone going to tell me what happened?"

"You almost died, Gracie," Peter said.

"It certainly feels like it," Grace replied. "But I mean Margot and Andrew and the painting . . . Did we get them?"

"The police caught Margot trying to get on the bus to London. They recovered the painting, and she gave them a full confession," Jack said.

"Clarence had been using her to get information on German targets where his business interests were threatened. And paying her well, I would imagine," Peter said, disgust lacing his tone. "But she wanted more money. She forged *The Blue Lady* and threatened to rat him out if he didn't vouch for it as the original when it went to auction."

"Oh." She wouldn't have thought vague old Margot had it in her. Then the memory of Margot's ferocious face coming toward her at the top of the cottage stairs came back with full force. "Did she have any help?"

"She was occasionally paying a dispatch driver to courier things to Clarence," Jack said.

Millar. She vaguely remembered seeing him with Margot at the cinema. "Poor Charlotte."

"And Worthington's feeling a bit shamefaced. He didn't realize she was pilfering the information from his desk," Jack said.

"Well, it's so messy. I don't suppose he would have." Grace gave him a wry smile.

Questions filled Grace's mind. Befuddled by medical treatment and distracted by the throb in her arm, she couldn't entirely compute what they were saying.

"But why involve me through the newspapers? I don't understand."

"Maybe this can help explain it." Wilson entered, looking more tired than Grace remembered seeing him before. He carried a folded copy of the *Evening Standard*, which he handed to Peter. "How are you feeling, Miss Deroy?"

"I've felt better."

"Very droll. You gave us all a big scare, you know? Some more than others." He glanced at Jack.

A long, low whistle from Peter stole her attention. He was looking over the front page of the newspaper.

"What does it say?" Jack asked. He still hadn't let go of her hand.

Peter glanced up. "The headline is 'Dastardly Duke and the Fakey Blakey.'"

"Read it to me," Grace said.

"'The corridors of power were in uproar today when Andrew Hastings, Duke of Clarence, was arrested for espionage. Sources within MI5 have confirmed the duke, most recently in the courts helping this newspaper defend allegations of libel, confessed to bribing an Air Ministry worker to obtain information about intended targets that he then leaked to business interests in Germany. Not only is it alleged the duke scurrilously conspired against our nation, he also sought to bring this newspaper into disrepute by feeding false stories about a relationship with one Miss Grace Deroy, daughter of RAF Air Marshall Sir Henry Deroy, to our reporter. Miss Deroy brought a case against the *Evening Standard* before the courts last month. The matter will now be settled privately.'"

"Is that an apology, do you think?" she said. "Keep reading, Peter."

"'However, the duke's dastardly deeds don't stop there. The *Evening Standard* has learned the duke, a longtime art aficionado and bona fide collector, knowingly authenticated a forgery of Alexander Blakey's famous portrait *The Blue Lady* at Sotheby's earlier this year. On the basis of his authentication, the painting fetched over one hundred thousand pounds for its anonymous seller—thought to be Blakey's sister, who was recently institutionalized for unrelated issues.'"

Peter scanned the rest of the article and summarized it for her. "They spend a lot of time excusing themselves for printing the stories about you, Gracie, and 'apologize unreservedly for the anxiety we caused Miss Deroy, whose character we now understand was never doubted by intelligence authorities.'"

Jack snorted. "That's not entirely true, is it, Wilson?"

"You can't blame us for suspecting her in the first place. She did prove to be the missing link after all." Wilson defended himself. "Clarence confessed he only realized your connection to Bartondale after he saw you at Sotheby's. They worked together to make you look unreliable and guilty so suspicion would naturally fall on you. He said the story in *The Times* gave him the idea, but the *Evening Standard* reporter was more gullible."

"Will he go to prison?" Grace asked.

Wilson nodded. "He's in Holloway now. He might be a duke, but treason during wartime is a serious matter. I can't imagine he'll get off, not without very expensive lawyers."

Having seen firsthand the caliber of his lawyers, Grace didn't hold on to hope that he would face justice anytime soon. "What about Margot? I can't believe I never realized she was Alexander's sister."

"She is quite a complex case. Resented her brother's success but also wanted to share in it. She painted the forgery and demanded to expose Clarence if he didn't help her sell it."

Grace's head felt like it might burst, but she was afraid if she mentioned it, they'd leave. She wanted them here to talk everything through.

Jack was too good a doctor not to notice. "You need more sleep now, Grace. You need to rest."

"But I want to talk more," she pleaded.

"There'll be time for that. I promise." He kissed her hand as her brother said goodbye by kissing her forehead.

She must be stronger than he thought because she didn't drift straight back to sleep. She kept thinking long into the evening.

"You must be feeling better," Jack said, leaning against the doorframe of her hospital room the next day.

He almost regretted speaking. She looked so beautiful that he wanted to drink in the image of her standing by the window, fully dressed and drenched in morning sunlight. More color than yesterday too. A good sign.

"Thank you. I am."

Out of habit he wandered over to the end of the bed between them and picked up her medical chart. Then he thought the better of it. He wasn't actually her doctor, after all, and it would be intrusive to read more. Besides, he didn't want to think of Grace as a patient. It brought back images he wanted to banish of her lying unconscious on the stone floor of the kitchen, wearing clothes soaked in her own blood.

"I wouldn't be here if it weren't for you."

He looked up from where he'd hung the chart and nodded. He knew that better than most.

"I'm so happy to see you up and at 'em, Grace."

Happy? Up and at 'em? The understatements of the war!

He crossed to the window and took Grace's hand, but the closeness didn't make him any more articulate.

Why was this so hard?

The moment he asked the question, he knew the answer. This was hard because he couldn't read Grace. She wore her mask of passive politeness. The one she had been perfecting all her life. One she once used to drop when he was near. Her expression was perfectly pleasant, but also blank. A rock grew like a tumor in his belly.

"Thank you for saving my life, Jack." She withdrew her hand and crossed to the other side of the room.

Nothing had changed for her. The trauma of seeing her nearly die had brought his feelings into clearer perspective, deepening the love born the moment he saw her and that had grown to maturity over the summer.

But her experience was entirely different from his. She'd been unconscious through every one of the grueling minutes it took for the ambulance to arrive. She probably still mistrusted him for his betrayal. Perhaps given time she would process everything and change her mind. But he didn't have a lot of time at the moment.

"I have to go. New posting. Uncle Sam finally found out about my medical training. They want to use me at Camp Griffiss in Sussex."

Nothing. Absolutely nothing changed on her face. No emotion. No sorrow, but at least no joy or relief either. What was she thinking behind that blank-slate expression?

He forged on. "I know things between us are complicated." He weighed his words carefully. "But I was hoping you'd let me write to you."

"Yes, of course." Polite, aways polite.

"Grace, I want you to know that I wish we hadn't met in the way we did. I-I'd like to start over, with honesty instead of lies."

Maybe, just maybe, a flicker of feeling crossed her face. But he guessed she wasn't ready to trust just yet.

"I need some time, Lieutenant." Not using his name hurt worse than a slap.

He nodded, straining his face against the tears that pricked his eyes. "Take all the time you need." The words were strangled in his throat. "Goodbye, Grace."

CHAPTER THIRTY-FIVE

21 April 1944

Jack listened through his stethoscope to the solid swish, swish of his patient's heart. "Take a breath in."

The man obeyed, and Jack moved the stethoscope to hear how the air traveled into a different part of his lungs. "Another."

He heard the rough, scratchy sound that, combined with the man's high fever and his gaunt look, told Jack pneumonia was the most likely cause of illness. He listened to several more places on the man's chest and a few on his back to be sure, before announcing his verdict and ordering a course of treatment.

"You need rest. And penicillin."

The soldier in front of him nodded weakly, obviously keen to get back to his bed. He shuffled to the exit, and Jack ordered the next man in.

"Doc, I got a rash."

At least the work was varied.

Working double shifts in the busy clinic at the US Army camp—headquarters to Eisenhower himself—Jack barely had time to think about Grace. In the fleeting gaps between patients, he brushed up on the skills he'd tried so hard to forget. Anything to stop his mind wandering toward her. Wherever she was right now. Which he didn't know, because he still hadn't written to her.

"Next patient."

His eye caught on the brightly colored clothes. Definitely not olive and khaki. Jack's eyes flicked to the patient's face.

Not a patient. Teddy Deroy. He looked like a man on a mission. "You need to write to Grace, Jack."

Jack busied himself with paperwork, hoping to give himself time to process the swell of emotion seeing Teddy brought on. "Court-martial went well then?" Since Teddy wore civilian attire, Jack assumed he had avoided jail but been discharged. "

"Alarmingly well. I think Father's influence ultimately saved my neck. Old Ed helped, of course. And Grace has people who owe her favors too."

"How is she?" Jack asked the question burned onto his heart, trying not to sound desperate for the answer. His voice betrayed him with a tiny crack.

"She's feeling well. Taking some leave from the WAAF. But I think she'd be better if you wrote to her, the way you said you would."

"I don't think she really wants my letters, Teddy."

Not that he hadn't tried writing a few. More than a few. He'd written more unsent letters than was responsible, given the paper rationing here.

"Are you really giving up on her, then?"

He didn't think his heart would ever give up Grace Deroy. He would hold her there forever. But he couldn't explain that to Teddy. At least, not in a way that didn't make him sound crazy.

"The thing about my sister is that she has an infinite heart. When she loves, she does it deeply and passionately and without limits. I'm sure that's what Blakey exploited."

Jack refocused on the patient record in front of him, even though his pen didn't move.

"I think she loves you, Jack."

Jack swallowed and closed his eyes against that hope.

"Doc?" A man waiting at the clinic door stole away the picture of Grace that was forming in his mind, reminding him there were patients waiting.

"I gotta work."

Teddy left with Jack's promise that he would think about writing to Grace.

Which he did, well into the night as he lay in his lonely army cot, a dull lamp illuminating letters from the last few months. His unsent ones to Grace, as well as the few he had received from the States. He read them all through, including one from Robert Delany. His reply to Jack's letter about having met a woman he felt as strongly about as Dorothy had arrived just before Christmas.

At the time, so soon after Grace had politely sent him on his way, his father-in-law's words had felt like salt rubbing into his wounded heart.

> *Dear Jack,*
>
> *When you first walked into Dotty's life talking about signs from God, Maude and I warned her she should have nothing to do with you! But your persistence, your faithfulness and dedication to the task of honorably courting her despite all the obstacles we put in your way, won us over. Walking Dotty down the aisle toward a man who had so abundantly proved his ability to love, cherish, and adore her remains one of the happiest days of my life. Even now I am proud to call you my son. I won't pretend to know why God would take Dotty from us so soon after that day. But I know this. Neither your love nor your skill could keep her here if the Lord was calling her home.*
>
> *Dotty wouldn't want you to stay mired in grief. She would be as happy as we are to hear that you have met someone else. It is right and good, Jack. We will pray that the woman in question sees sense when you tell her you love her and that this war is short, so you can be together.*
>
> *Don't lose heart, Jack. God is faithful. Even in the insurmountably tragic moments when we cannot see His hand at work, He never forsakes us.*
>
> *Yours Sincerely,*
>
> *Your father, Robert Delany*

Now, Jack mulled the older man's letter over. Robert Delany had always been a man of few words, but he chose them well. God had been faithful. He'd saved Grace's life. Even if she had sent him away, Jack couldn't deny that God had answered the cry of his heart.

He whispered another prayer now. An appeal that God help him know what to do. An answer hit him immediately, in the form of a desperate desire to tell Grace everything. So he picked up a pen and took out a fresh piece of paper.

⎯⎯⎯⎯⎯⎯◂∞⟩

"Which one first?"

Sarah had laid the two items of post on the kitchen table, ready for Grace when she arrived home. They must have tormented Sarah all afternoon, because she'd pounced on Grace and dragged her to the kitchen table as soon as Grace had opened the front door.

When she saw the address of the thicker envelope, her mouth went so dry, she could barely swallow. It must be from Jack, and what with the way Sarah was looking at her, Grace suspected she knew that as well. The Hackney postmark on the thinner one told them it would provide answers about Olive's parents.

Grace reached toward the larger envelope, but her hand changed direction at the last moment to grab the thinner one.

"Should I get Olive in from outside?" Sarah asked.

"Let's see what it says first." Grace edged her finger under the flap and tore it open. Her eyes skidded across the page, and she read to Sarah without stopping to think.

"It's from my friend, Katie. The one we met that day. Remember? She says she's met the Brooks. A coincidence, she says, but that we should be hearing from the Red Cross any day now. Oh dear." Grace laid her hand over her heart. It ached as she read the next paragraph.

"'Things have been difficult since my little Betty passed away, but when I met them, I spilled everything I learned from you that day. They seemed to go straight to the Red Cross. But bureaucracy can sometimes take an age, so I wanted to write to you straight away.'"

"Well, that's good news . . ." The words died on Sarah's lips.

Was it good? They had both grown quite fond of the child. It was Olive who'd raised the alarm when Margot had attacked them. She'd been up a tree in the garden, imagining one of her pirate capers. Margot had no idea the child was watching the whole thing through the kitchen window.

Clever Olive had run to the butcher shop to get help and informed the police that Margot put drops in Sarah's teapot while it was brewing. The constable himself said that if it hadn't been for Olive's thorough description, they might not have caught Margot before she boarded the bus. Any frustration Grace and Sarah had ever felt evaporated right then and there.

"It is good news." She reassured herself with those words. "Shall we tell her?"

"I'll go get her, shall I?"

"Yes please." Grace's own voice sounded absent and vague. Her mind had moved on to the next envelope. The one from Jack.

CHAPTER THIRTY-SIX

16 May 1944

*D*ear Grace,
    I know this letter will come out of the blue for you since you haven't heard from me in six months. I didn't know if you really wanted me to write. I beg you not to burn this without reading it. Please just give me the chance to explain one last thing to you.

    We're preparing for something big. I can't say what, but it'll be soon. It's war, so there are no guarantees that I'll come safely through it. I need to tell you something before I go, so that if I don't return, you can know that I love you, despite the way you must despise me.

    I told you once about how when I met my Dotty, I had a sign from God. He lit her up with sunshine on a summer's day so that I would be in no doubt she was the one I was meant to marry.

    I never told you that I had the same sign the day you got into that car, flushed and beautiful from running down the laneway. It's what paralyzed me in our first few conversations.

    Please forgive me, Grace. I love you. More than you will think possible after everything I've done. I know that I don't deserve it, but I will go into what's ahead with one prayer on my lips: that you understand just how much I love you. I long to see you again, to hold you, to prove to you that I am more than the man who lost your trust.

    Jack.

PS: So you know I have been thinking of you all this time, I've included all the letters I wrote and didn't send over the past few months. Now that you've read this, you can burn them all together if you would rather erase me from your life entirely. J.

———◦◦∞◦———

"What do you think?" Grace asked Maggie, to break the silence hanging between them after Maggie had read Jack's letter. Grace practically had it memorized after reading it so many times in the last few weeks.

"Did you read all the other letters?" Maggie asked.

Grace nodded. "There were twenty-three." A theme and variations on contrition.

"And you're still unsure?" Maggie could ask a question in way that made the answer so clear. "You once told me that I should give Alec a second chance. It was the best piece of advice I ever received." She patted the belly that was now swelling under her too-tight WAAF uniform. She would have to resign from her duties soon. "And Alec didn't even save my life or anything."

"To be fair, he also didn't spy on you and make you reveal your most deeply held secrets so he could turn them over to military intelligence." Grace sniffed.

"Did he really make you reveal your secrets? The way you tell it, he could barely form words in the beginning." Frown lines ran deep across her forehead.

"I miss him, Maggie. I think I love him." Those twenty-three letters, where he tried in various ways to explain, to apologize, to beg forgiveness, to bridge the gaping chasm between them, had shown her that.

Her friend reached her arms out, and Grace willingly sank into the embrace.

"Then tell him. It's war, Grace. There are no guarantees. But don't let him go into it wondering how you feel. Not after a letter like that."

———————◦⃝◦)

Alvin's low, appreciative whistle was the first thing that alerted Jack to the presence of someone approaching. Even then, he didn't lift his eyes from the book he was reading under the shelter of a tree while friends picnicked by the river. Alvin was too often whistling like that at women, and Jack didn't want to indulge him. There were too few moments to relax amid the swirling preparations for war, and he didn't want to waste this one. Besides, Hercule Poirot was just about to announce the identity of Arlene Marshall's murderer.

"Hello, Jack."

A crisply articulated voice made him forget all about the book. His eyes shot up to Grace standing in a pool of light, the sunshine making a hundred honey-colored patterns in her hair. The vibrant blue of her dress—not her uniform, he noted—made the rest of the spring day around him feel like a black-and-white photo. He might be tempted to give the same whistle as Alvin, if he could breathe. But she had stolen that ability away.

From the look on her face, the way her lips quirked up a little and her eyes challenged him, she knew she had that effect. It was almost as though she were daring him to speak. But how could he speak when his heart was jumping in his chest like this?

He continued to stare as he stood, allowing himself to smile as he committed the glorious image of her bathed in sunlight to memory. He knew that even if she had come to slap him in the face and tell him never to write letters like that again, this picture was one he wanted to take with him into whatever lay ahead.

"Well, if you're not going to talk to her, I will." Standing next to him, Alvin leaned in, arms crossed over his chest, as he stared at Grace in admiration.

Jack quickly found some words. "No you don't."

He slapped his book into Alvin's chest without looking at him and headed toward Grace. What was she thinking? Her expression was unreadable, but she was here. That was enough just now.

"I guess you didn't burn my letter?"

She smiled. The encouragement made his heart jump a beat.

"I read it. I read all of them."

"And?"

"You might get tongue tied sometimes, but you certainly have a way with the written word when you set your mind to it."

Now that they were face to face, her gaze didn't seem so challenging. But there was a depth to her hazel eyes he hadn't seen before. He could smell her delicate perfume when he breathed in to speak again. "I meant every word."

He'd laid everything out in that letter, but should he reiterate it now? Apologize for the deception? Plead for her forgiveness? Tell her he loved her? Once again he had no idea what to say next.

"I know. And your final letter practically contained a proposal."

He nodded. "I suppose it did."

"And you meant every word?"

They were so close that he could see the doubt creep into her eyes, even though the rest of her expression didn't change. "Every word, Grace. I'm sorry we met the way we did, in circumstances that meant we started our relationship as a lie. But I don't doubt that God was there lighting you up for me. I can only pray now that you can love me after all I've done."

She reached up to lay her hand on the side of his face. He leaned into its warmth, closing his eyes against its gentleness.

"You have more important things to be praying about."

He opened his eyes at the truth she spoke. A big offensive was coming, and he could be deployed any day now. Perhaps the Allies would rout Hitler and his forces. Perhaps they would die trying. He should be praying about that. Praying for his soul and everyone else's.

"Probably." Her touch had made his voice raspy. "But the only thing on my heart is you."

Her hazel eyes softened at his words, doubt replaced by tenderness and love.

"Well, I'll tell you what. You come back to me after this is all over, and I will let you spend the rest of your life convincing me that we are meant to be together."

"Really?" Emotion flooded him—although he couldn't say which one. All of them probably.

"Really."

He closed the distance between their lips, snaking his arm around her waist and pulling her into him. The hand of hers that had been pressed against his face ran around his neck and held his face to hers. The swirling preparations of war were completely forgotten, replaced by the bliss of her touch and heat in his veins.

"Kissing a dame in broad daylight! Well, that's something I never thought I'd see from goody-two-shoes Jack Marsden."

Alvin.

The moment was ruined, but it was probably for the best. When they broke apart Grace looked flushed and Jack looked giddy, judging by the smirk on Alvin's face.

"Oh, don't stop on my account," Alvin teased.

"A friend of yours?" Grace said.

"Nope. Don't know him."

Creases formed in the corners of her eyes as she chuckled, alight with joy. Jack reluctantly stepped away so he could introduce Grace to Alvin properly. Alvin shook her hand.

"I'm glad you're here. He can stop moping now."

Grace grinned at Alvin but swiftly turned her smile back to Jack.

"Well, you know what you have to do now, don't you? Go and win the war please. And, Alvin, make sure he comes home in one piece."

Alvin tipped his cap and sauntered away as Jack pulled Grace in for another kiss.

CHAPTER THIRTY-SEVEN

21 May 1945

Grace hurried out of the cinema, wiping away tears. Abbott and Costello were meant to be funny, but she couldn't even muster a smile. She blamed the newsreel. Seeing footage of US forces liberating prison camps in Germany didn't set her up well to enjoy a movie, especially when she had inside information that the newsreel didn't—or couldn't—tell the public.

Over the last year, Jack's letters had arrived sporadically, with big black censor marks all though them. It felt strange at first to know someone else had read his letter before her. They only removed details and sentences containing strategic information about military activities, but they still read through the whole thing. She blushed to think someone had read the intimate details he'd shared about himself, his words of longing for her.

The letters had changed in tone as the year progressed and he saw more of what the Nazis had done to Europe. As he went deeper into occupied France and then into Germany itself, the letters became less frequent. She begged God every night to bring Jack back home not just alive but with his spirit intact.

Somehow Jack's last letter had slipped through the censor's net.

Maybe with the war in Europe drawing to a close there was less need to protect the secrets of the advancing Allies. Or maybe someone just got sloppy. Whatever the reason, the letter arrived just as he'd sent it, without a mark on it. If the censor had been doing their job, full paragraphs would glare up at her as solid black.

> *I normally spare you these details, my darling, but I have to write this down as a way to comprehend what I am seeing, and since the censor will likely protect you from the worst of it, I will speak honestly to you about the evidence of organized depravity I see here every day . . .*

He described caring for emaciated men, women, and children who had been prisoners at Nazi work camps. Nursing starving people back to health. Losing patients riddled with typhus and dysentery. Seeing marks and mutilations on innocent bodies. Piles of corpses. Mass graves. He didn't hold back, relying on the censor to keep his descriptions away from her eyes. Instead, she'd felt the full force of his testimony.

The newsreel only gave a quick glimpse into the reality Jack had described, but her brain couldn't let go of the images, even when the movie had begun. She now dragged her heavy heart to the restaurant where she was supposed to meet Sarah.

A flash of olive and khaki caught her eye. Two US GIs sat talking over coffee. Not Jack, of course, but whenever she saw the uniform, it was like her heart gave an extra beat for him, wherever he was.

She scanned the room. Sarah sat alone at a table that must fit six or seven people. Grace hurried to her.

"You're early, miss." Sarah glanced toward the door, slightly panicked.

"Hello to you too." Best not to mention why she'd left the cinema before the end of the film. "Have you eaten?"

Right now she wanted to get home, put on the gramophone, run a scalding bath, and try to forget the world around her.

"Not yet, miss." Sarah kept glancing around. Perhaps she was planning on meeting a sweetheart here while Grace was watching the film.

"Are you meeting someone?" The way Sarah's eyes widened made Grace certain she was right about Sarah having a date. "You secret thing you! You said nothing about having a date planned, and now I've blundered in. Who is it? Do I know him?"

"Oh, you know him," Sarah said with a grin. But she wasn't looking at Grace. Her eyes were fixed on the front door of the café.

Grace spun around to see who it was.

Her heart nearly leapt out of her chest when she saw Jack holding the door open for a mother and child as they exited. His eyes raked across the room eagerly and expectantly. When they fell on her, his face, more weary than when she had seen him last, lit up in a grin that made her heart swell.

She should stand up and run to him, but she couldn't. All she could do was sit rooted in the one spot, her eyes drinking him in while he made his way through the bustling restaurant. Her body managed to move itself when he neared. She threw her arms around his neck.

He was here. Home. Real. Alive. And in her arms.

She pulled back to look at him, her arms still looped around his neck, to study the face she had only dreamed about for the past year. It had more lines, and she longed to trace every one of them with her lips. Instead, she drank in his scent of coffee and spices.

"You're here," she murmured. Had this been what it was like for him the first time they met? All her thoughts and feelings raced around her head, and she couldn't frame words to fully capture them.

"Yes. I'm here to take you up on your offer."

"What do you mean?"

"You said if I came back, you'd let me spend the rest of my life convincing you that we belong together."

"I did, didn't I?" She became aware there were tears streaming down her face. His too. "Well, go on then."

He crashed his face into hers for a kiss that would have gone for much longer if they hadn't been in a crowded restaurant.

"That's enough convincing for now, sister dearest."

Grace was so wrapped up in Jack, she only noticed now how many others had arrived at the table. Peter and Teddy were there. Maggie sat next to Sarah, smiling broadly. Olive materialized too, with her parents.

"What are you all doing here?"

"We are throwing you an engagement party, dear friend," Maggie said.

"Well, technically, we aren't engaged, you know." Grace sat down when Jack held a seat out for her.

"He kisses you like that and you aren't engaged?" Teddy teased. "I should beat him up for being so bold."

Laughter washed over the group.

"Well, go on then." But Peter wasn't looking at her. He was eyeing the man sitting next to her so intently, she turned to look at Jack. And came face to face with a ring.

"Grace Deroy, will you marry me?"

Words stuck in her throat. She nodded out her yes through blurry eyes.

He slipped the gold band with a champagne-colored diamond onto her finger and pressed another kiss to her lips while everyone around them cheered.

"I hope you didn't mind that I asked in front of everyone. I had a different plan, but Peter wouldn't hear of me proposing without a ring," Jack said, one arm around her shoulders, like he couldn't bear to let her go.

"It was perfect. How did you even get this?" She admired the ring, turning her hand to enjoy the way the light caught on the stone. It seemed so extravagant.

"It's one of your mother's."

"You asked them?" Her heart melted at the thought of him with her parents.

"I had lunch with them yesterday. Peter arranged it."

Thank you! she mouthed to her brother.

Her heart was on fire with happiness. The ring on her finger, her love next to her, her friends and family surrounding her, and peace at last declared. She couldn't want more.

Her contentment multiplied when the others went their separate ways and she had Jack all to herself. His arms slipped around her as they lingered under the glow of streetlights—streetlights!—that didn't need to hide from the Luftwaffe anymore.

"When can we get married?" he murmured, arms about her waist.

"I happen to know that I can make a wedding happen in just three weeks if you're sure. You've only just got back, and I know that you've seen some terrible things. You might want to . . ."

"I've never been more sure." He cut her off. "Of anything. And I don't want to wait."

Neither did she, not when he kissed her like that.

"Who shall we invite then?" She took his hand, pulling him along the street.

"All the people from tonight. And all the people who brought us together."

"Wouldn't that mean we invite Wilson? What did he keep telling you? To get closer?"

"I suppose so." He laughed, pulling her near. "Although he's such a man of mystery, where would we even send the invitation?"

"Maybe we'll have to name our first child after him or something." His hand in hers tensed, almost imperceptibly, but she regretted her words. How could she ruin the moment by drawing to his mind the wife and baby he'd lost? "I'm sorry. That was insensitive."

"Don't be sorry, Grace. That is the past, and I want all those things for our future."

A smile played at her mouth. "What? A child called Wilson?"

"A wife called Grace." He paused under another streetlight to wrap his arms around her waist again. "Are you going to like being Mrs. Marsden?"

She kissed him in a way that would leave no doubt in his mind about her answer.

EXCERPT FROM *THESE LONG SHADOWS*

King's Cross Station, London, January 1946

The bitter taste of coal dried out her mouth. Katie Ables twisted the thin gold band on her left hand, watching the train pull up in a hiss of steam. She would have preferred to come to the station alone to see her husband again for the first time in two and a half years. But her mother insisted she come too. She'd brought along four of Katie's seven siblings, the youngest of whom were now chasing each other around the platform, narrowly missing luggage trolleys.

"Don't fidget, Katherine," her mother said over her shoulder.

Katie hated being chided like she was a girl when she was, in fact, a married woman of almost twenty-two. But there wasn't much she could do about it when she was still living with the woman. She dropped her hands to appease her mother, but her insides twisted. Questions she'd already asked herself a thousand times wove through the nerves in her belly.

What would happen when Jonty stepped off the train?

Her eyes traced through the crowd alighting from the train,

looking for a glimpse of blue. Maybe he wouldn't be wearing his uniform. It had been so long, and she wasn't even sure if he had been properly demobilized or not. Her eyes darted about as her mother chastised her brothers for their hijinks. Even in the clouds of smelly steam, he shouldn't be hard to spot with his shocking red hair and lopsided mouth.

They'd already been here for half an hour. Tightness rose from her belly into her chest. What if he hadn't come? He might have changed his mind since he wrote the letter, made another unexplained detour. She gnawed at her bottom lip.

Her eye caught on an RAF uniform. Not Jonty, but she followed the airman long enough to see him drop his duffel bag and hold out his arms for a woman in a plum-colored suit to throw herself into them at a squealing run. They clung to each other for minutes on end, her head over his shoulder, before they found each other's lips. They kissed long and deep, in full view of the whole station, like in a novel. Katie's heart skipped a beat for them. Her meeting with Jonty would never be as passionate—even if her whole family wasn't watching on.

They'd told everyone they fell in love working together in the armory at RAF Bottesford. Jonty would tell the story, joking that he initially fell in love with the speed at which she could load the ammunition into the belts, but soon realized the speed of her fingers was nothing compared to the beauty of her face.

It was kind of him to lie so comprehensively.

The truth wasn't so simple.

She could still hear his gentle Scottish brogue proposing to her. "Marry me, Katie. We don't have to tell anyone that the bairn's not mine."

A crashing sound on the platform behind her stole her attention away from her search. She spun around to see that her youngest brothers had somehow managed to cause a luggage trolley to topple over.

"Boys! Behave!" Her mother called out to Katie's brothers as she hurried over to help restack the trolley and apologize to the glowering station attendant. The boys stayed contrite for approximately two seconds before they began their games again, farther down the platform. Katie should help her mother deal with the suitcases, but she turned back to keep scanning the crowd, ignoring the creeping worry that he might not show. She took out his last letter from her coat pocket to double-check the details, even though she knew she was right where he'd told her to be.

Kings Cross station. Platform two. 11.30 a.m.

What if he didn't come?

It had been so long since she had thought about the future with any hope that she didn't know how to now. She prepared herself for the mortification of going home without him, for the conversation with her mother, for what she'd say to the rest of her siblings when she arrived home without Jonty. For almost three years she'd been honing the steel inside her to get through each day alone. If he didn't show, she would keep doing that.

"Katie?"

Jonty's unmistakable accent came from behind her. Time stopped. Every muscle tightened. She took a deep breath to steady herself and turned toward his voice.

For the first time ever, she was glad for his scarring. She might not have recognized him otherwise. His hair was cropped so closely that she barely saw its color. Jonty was never plump, but he'd lost even more weight in the years since she'd seen him. His uniform sat like it was on a hanger, not a body. His cheerful spirit used to fill his whole body, giving him the air of an irrepressible puppy. Now he stood still. The stark difference hit her hard, like a slap to the face.

Of course he had changed. It had been almost three years since they'd buried the baby girl who had been their reason for marrying in the first place. Three years since that dreadful night when, numb in her grief, she'd screamed at him to leave and never come back.

She'd heard about how war had turned previously tender men into scoundrels who beat their wives. How amiable ones became sullen, sulking into a bottle all day. But Jonty's letters felt so remi-niscent of his first proposal. He'd begged for them to reconcile and not divorce the way so many others seemed to be doing after making hasty wartime unions. But he left the final decision up to her.

"You choose. But I promise you'll never have cause to fear me. Never again."

His sincerity ultimately convinced her to show up today de-spite the lingering doubts intertwining with her unanswered ques-tions. Why did he take so long to come back to England after the war had ended? He had only explained his delay in the most vague terms. Something about unfinished business. How could they pos-sibly find a way to start again after everything?

He moved first. She noticed an unevenness in his gait as he closed the distance between them. With that limp, the scars on his neck seemed more pronounced in the way that they pulled his expression over to the left.

She didn't throw herself at him, like the woman in the suit had thrown herself at her husband. Theirs wasn't a sweeping romance, after all. But she was also worried she might knock him over if she did.

"Hello, Katie-my-love," he said, eyes searching hers and so in-tense she glanced at the ground to avoid them. From the moment they were married he'd called her that, running the words together as though they were all part of her name. It had felt strange at first, because the name, like their love, hadn't grown from anywhere. The nickname was the result of his decision and determination—like stating a fact. Now, it was the most familiar thing about him.

She knew her mother and siblings were watching from a few paces behind, so she tried her best to smile. She'd conceived pos-sible things to say last night, as she lay awake next to her younger sister. Practiced them under her breath as they trooped through the rubble to get from their home in Hackney to King's Cross. But none of them came to her dry mouth now.

"Hello, Jonty" was all she managed, glancing back at her mother and brothers. Anything to avoid meeting his eyes.

A smile stretched over his thinned face, and he reached out to take her hand. She flinched and pulled away out of instinct. Did her mother notice? Jonty held his smile in place, and only she saw the disappointment flicker in his eyes.

"It's good to have you home."

She tried with all her heart to mean what she said.

Coming Soon!

For release details, go to

https://jennifermistmorgan.com/these-long-shadows.

AUTHOR'S NOTES

Thank you so much for reading *The Mapmaker's Secret*, the second in my On Victory's Wings series. If you are like me, the first thing you want to do after finishing a historical novel is check where the author clung to history and where they deviated from it. So let me explain that while the concept of Bartondale is real, the details are fictional.

During the war, many country houses around England were requisitioned to play a role in the war effort. These houses went on to perform a myriad of functions. They became military headquarters, code-breaking facilities, safe havens for evacuees, training centers for saboteurs and spies. Due to the binding nature of official secrets, the work that went on in some of these houses wasn't revealed until generations after the war.

The story that captured my imagination was that of Hughenden in High Wycombe, Buckinghamshire, once the country house of Victorian-era politician Benjamin Disraeli. Renamed "Hillside" during the war, the house was used as a place to make maps for RAF Bomber Command. The purpose of the work was so secret that it wasn't until the 1990s, when a National Trust tour guide overheard a grandfather telling the story of his war work to his grandchildren, that the story became widely known.

While Grace's home is inspired by Belton House near Grantham, the institution "Bartondale" is inspired by Hillside. I don't intend it to be an exact replica, but I did borrow many details from the accounts of people who worked there, including the idea that very few knew the entire story of the work. I also borrowed details from accounts of workers in other photographic intelligence units in the RAF to create the world within Bartondale's walls. I had to reduce the security level somewhat, in order to be able to place an American "spy" in the facility. Needs must when you write romance.

You can find other historical notes and ask questions about the historical details at jennifermistmorgan.com/mapmakers-secret.

If you enjoyed the book, please consider leaving a review at your retailer or on Goodreads. Your reviews help others find the book.

ACKNOWLEDGMENTS

First and foremost, I have to thank my family. I simply couldn't have written this without their generous patience and the time they give me to spend crafting imaginary friends. A writer on a deadline is a somewhat crazed, selfish creature who cannot think beyond the words in front of them. Thank you for your kindness when I am in this state. This one is for you.

Thank you to all the others who made this book possible: Bronwyn, my first reader, for generously copyediting the first draft. Dori Harrell, editor extraordinaire. It is a joy to collaborate with you. Cover designer Roseanna White: thank you! It's so beautiful! My agent Rachel McMillan for her continual support. Dear friend and de facto medical consultant Amanda, who doesn't mind taking random phone calls where I begin by launching in with "I need to stab someone . . ." and who is kind enough to proofread manuscripts even when she is undertaking an international relocation or recovering from a sledding accident.

And to the readers who loved Grace in *Heart in the Clouds* and were devastated to learn of the aspersions cast over her reputation! I hope you enjoyed the story. To God be the glory.

MORE FROM
JENNIFER MISTMORGAN
HEART IN THE CLOUDS

RAF Bottesford, November 1942: Maggie Morrison joined the Women's Auxiliary Air Force for a free ticket into the romance she craved, away from her sleepy life as a vicar's daughter. But the men of Bomber Command are careless with the hearts of women. She hides the pain of her broken heart and mother's sudden death behind calm confidence on the airfield radio, as the last voice men hear before they fly into danger.

Australian pilot Alec Thomas is a gambling man on a winning streak. Every night when he flies with RAF Bomber Command, the odds of surviving are fifty-fifty. And every night so far, he's made it back to English soil. But as the battles over Europe intensify, Alec's luck feels less certain.

When Alec bets with his crew he can get Maggie to kiss him before the year is out, he has no idea it's the most important wager he'll ever make. But pursuing her leads Alec to reexamine everything he believes about his so-called luck, prompting him to question what—or who—is behind it all. Even if Alec can win his bet, can his risk-taking ways win her heart? Or will his luck in the brutal air war over Europe run out before their first kiss?

If you enjoy gripping wartime romances by Sarah Sundin and Roseanna M White, you'll love this heart-stopping story of love, chance and consequence. Go to: https://jennifermistmorgan.com/heart-in-the-clouds/.

READ *FINISHING SCHOOL* FOR FREE

Inverness, Scotland,1944: In her final weeks of training at a Special Operations Executive Finishing School, Amy Snee's last chance to redeem her career is to parachute behind enemy lines as an SOE wireless operator. She just needs to master Morse code.

Stuart Lewis teaches radio operations, knowing that his bright, brave students won't last more than six weeks behind enemy lines. Can he bring himself to teach Morse to his high school crush, when it means losing her forever? Or can he give her a fighting chance at love?

With rigorous historical detail and compelling characters, this sweet historical romance will delight fans well-crafted close-door romance.

This novella is only available by signing up to Jennifer's monthly "Nom de Plume" newsletter at https://jennifermistmorgan.com/subscribe/.

Printed in Dunstable, United Kingdom